T0125809

ESCORTED

What Reviewers Say
About Renee Roman's Work

Where the Lies Hide

"I like the concept of the novel. The story idea is well thought out and well researched. I really connected with Cam's character..."
—*Rainbow Reflections*

"[T]his book is just what I needed. There's plenty of romantic tension, intrigue, and mystery. I wanted Sarah to find her brother as much as she did, and I struggled right alongside Cam in her discoveries."—*Kissing Backwards*

"Overall, a really great novel. Well written incredible characters, an interesting investigation storyline and the perfect amount of sexy times."—*Books, Life and Everything Nice*

"This is a fire and ice romance wrapped up in an engaging crime plot that will keep you hooked."—*Istoria Lit*

Epicurean Delights

"[*Epicurean Delights*] is captivating, with delightful humor and well-placed banter taking place between the two characters. ...[T]he main characters are lovable and easily become friends we'd like to see succeed in life and in love."—*Lambda Literary Review*

"Hard Body"

"[T]he tenderness and heat make it a great read."—*reviewer@large*

"[A] short erotic story that has some beautiful emotional moments."
—*Kitty Kat's Book Review Blog*

Visit us at www.boldstrokesbooks.com

By the Author

Epicurean Delights

Stroke of Fate

Hard Body

Where the Lies Hide

Bonded Love

Body Language

Hot Days, Heated Nights

Escorted

ESCORTED

by
Renee Roman

2022

ESCORTED
© 2022 By Renee Roman. All Rights Reserved.

ISBN 13: 978-1-63679-039-8

This Trade Paperback Original Is Published By
Bold Strokes Books, Inc.
P.O. Box 249
Valley Falls, NY 12185

First Edition: February 2022

Credits
Editors: Victoria Villaseñor and Cindy Cresap
Production Design: Susan Ramundo
Cover Design By Tammy Seidick

Acknowledgments

Thank you to everyone at Bold Strokes Books for ensuring authors remained visible to readers everywhere by holding virtual events and being successful at reaching our audience. I'm sure it wasn't easy, but you made it look like it was.

A huge thank you to readers everywhere who continued to read our stories, and I hope they brought you comfort in whatever form you needed to get you through the tough times.

Dedication

Knowing what you want is the easy part.
Finding it where you least expect is magic.

We are all magicians.

CHAPTER ONE

Ryan Lewis pulled her hand down her face. Long hours had never bothered her, and they still didn't, but some other force was at work here, and for the life of her she couldn't put a finger on it. She eyed the Keurig on the credenza before glancing at the clock. Coffee after nine was a first-class ticket to a sleepless night, and she'd had enough of those over the last month to keep her seated. A rap on her open door deflected her from the reasons why.

"Come."

"You're here late, boss. Problems?" asked Lane Michaels, accountant extraordinaire and one of Ryan's right-hand women, before dropping into the soft leather chair facing her desk.

Lane was one of the few people Ryan often confided in. "No. There's been an influx of new clients and they all want to be serviced yesterday." Ryan tapped on the printed spreadsheet of all her employees. She'd already noted a lot of the recent requests were for a particular type of service that the Agency provided, but there weren't enough escorts to meet the demand. If she was going to accept more clients, she would have to bring on more staff.

"How will the books hold up if I hire a couple more escorts?" The process of vetting newcomers was a royal pain in the ass, though she'd never hire anyone without the extensive background checks and unorthodox interview process she insisted on for every applicant. There were too many psychos in the world to take people at face value. *Maybe I need to stop watching so many crime shows.*

"The Agency's in good shape. Recent numbers indicate you could hire a dozen and still be well in the black." Lane smiled.

Aware how much she liked staying on dry dock, Lane made sure they avoided the red tide when it came to the business. She groaned nonetheless. "A dozen would kill me. Are you in a hurry to collect your share?" Since she had no family or partner to provide for, her will outlined that Lane, along with her best friend and business partner, Drake, would split control of the business should something happen to her. Drake held the edge and ultimate decision-making powers, though Ryan hoped she'd give serious consideration to Lane's innate ability to predict the future when it came to earnings.

"You hurt my heart." Lane held a hand over her bound chest.

"Bullshit." She laughed. It was time she went home to her empty condo. Maybe Chester, the stray she'd rescued from the dumpster beside the building last winter, would be happy to see her for a change. "Is there a reason for your impromptu visit, other than being unable to stay away?" The ongoing joke between them, of Lane teasing her by saying if only Ryan was a little less butch she could really go for her, often helped her mood.

Lane stood. "You wish. We need to think about some new locations. With the increase in appointments, we're running up against tight accommodations, unless you want to start putting time limits on clients."

Ryan frowned. "No. We're not a prostitution ring. We don't provide by the hour services, and we never will. Any suggestions?"

"You're in luck. Several new high-rises are opening up. One is on the east side of Saratoga Lake, and the other in Greenfield Center. Because of our reputation as a great leasee, we can opt in before they go on the market. I'll send you the specs. Let me know what you think next week." Lane turned to leave. "Ryan?"

Looking up, she pushed back from her desk. Lane only called her by name when there was a personal component to their conversation. "Yes?"

"Have some fun this weekend and then get some rest. Don't let the business be your life."

She wanted to be angry, tell Lane it was none of *her* business what she did with her time, but they'd been friends too long to deny what she knew to be true. "I'll try."

Lane studied her for a minute, then nodded. "Good night."

Fuck. As much as she may not want to admit it, Lane was right. Life behind her desk, even if it was a very nice mahogany desk, had never been the life she'd envisioned for herself.

"And then I said to my asshole husband, if you think for a minute I'm hiring some young thing to clean the house you may as well sign the divorce papers now."

Daniella Brown continued to clip at the overprocessed dyed blond hair of her client while she ranted on about her lowlife spouse. The same spouse who paid for every indulgence imaginable to keep said wife happy. So what if he wanted a little eye candy? For all the money she spent on herself, the woman in the chair would only get looks from people who couldn't believe someone actually *wanted* to be a plastic imitation of a model. And not a very pretty one at that. Dani put down her scissors, blew out the hair, slapped in some product, then smiled into the mirror.

"All set, Mrs. Roberts." She whipped off the cape with a flourish.

Leaning forward, Mrs. Roberts looked at her reflection and pulled a strand here and there before smiling back. "You're a miracle worker, dear."

That she was. If the woman did one more process to her over-bleached, over-permed hair, Dani couldn't guarantee there'd be anything left to work with. She had made it clear she wouldn't do anything more than wash, cut, and style in the future. If the woman got stares now, she would be outright gawked at if she looked like a tufted mannequin. "Thank you." She wrote out a fee form and rang the total up on the register. "That will be eighty-four dollars."

Mrs. Roberts handed her a crisp one-hundred-dollar bill and gave her an air kiss. "I'll see you in a couple of weeks." She breezed out the door, her fake ass bouncing along behind her.

Sixteen lousy dollars to put up with her shit. It wasn't nearly enough. "George, I'm out of here." Dani called to her boss before sanitizing her station and instruments, then handed a twenty to the shampoo girl, and left by the back door. She'd learned that little trick when one of her clients practically chased her down the street while demanding she absolutely had to have her hair colored "right now." Safely in her car, Dani grabbed the wheel, and let her head fall back against the rest. Most of the time she loved her job, except when she had to put up with the likes of Mrs. Roberts. It was times like those she pictured stabbing herself in the eye with her rattail comb in order to escape. Likely, she'd bleed out before the woman even noticed.

The idea of staring at four walls rarely bothered her, but today had been more than stressful and her tips, while good, were nothing to brag about. Being on her feet for over eight hours hadn't helped improve her mood. Dani woke up the screen on her phone, scrolled through her contacts, and landed on one that made her smile.

"Hello."

"Please tell me you don't have a hot date lined up and you can hang with me for a while."

Mark laughed. "How could I pass up an invitation like that? What's going on, babe?"

"Would you believe I'm missing you?"

"Well...maybe, but that's not why you called," Mark said, a tease in his voice.

Dani sighed. Mark knew her too well to pull one over on him. They'd struck up a fast and hard friendship when she'd stuck up for him in high school. The macho boys, mostly on the football team, called him fag and queer. He never gave them the satisfaction of letting the hurt show, instead making quips and larks about their small brains and muscle-bound reach, though none of them were smart enough to figure out the insults being hurled at them. "Sitting on the pity pot alone has lost its appeal. Care to join me for a drink and comfort food?"

"Of course. Give me thirty minutes to finish what I'm doing, and I'll meet you at Green's."

"Thanks. You're a life saver."

"Darling, aren't I always?" Mark's empathetic tone let her know he didn't mind at all.

Green's Pub was housed in a nondescript brick building on a nondescript road outside of town. The local crowd took over the bar on a nightly basis, which was fine by her. The dining room was quaint and cozy, the fireplace old and well-used. Even in summer a small fire burned most nights, and while the ambiance wasn't lost on her, it did nothing to calm the tingle that traveled along her spine. After ordering a beer for herself and a whiskey sour for Mark, she perused the worn, faded menu. There wasn't really a need to look at it other than to occupy her hands until Mark showed. She knew every item listed along with the rotating specials. If she was on her game, tonight's offering was a roast beef club on sourdough with seasoned waffle fries and a homemade dill pickle. What did that say about her life? If she had her way, there'd be some real excitement, and she wouldn't be sitting alone in a sedate pub waiting for her best friend on a Saturday night.

The front door opened, and Mark strode in with a flourish, his bright green scarf flapping behind him. "Girl, where the hell did all that traffic come from?" He sat down in a huff, then smiled when his drink appeared. After a sip of foam, he sighed. "Now, tell me what's got you in a funk."

Dani trailed her finger down through the sweat forming on the neck of her beer bottle. "I can't stop thinking about sex."

He snorted. "Join the club, honey." Mark liked sex. A lot. He refused to be judged for what he considered something as natural as breathing. His sometime boyfriends didn't seem to mind they had to share him, and Mark claimed there was plenty of him to go around.

"Not just sex. Sex with a woman."

"Oh no, are we back to that again?"

It was true. Dani had been playing around with the idea for months now. Every time she saw a woman who rode the edge of gender—the masculine-of-center-type edge—her pulse jumped, and her body responded. Her nipples would harden, and she'd squeeze her legs together. She didn't need a degree to know what that meant.

Dani was attracted to women. Granted, she had no experience, but it wasn't like she hadn't tried to check out dating services. Some of her friends warned her to be careful who she got involved with. Christ. Dating hadn't even been on her radar yet and she was already questioning how wise it would be to sleep with someone she might not even end up liking. She was crawling out of her skin to get to actually kiss a woman, touch a woman, *feel* a woman, and be felt by one. It was like an obsession that grew out of being denied; knowing you couldn't have something made you want it more, and soon it was all you could think about. Just thinking about it now had her wet and wanting. "You make it sound like I've no chance in hell."

Mark touched her hand. "It's not that at all. You're fucking hot and you know it."

She was average at best and was about to argue that point when the waitress appeared, and she bit back the sharp response.

"What'll you have?"

"I'll take the special, and we'll share an order of onion rings."

"Presumptuous little thing, isn't she?" Mark displayed a killer smile, his tone laced with sarcasm. "I'll have the smothered burger, medium well, hold the ketchup, and a side of mayo."

When they were alone again, she continued. "Then why is it so hard for me to find someone?" She looked everywhere she went. In the salon. On the street. She found herself staring at the driver of the car next to her when she was at a stop light. But not knowing what she was looking for, or with who, left her frustrated and unsure what to do about it.

"What about personal ads?" she asked. "Do women do that? Maybe I should take one out with a catchy phrase." She thought for a bit before sharing her idea with Mark. "How about, 'Horny single woman looking for a woman to kiss.' That ought to get a response, don't you think?"

Mark's lips pursed. "I've told you, it shouldn't be like that. Not when you don't know what you're getting into." He studied her as they both drank. "I'll tell you what we're going to do. There's a queer friendly bar that opened a few months ago and I've been dying to check it out. How about we go together, and if warning bells aren't going off in my head that the place is a meat factory in disguise, we'll see what strikes your fancy." He waited while their food was delivered.

She snagged an onion ring. "That visual isn't appealing at all."

"I forget how naive you are. It's a cliché, but never mind my terms of endearment when it comes to hot bodies on display." He lifted the bun, coated it with mayo, pressed it down, cut his burger into quarters, and daintily picked one up before he took a bite.

"So we go check out what's being offered?" At some point over the last few months, Dani had taken time to examine her emotional state during high school. Specifically, freshman year while at gym class. When it came time to shower, she'd been understandably shy. It was her first time being naked in the presence of other girls. That wasn't the reason her face became heated though. The surreptitious glances she'd stolen of their breasts and the dark curls between their thighs, made her belly tighten in a way that was both exciting and forbidden.

Mark chewed and nodded. "Both sexes are guilty of boasting about having the skill to deliver on fantasies, but very few actually have the knowledge, and being a newbie you need to be careful. You could end up in a bad situation. Even worse, you could be hurt— physically *and* emotionally. Trust me, you don't want to go there." This time Mark shoved a huge chunk of his burger into his mouth as though trying to destroy a bad memory.

She wondered how he managed to chew around the massive hunk of meat. It took her a second to make the correlation and she quickly looked away, not wanting to think about what Mark was capable of fitting in his mouth...or swallowing.

"You sound like you have firsthand experience. Pardon the expression."

He rolled his eyes. "More than once, and they weren't pleasant at all. I'd rather you not subject yourself to anything like that."

The bars were probably the last place she should be looking to hook up and explore her sexual cravings, but her options weren't expanding, and no one was pounding on her door. Maybe she should give the internet another try, though the thought of meeting catfishers and ghosters wasn't only frustrating, it left her feeling desperate. Mark said there was an "ever-expanding sea of sex-craved and horny" people lurking in chat rooms and on dating sites. She just wasn't sure she wanted to take that route. The idea of baring her soul to a total stranger scared and intimidated her. What was she supposed to do? Walk up to a woman she thought *might* meet her mental image of hot and say, "Hi, I'm Dani. I'd like you to fuck me and I want to do the same to you, but I'm a virgin when it comes to women."

On the one hand, sleeping with a stranger, someone who didn't know anything about her and didn't know how awkward she might be in bed sounded exciting, but the possibility of finding herself in a creepy or dangerous situation tamped down her desire to sleep with just *anyone*. No, dating might be safer, but establishing a relationship only to discover she'd wasted her time by picking a totally incompatible person might permanently turn her off to the whole idea of freely exploring who she was, not who she'd always felt she had to pretend to be. She wasn't sure about much except her clit was going to shrivel into a dried raisin if it wasn't used soon. *Oh God, could that happen?*

Dani crunched on another onion ring. There had to be another way. She'd gone to one bar where she thought queers were as welcome as straight patrons as long as they could pay their tab. A few guys had tried to make a move on her, and although she'd dated boys through her teen years, it had been more to appease her parents than herself. Then, as a young adult, she'd finally let a couple of guys take her to bed, but she hadn't enjoyed it because nothing they did felt natural, and they'd rushed through the act that was over before she'd barely warmed. The whole experience was unpleasant, and nothing like the novels she'd read. She hadn't even been sure she'd orgasmed and had proven her theory once she started masturbating, but what she really wanted was to share the experience with another person. A warm, caring person who actually wanted to please her rather than just get off.

"What makes you think this will be different from the other times I've had sex?"

Mark tapped her hand. "You weren't at all into it, honey."

That was true. She hadn't given up though and went back another time. Two different women had approached her. One wasn't at all shy about wanting a quick fuck and was way too friendly for having just met. Dani had been polite in turning the woman down because she had strange vibes from her that made her wary. The other one reminded her of a schoolgirl, all giggly and well into her liquor. Dani wasn't a snob, but someone with a little sophistication would have been nice. Mark said she shouldn't give up based on a couple of underwhelming events.

"I guess I'm stuck with manual relief until I figure it out."

Mark swallowed the last of his burger and licked the drippings from his fingers. "That's a guaranteed result at least." He finished his drink and patted her hand. "Let's make a plan for a girls' night out. Until then try not to get too discouraged. When it's meant to happen, it will."

Dani nodded, but she wasn't so sure. She'd been waiting for months and her anxiety level about finding what she wanted grew exponentially every day.

Chapter Two

How much experience do you have with BDSM?" The salt-and-pepper-haired woman's lips moved in a seductive grin. "I'm fifty-three, Ms. Lewis. Let me assure you I have extensive experience in providing all forms of pleasure. Would you like a demonstration?"

Ryan inwardly grinned, though she wouldn't do so outwardly so as not to encourage thoughts that Beck was a shoo-in for the position. "That will be part of this interview, of course, though I'll only be observing." She had all she could do not to laugh at the momentary surprise on the applicant's face. To her credit, Beck Simon recovered quickly. She pulled a sheet of paper from the folder in front of her. "This is an acknowledgement stating you were not solicited for the position you are interviewing for and that any conditions verbally stated or provided in writing during and after the interview process are confidential between the Agency and the applicant. Any breach of such information will result in immediate dismissal and legal action, including but not limited to, monetary damages as a result. Please take a minute to review and then sign it."

Ten minutes and several additional nondisclosure documents later, including one regarding no personal relationships with clients, Ryan picked up her office phone. "Anna, would you be so kind as to escort Ms. Simon to room four?" She stood and extended her hand. "This will be the last we speak until a determination has been made based on your qualifications."

Beck appeared confused. "Thank you," she said. "I thought the process would be longer."

"You aren't finished, but I won't talk with you anymore today. I'll observe your interactions with my screener and when I'm satisfied I've seen enough, you'll be free to go." A knock on the door was followed by her assistant's appearance.

"Ms. Simon, if you'll follow me, please."

Beck didn't look nearly as confident as she had when she strode into her office half an hour ago. Ryan sat to make notes in the file open on her screen, sealed it with a password, then fixed herself an espresso. A few minutes later, she strode down the hall to the room where Beck had been led. Beck had stripped to her boxers while the screener wore a garter belt with black stockings and a bustier of butter-soft leather. Ryan took a seat in the finely-crafted leather chair in the corner. An armoire was open on the opposite wall and held an array of pleasure toys and instruments, as well as a variety of bondage items. Escorts hired to provide sexual pleasure in whatever way a client desired had to be well versed in how to use what was at their disposal. Every apartment the Agency leased was similarly equipped.

The screener, a woman whose name only Ryan knew, made eye contact and Ryan nodded for them to begin. She left thirty minutes later. Her nipples were hard and her clit thrummed, however, there was no desire to orgasm. She'd learned to control her own urges and her body was tightly leashed, a skill she'd developed over the years. As an orphan child who moved from one foster home to another, she'd learned to hold her sometimes volatile emotions in check. It was difficult enough to acclimate to each new environment without causing more problems for herself. As an adult, she'd perfected her control while providing sexual pleasure to women. A client always came first, figuratively and literally, unless they requested otherwise. After a little while, the heat in her lower belly would subside and she'd be fine. This was her business, and she was the quintessential professional because she had to be. She didn't feel the least bit sorry for making Beck nervous when she'd entered the room, but Beck had soon regained her footing and focused on what she was doing.

An in-control dominant, or submissive, was a prerequisite. Her techniques, while much different from Ryan's, had nonetheless been effective. She'd confer with the screener, though she was confident Beck would be a fine addition to the Agency. She had an edge to her that would be in demand after clients got to know her.

"Anna," Ryan said over the intercom. "Please have the screener drop by my office when she's free."

"Of course, Ms. Lewis."

She shook her head. Anna was a fantastic assistant, but no matter how many times Ryan told her to call her by her first name when they were alone, she wouldn't give in. Anna insisted they maintain a professional appearance at all times, no matter if there was anyone to witness their interactions or not. While she waited, she had her own screening to perform on the client inquiries waiting in the business email inbox, a task she was growing less interested in every day. It wasn't that she was tired of running her very profitable business. Nothing could be further from the truth, and the freedom she had to do what she wanted, when she wanted was a definite plus. She was the CEO after all, and the success or failure fell squarely on her shoulders. There was something else going on and she didn't have a clue what it might be.

❖

"So, we're going to do this, right?" Dani shoved essentials into her small cross body bag and tried to calm her tattered nerves. Strung out for the last four days in anticipation, she'd gotten little sleep thinking about going with Mark to check out women.

Mark cocked a hip. "Am I going to have to slap you to calm you down?"

She laughed nervously. "Of course not. I'm just…excited." That wasn't entirely true, but it was the best she could do. She hadn't done anything out of the ordinary and still her parents' stern tone droned on in her head. Words like *disgrace* and *what would the congregation think* constantly reverberated in her head every time she went to explore who she was.

"Don't pee yourself before we get there. I should have gotten some puppy pads when I offered to be your chauffeur. Leather doesn't do well where bodily fluids are concerned."

She stared at him until he stopped looking at his manicured purple nails. "I don't want to know how you're an expert on leather and fluids."

Mark gave her a sagacious grin. "Can we go now?"

"Okay, okay. I'm ready." Dani glanced in the hall mirror and gave herself the once-over for the fifth time since Mark's arrival. He shoved her firmly out the door.

"Whatever's going on in that pretty little head of yours I need to know so I can run interference if you get in too deep."

"I'm okay. Parent-speak going on in my head is all." She swallowed down the internal audio assault and concentrated on the scenery whizzing by at a less than safe speed. Everything Mark did was with purpose. At the moment, she imagined it was getting to the bar so he could have a few drinks under his belt before switching to nonalcoholic beverages for the rest of the night. That was his MO. Hard and fast.

"Well, stop it. You're an adult living on your own. You can do whatever the fuck you want, with whomever you want." He patted her thigh for emphasis.

This was why she loved him. "I'm sorry I hid you from my parents. It was wrong of me." The thought was more than sobering. Every once in a while, she relived the days she had to sneak around, knowing if they took one look at Mark in eyeliner and effeminate clothes they would have grounded her until she was twenty-one, or dead. Whichever came first.

Mark gazed at her, empathy in his hazel eyes. "I know, honey. Not everyone can deal with this much sex appeal," he said, making her laugh. "All our classmates knew your folks were as straightlaced and uptight as they come." He took a minute. "And in spite of all that, you were still my closest ally." He squeezed her hand. "I'm not sure I would have survived high school without you." Mark's mood rarely became somber, but the shadow of pain that flashed there was one she recognized from her own mirror too often.

"You're resilient to the core and you know it, but I'm glad I met you. It was perfect timing."

"That it was."

"Now you're going to show me how to meet women." Deep down, Dani didn't doubt where her body was leading. All she had to do was get the rest of her on board.

Dani shook her head. One drink in and working on the second and she was exhausted. She didn't want to be rude, but the woman who'd come up to her had been vociferous and cocky. Too self-assured and too egotistical for Dani's liking, especially since she was just dipping her toes in the water. Whether women or men, those type of people were a turnoff.

"Tell me again what you're looking for." Mark was savoring his last cocktail of the night before switching to soda. They'd been sitting at the end of the bar where there was a good view of the long expanse and the dance floor. Men and women in mixed combinations milled about the large open space. Some were laughing, some dancing, and quite a few flirting.

She sighed. That was part of the problem, even she didn't know what would make her heart beat faster. "This was a bad idea."

"Girl, we're just getting started." Mark sucked up the last of his whiskey sour and ordered a ginger ale with lime. "Here's what we're going to do." His eyes sparkled with excitement. "I'll point someone out and you tell me what you like or don't like about her."

"Okay." She motioned the bartender for a refill.

"Three o'clock on the dance floor, the woman with the redhead in CFM boots." He gave a discreet nod.

She wore faded jeans, an oxford shirt, and Nike athletic shoes. Her features were soft and her body matched. She wasn't unattractive, but Dani had no reaction at all. "Not even close."

"So, give some help here. Taller, shorter?"

"Taller, and lean. Not skinny, but..." She couldn't come up with the word she was looking for.

"Carved?"

A shiver ran down her spine. "Yes." Dani closed her eyes. Unlike the romance novels she'd hidden and read as a teenager, her more recent fantasies were all lesbian ones. "Handsome, maybe a bit roguish. And…sophisticated." When she looked at Mark he was smiling.

"Girl, you want a Greek goddess of the androgynous type."

She sipped her martini, the pungent aroma of alcohol made her nose wrinkle, the sharp pomegranate tingled on her tongue. "I have no idea what you're talking about." The dating sites she'd cruised were full of women just like her. Ordinary…and mostly straight or bi…except for Tinder, from what she could tell. Her fantasy women, however, were anything but either of those, and none had descriptions like MOC, femme, or similar. That would have made the endless scrolling a lot more efficient

Mark casually glanced around the bar, seeming to take in everyone and everything at once. He had a talent for it. One Dani wished he could teach her.

"There, at the end of the bar. Tall, dark, and luscious if you like that kind." His eyebrow rose in question as Dani tried to focus.

The woman's face was sharp angles with high cheekbones and a strong chin. She was roguishly handsome. Collar length charcoal hair shone in the overhead cam lights. The color of her eyes was hard to see from where Dani sat, but she caught a shimmer of ice blue, bright and dazzling as she laughed. She wore a suit jacket over a red silk dress shirt, open a couple…three…buttons to reveal the shadowed curve of a breast. Long fingers wrapped around a bottle of Stella as she chatted up a pretty woman who sat on the stool next to her. She wished she could trade places. Her pulse quickened, her gut tightened, and when the woman smiled, her clit jumped. Visions of what the woman would do to her, command of her, demand of her body, made her sway.

"Whoa, girl," Mark said as he held onto her arm. "Bingo. Once you get your shit together you should go talk to her."

She wiped the sweat from her upper lip and reached for her drink even though her hand shook. "What would I say?"

Mark rolled his eyes. "Jesus, you're pathetic." He sucked his beverage through the narrow straw. "Let's get horizontal?" His brows were drawn together as he thought. "You're the woman of my fantasies. Want to make my dreams come true?"

She snorted, then quickly looked around. "Do those lines actually work?" Dani didn't think a woman like the one she kept glancing at would fall for a clichéd come on.

Mark shrugged. "It works with guys." He smiled sheepishly.

Dani looked over Mark's shoulder and sighed. The woman was leaving, her hand at the small of the back of the woman she'd been talking to. Maybe they'd come together, or maybe they had just met, but either way fantasy woman was no longer an option. "She's leaving, so it doesn't matter."

"Damn. You've got to stop dragging your feet. When you see what you want, go for it."

If only it were that easy. She finished off her drink and let the nice buzz she had buffer her disappointment. Since her prospects looked bleak for the immediate future, Dani turned her attention to Mark. "Dance with me?"

"Babe, that's one request I'll never turn down."

If only she could be sure the next person she approached would be as willing.

Chapter Three

"Oh my God. All I can tell you is that one night was worth every penny, and then some." The woman thought she was whispering. Dani knew the entire room of customers under hoods had likely heard her since they were all turned in her direction, eyes wide.

Her best friend sat next to her with her mouth shaped in an expressive "O." "I didn't think there were services like that. Did they show you a clean bill of health? You can't be too careful these days you know."

Dani lifted the hood and checked one of the foil wraps in her client's hair. The hair appeared sufficiently bleached and now she could listen more intently.

"For goodness' sake, Marge. She's not a hooker. Trust me, the price alone guaranteed I didn't have anything to worry about except having a good time."

"Come with me, please."

Marge disengaged herself from her seat and followed them to the empty chair next to Dani's station. "Are you going to make another appointment?" the friend asked, her eyes full of avid interest.

"You bet your ass I am." The woman smiled. "Just as soon as I can."

Curiosity piqued, Dani spoke up. "What are you two so excited about?"

Marge became animated. "Have you ever heard the song, '867-5309/Jenny'?" Dani nodded. "Well, it's real. Not as in that's the actual number, but there's a place you *can* call for a good time."

"She's right. A very, very good time." Foil head piped up. The wealthy woman, who owned a few horses and raced them at the Saratoga Race Course, known as the "Track" to locals, looked more like something out of a sci-fi movie than a high-society one.

Dani wasn't sure what to make of their goings-on, but that didn't mean she didn't want to find out. "Care to share your secret?" She smiled sweetly. Her mother had insisted she be polite and "act like a young lady should" in every circumstance.

The client smirked at her in the mirror. "I'm not sure you can afford that much..." she paused before continuing. "Uh..." She lowered her voice. "Attention. Whatever you need. That is, if you like women." She pulled her wallet from beneath the cape and rummaged until she found a black matte finish business card with white lettering and handed it to her. "You'll have to save a year of tips, honey, but it'll be worth it if you do." The woman's smile was a bit smug with some mischief mixed in.

Dani cringed at the lipstick smeared on the woman's teeth. The card had two lines. *The Agency* and a phone number. Now her curiosity was all in. Women. Maybe this was her lucky day after all. She tucked the card in her pocket. "Thanks."

"Oh, honey, you don't have to thank me. You'll be thanking whoever shows up. Trust me." She laughed.

For the next hour, Dani tried to keep her focus on the head in front of her. Rinse, wash. *Women.* Apply toner. *Sex.* Cut and style. The tingling returned. The card felt hot against her skin, but that was impossible. Wasn't it? Finally done, she rang the woman up. "That's one forty-eight."

The woman produced her credit card then pulled a fifty out of her wallet. "I'd like to contribute to your fund." She waggled her brows, and Dani laughed before taking the money.

"I appreciate the donation."

The woman grasped her hand. "Don't be afraid to make the call. I'm sorry I didn't do it sooner." She started to turn away. "Please don't share that with anyone else. The business runs on a referral only basis and each client can refer only once. You're mine."

Dani stared after her. The fantasies she'd been having were becoming more vivid. More real. Without anyone to act them out with she was in a constant state of arousal and her frustration level was through the roof. Mark had warned her to stop trolling bars because the kind of woman she was looking for wouldn't be there. Even in today's culture with the popularity of queer-friendly establishments, the old standards still sometimes rang true with straight men who thought two femmes getting it on was hot, but two androgynous or butch women were not, simply because they threatened their masculinity. So, she'd taken Mark's advice and started picturing the future and what she wanted it to look like instead of carousing on her own.

Problem one: she didn't even know if she'd like having sex with a woman, though as each day passed she doubted that was true. Problem two: she had no clue what she wanted life to look like tomorrow, not to mention a year from now. While she wanted her growing physical needs remedied, Dani would someday like to have what other couples were making happen. A stable job, a nice place to live, someone to share the highs and the lows that life presented and having fun doing it. For now, she'd push the distant future to the background and focus on today.

She pulled the card from her pocket and ran her fingertip over the embossed print. Even the texture was enticing. *For Christ's sake.* She had to get a grip. Dani tapped the card one more time and slipped it into the slot on the case of her phone. The idea of soliciting someone to deliver her dark fantasies excited her in a way she'd never thought possible because she still wondered if her fantasies would ever happen or if they would remain elusive. And for every reason she found to pursue sexual fulfillment, she questioned if she'd have the nerve to express her desires when, or if, the time came. It was the idea of telling someone what she wanted and *how* she wanted it that made her think it wouldn't happen.

She stuck the fifty-dollar bill next to the card. If her client was telling the truth, she was going to have to do a lot of ass kissing in the next few weeks if she had any hope of making a call to the Agency.

❖

Ryan wasn't herself. Some vital part of her orderly and precisely balanced world had tilted off its axis and the feeling was disconcerting. She stared at Drake while she talked with the bartender who knew them both by name. Drake's long blond hair and piercing green eyes might have confused some people at first glance, but the well-tailored suits, lean body, and lack of an Adam's apple should have made it clear she was a woman. Ryan didn't even need to mention her ever-present swagger, a dead giveaway to her androgyny. She often teased her about being a female version of Chris Hemsworth or a young version of Brad Pitt. Naked, there was no mistaking Drake was all woman, and she garnered a fair share of gasps in the women's locker room at the gym whenever she strode from the shower, unashamed by her body on display.

When she took the stool next to her, Drake pulled her close and whispered in her ear. "When was the last time you fucked purely for pleasure without your head caught up in how a woman's talents stood up to the caliber of the Agency?" Drake let go and sipped her bourbon. Jazz music played in the background soft and seductive with a hint of anticipation.

"It's been a while." Why Ryan had agreed to double-date with her best friend was still a mystery. She didn't date. Ryan made an appointment, sometimes with dinner as a prelude, but the end result was always the same—a satisfying orgasm, or two. That's how it ended. Always how it ended. A little polite conversation because she wasn't a neanderthal, but she refrained from snuggling while in a satiated state, and definitely didn't engage in small talk. Uncomplicated, just the way she liked it. She would have liked some kink now and then, but the kind she craved was passionate, intimate, amazing sex and for that to happen, at least for her, she'd need to *know* the woman, not just fuck her. Unlike many of her clients, who just wanted the fantasy without the emotion.

Somewhere among the years that had unceremoniously ticked by, sex had become a necessity rather than a pleasurable interlude. Gone were the days when heat and passion drove her to find a way to curb her insatiable lust and appetite to give and take satisfaction, however she found it. Somehow, she'd lost that edge, the drive that she craved to experience. When she was younger and sex was an uninhibited exploration, she thought the girls she slept with were interested in *her*. They'd mostly just wanted a victory, having slept with someone who looked like she did and who was unafraid to ride edges most women backed away from. A lot of those women were married thrill seekers, or virtual virgins, or had never had an orgasm. Those were things she and Drake knew how to give.

She got her MBA degree as was expected of her, and though she hadn't minded because her adoptive parents had given her a much different life from the one she'd gotten accustomed to as a child, she didn't want the same things her adoptive siblings had wanted. Oh, she'd gladly taken her family's monetary gifts, before working her ass off to establish the Agency. Sex was always in demand, and having places to go for satisfaction went as far back to ancient Rome, but Ryan and Drake had a vision of what a modern, safe place to explore sexuality and sensuality of every level would look like, and it had turned into something so grand she was still in awe.

Disconnection had to be part of the service she provided because getting personally involved with clients was forbidden, a rule she'd instituted from the start. But with that disconnection came disinterest and what she once found exciting now felt mechanical.

"Want to tell me why you haven't been with anyone in a while?" Drake wouldn't back down.

She finished her twenty-one-year-old scotch. "I've become complacent about sex. It's remote." Ryan glanced away. "I feel..." That was the problem, she didn't feel anything.

Drake nodded, her gaze empathetic. "How long have I known you? A couple of decades?"

"Sounds right." She motioned to the bartender. Deep discussions were less painful when her conscience was dulled a little.

"In all that time, I've only once ever seen you emotionally stirred by a woman, not ones you've slept with outside of the business. Why?"

Her breath froze in her chest. Pain—like the kind that made her wish, if only for a minute, Drake hadn't gone there. Hadn't awakened her deepest secrets. She was bleeding in front of the one person she didn't want to ever again witness her agony. Being Ryan's friend at a time when Ryan cared about nothing and no one had cost Drake something, though she denied the emotional scars left in its wake.

After all this time the driving force to live a charmed life was slowly being drained from her. Ryan had hoped she'd mastered the disconnect that had been her shield against anything or *anyone* touching her. Drake grabbed her arm, worry transforming her usual serene features into pinched concern.

"Ryan. Ryan, I'm sorry. I would have never—"

"It's okay." She heard herself say as she pulled away from the memory. "It was a long time ago, though I don't care to relive it." That was the single most honest thing she'd ever shared with anyone, or ever would.

"Fuck," Drake mumbled under her breath.

She squeezed Drake's shoulder. "Don't worry about it, Drake. You weren't wrong. I don't let myself connect to women." She forced a grin she didn't feel. "That doesn't mean I don't enjoy them. Isn't that why we're here?"

"Yeah."

"I can't wait to see the woman you've chosen for me." Ryan laughed when Drake cocked a brow.

"I'll be interested in finding out how I did. But since they're here, that conversation will have to wait."

Drake went to greet the two women who stood at the entrance of the posh lounge located on the first floor of the Adelphi Hotel. Both women were beautiful. The taller of the two was blond, with high, firm breasts and long, lean legs. A classic beauty. The other woman exuded darkness. Short, black hair, dark eyes outlined with just enough makeup that said, "I dare you." Her alabaster skin was a vivid contrast to the black outfit. Her body compact, though not in an unappealing way. She looked a bit dangerous. Drake's type. Ryan emptied her glass and stood.

"Ryan, this is Carol." Drake indicated the blonde.

Ryan took the woman's hand. "Hello."

Drake wrapped her arm around Carol's waist and pulled her closer before turning toward the other woman. "And this is Trish."

Trish held out her hand as her gaze traveled along Ryan's body before their eyes met.

"My pleasure, I'm sure." Trish's voice was deeper than expected. Her eye color was hard to discern in the muted light, blue bordering on midnight maybe.

Her clit was already hard, pressed beneath the material of her Jockeys. Something about Trish warned her against familiar touching. The clear signal of being a femme top stirred her lower belly into a tight knot. Ryan didn't like to give up control and had rarely ever let anyone take what they wanted from her. Maybe it was time she did. "Would you like a drink before dinner?" She kept the tone of her voice cool. Aloof. Inside, every nerve twitched with unexpected longing.

"Whatever you're having is fine." Trish slid her hand away, but not before the tip of her middle finger drew a line of fire down the center of her palm.

"Scotch."

One brow rose on Trish's otherwise composed face. "Not blended, I hope."

She laughed, the tension in her body easing a bit. "No. Never." Trish nodded. She turned to Drake and her date. "Drinks?"

"None for me." Drake didn't like having sex with an alcohol buzz, except on rare occasions.

"Pinot Grigio, please." Carol smiled, then glanced at Drake.

Ryan internally grinned. Drake was going to take everything Carol had to offer, and then some. She could only imagine what was in store for her.

CHAPTER FOUR

After a leisurely dinner where Ryan let her mind drift and didn't think about anything but enjoying the banter going around the table, Drake handed her a key card.

"Have fun for a change."

The heat in Trish's open appraisal wasn't meant to be missed and she led her to the elevator alongside Drake and Carol. As they stood in silence, she wondered if this interlude, with this woman, would reestablish her equilibrium. A mirthless tone announced their arrival and while Drake and her date turned left, she turned right.

As the door swung in, she took a breath and told herself there wasn't any reason not to enjoy what was about to happen. Sex often settled her and what better way than with someone who didn't know her and didn't need to for what would take place between them. Casual, uncomplicated, unemotional sex. That's all she needed.

"Can I get you anything?"

Trish's brow lifted and her eyes narrowed. "All I need is a bed, with you naked in it," she said, then produced leather wrist cuffs from her oversized bag. "And these."

Her body tensed. Control was her thing, even Drake knew that. Yet, Drake had matched Trish with her for a reason. She didn't switch often and never with a client. She could hear Drake's voice telling her tonight was for personal pleasure, and maybe if she let someone else, someone who she'd probably never see again, take control, she would let go of whatever *else* was bothering her. It didn't take her long to get into position.

Despite the cool, luxurious sheet beneath her, Ryan's body was covered in a fine layer of sweat. She didn't struggle against the restraints wrapped around her wrists and ankles and secured to the opulent four-poster bed. It took her even less time to admit being in the unfamiliar position was exciting, as was finding out that Trish's idea of fun meant teasing her into submission. Her blood raced through her veins and the sensation pushed her to *want* to let go and enjoy what Trish was offering.

"You can always use your safe word. There's no shame in knowing your limit." Trish ran the tip of her finger along the throbbing shaft of her clit, just enough to make her breath catch.

"I doubt you'll ever hear me say it, but you're welcome to try." She'd told Trish her word when they'd started, as she had with other women who thought they could break her. None had succeeded, and Ryan had no intention of giving in tonight, even as her body trembled with need. She'd fought against coming so many times already she wasn't sure she'd ever come again. Trish laughed. Confident and masterful, Trish had what it took to be a great top and she considered how well she might fit in at the Agency. She laughed to herself. Drake had said as much. That was just before Trish began to jerk her off in stops and starts. The lack of rhythm drove her closer to the edge. Searing heat ran down her legs. The battle was lost. She focused on Trish's hot gaze and exploded, covering Trish's hand with her essence, her legs steel against the soft bedding. All without a sound.

Trish straddled her hips and leaned close. "Damn. I've never watched anyone come so hard without losing control. You're good, Ryan. Very good. Drake warned me."

She swallowed, took a breath, and ignored how much she wanted her hands free. She needed to fuck Trish into oblivion and take her to the place she'd just been. She didn't do it often, but for tonight she could switch. "What did Drake warn you about?"

Trish played her fingers up her chest and flicked her thumbs over her tight nipples. "That you never give up control, not completely anyway." She leaned close. "I could never resist a challenge," she said just before their lips met.

Her mouth was hot and sweet, and Ryan pictured what it would be like to have that mouth on her cock if she were wearing it.

"I could tell. Untie me."

There must have been something in her tone that moved Trish into action. She sat up and rubbed her wrists, the return of circulation painful, but tolerable. Trish sat off to the side watching her every move.

"I hope you didn't expect to be the only one to have fun tonight." Ryan flipped her onto her back and pinned her down with her body. "What's your safe word?"

Trish's eyes grew large, inquisitive, but without fear. "Would you believe 'pansy'?"

She stopped herself before she snorted. "Whatever works for you." She ran her teeth down the column of her neck, bit at the hollow of her throat. Ryan covered Trish's swollen lips with her mouth and savored the taste of her until they were both breathless before she rolled her onto her stomach. Once she was tied facedown, she went to her bag, then pulled on her harnessed cock. A condom, lighter, and a white candle was all she needed.

"Is there anything you don't want me to do?"

Trish turned her head to be heard. "Don't make me bleed, and I don't like gags."

She stood at the foot of the bed. Her body had quieted, but her need grew exponentially, like her clit had in anticipation, and she wanted to take Trish to the place where the external world faded away until there was nothing but the sensations of her body and the disconnection of floating outside of herself. She straddled Trish's slender thighs, sharply slapping each cheek of her ass with enough force to make them pink. "Such a pretty color," she said as she smoothed her hand over the heated flesh. Once the candle was lit, she trailed wax one drop at a time from the small of her back to her shoulder blades and back down. Trish's moan was pleasure-laden, and Ryan's center stirred to life. Moisture pooled beneath her cock.

"Do you like that?" Her voice was thick.

"Yes, Master."

Ryan hadn't been addressed as a dominant in a very long time, and Trish doing so sent a shiver up her spine. She nipped at the tender flesh of her neck and painted a thin line of wax from the spot to the cleft of her ass. When Trish wriggled in response and with the candle nearly spent, she untied her legs. "Up on your knees for me. Show me your dripping pussy." Trish groaned and she helped her into position after loosening her wrists. She pulled her ass closer. "Head down, baby."

Trish's glistening center was on full display, and Ryan slapped her thighs before pressing her thick cock all the way in. Trish trembled beneath her. Ryan withdrew completely, then gathered moisture on her finger and traced Trish's puckered entrance, making her momentarily clench and Ryan's body shuddered at the natural instinct. Trish pressed back against her thighs, in a show of supplication and she pushed her fingertip inside. Her sex tightened when Trish took her deeper, but Ryan was leading now, and she still wanted to fuck her.

This time she entered her hot pussy fast and hard, making them both grunt. She was so close to climaxing she stilled. She didn't want to come. It wasn't her style or her preference. A sub always came first, literally and figuratively. After a mental check, her strokes shortened and the thrusts deepened, and Trish moaned and pleaded to be taken harder. Harder.

"Do not come until I tell you." Sweat dripped from her chin and splashed onto the wax pooled on Trish's back. Every time Trish's pussy tried to pull her in, Ryan backed away. Trish began to beg, her voice a strangled, whimpering sound amid the noise of flesh meeting flesh. Edging was one of Ryan's favorite forms of play, and since Trish had so thoroughly done with Ryan, it was only fair she returned the favor.

"Please, Master. I want to come." Trish tried to slam her ass against her, but Ryan was ready for her and held her away. "I *need* to come. Oh, God." Trish sobbed.

To her credit, she didn't halt their play, but Ryan knew she was a hair's breadth away. "So needy," Ryan rasped as she entered her hard and began stroking her clit, sending Trish tumbling over in a torrent of shouts and making Ryan's climax that much sweeter.

After removing the restraints, she gathered Trish's limp body into her arms as she whimpered and shuddered. "You're okay. I've got you." Ryan held her close, rubbed her back, soothed her body.

A short time later, Trish looked up. "What the hell did you do to me?" Her voice was raw.

"I gave you what I thought you wanted. If I hurt you, I apologize, but you could have stopped me." She ran her fingertip down Trish's cheek and followed the edge of her jaw.

"I couldn't even if I wanted to. It was too good. *You* were too good to stop." Trish ran a shaky hand through her sweat-soaked hair.

"As long as you're satisfied." Ryan thought back, way back, to the time when she'd been where Trish was now. Her dom had taken her to the edge in so many ways, so many times, that she'd come for what felt like hours. Even thinking of it now, her body stirred.

Trish kissed her softly. "I may not be able to move tomorrow, but I'm good."

With the intensity of their shared sexual appetites Ryan wondered if perhaps she'd found that connection Drake had asked about. As Trish lay against her still recovering, the answer was the same as the last few years. Physically, she always connected with the women she shared a bed with, but emotionally, the walls remained. Besides, how long would it be before the mere nature of her business and the work it entailed caused her partner to grow jealous, or vindictive over the women she slept with, though she hadn't taken on a client in a while. Her life was too complicated and too intense for most women to handle. Sooner or later they all walked away.

Dani poured coffee as she ran through her day's agenda, her game plan solid. Sitting at the counter, she watched the scene outside her window, which wasn't something she often thought of. Her neighbor across the courtyard rarely opened his curtains. As imaginative as she was, Dani conjured up all types of nefarious reasons for his actions, or lack of. Maybe he worked nights and slept days or was involved in a life of crime that he didn't want anyone to witness. Perhaps there was a bevy of lovers who had a lot to lose if discovered. Any life was more exciting than the one she was living.

She hadn't dated in months, and she wasn't looking for a relationship. The tight control of her parents, though intellectually different from that of a partner, had left her resistant to the confines a commitment would require. She was just beginning to enjoy the freedom of exploring who she was, and she wasn't about to give that up anytime soon. Her night out with Mark proved one thing. She wanted to experience being with women physically, if not emotionally, and she wasn't going to waste any more time staring out her window in hopes of finding some excitement.

"Christ." She needed to get a life. Her gaze fell on the business card tucked under the lip magnet on her refrigerator. "Fuck it." She keyed in the numbers, wishing there had been information available on the internet, but every search was a dead end. The Agency was likely a farce, but if that was true why had her client been so adamant about keeping it a secret? She felt a little guilty for not telling Mark, but after his repeated warning about sleeping with strangers she didn't want to hear it all again. It was time to act, not crawl under a rock and wait. She was done waiting. After several rings, a female voice greeted her.

"Good morning. This is the Agency. How may we help you?" asked the woman.

Dani hadn't planned on talking with a real person since most businesses had converted to robotic menus of "press one for this, press two for that" and so on. Her mind was a blank as she came up with a reason she'd broken down and called. Nothing felt normal about this call, but normal was the last thing she wanted. "I'm inquiring about the services you offer."

"Certainly. I'm Anna. Please provide your name, phone number, and the name of the person who referred you."

She gave the information and waited. The polite woman on the other end was definitely all business. Dani wasn't sure what she'd expected but she vibrated in her seat in anticipation. She was really going to do this. *Jesus.*

"Excuse me, Ms. Brown. I didn't quite catch what you were saying."

"Oh, sorry. Just thinking out loud." Dani shook her head as she face-palmed.

"It happens," Anna said kindly. "Here we are. Your referral is confirmed. Now, what would you like to know?"

"I hate to start off with the obvious, but what are your fees?"

"I assure you, Ms. Brown, being cost-conscious in today's world is an admirable trait. Our fees are based on the service required. The range is fifteen hundred to ten thousand dollars. You won't really know until you speak with Ms. Lewis, our CEO. She personally screens every inquiry. If you'd like to proceed, I can take your basic information over the phone. We believe personalized communication is much more pleasant than animated electronics."

She couldn't agree more. Yet, as her blood raced through her and her belly tightened, she hesitated.

"If you're still unsure about moving forward, we'd like you to know we provide an unconditional guarantee. If you decide to cancel at any time before the actual meeting, we charge a one-hundred-dollar cancellation fee. No questions asked."

Dani let out the breath she'd held. The last thing she wanted to do was pass out. "That's generous. What about after the actual meeting? What if that doesn't go well?"

"The Agency takes pride in satisfying our clients. We've never had anyone request a refund."

"Ever?"

"Ever, Ms. Brown. Would you like to proceed?"

Fifteen minutes later, she hung up after Anna assured her she would receive an email confirmation of her personal information and a release to her health care provider for proof of HIV and other communicable disease test results. Dani would also have a receipt for the one-hundred-dollar deposit, along with the reassurance that Ms. Lewis would contact her within twenty-four hours. Heat curled in her abdomen, the kind that wasn't going to go away. Anna had answered a few of her questions, including the assured health of all of the escorts, but mostly she deferred to the follow-up call. Now all she had to do was wait. She flicked her gaze to the clock and started. Where had the time gone? But she knew. She'd been fantasizing what she wanted out of this adventure. Anna encouraged her to not hold back. To speak her truth and give details because that was how the Agency guaranteed she'd be satisfied.

She snagged the grocery list off the fridge and found her keys. Groceries were on her to-do list, and just because she was going to make a date to have sex with a woman she didn't know, didn't mean she should starve herself, although a glance in the mirror made her think twice. *I'm fine.* And she was. She had curves and not one of the questions she answered had to do with her physical appearance. They centered around her overall health, mental status, and reason for calling. She'd been impressed by the respect she'd been shown. For the amount they charged she didn't expect anything less.

Applicant #04282. Ryan rubbed her eyes. She'd been at the computer way too long. Thinking about a meal and a drink, she almost left it for tomorrow until she caught a tag line, "Fantasy and lesbian virgin." Her heart did an extra beat. It was seven forty-five. If she opened the file, she'd do the interview. Another hour. Sighing, Ryan clicked on the intake summary for client Daniella, aka Dani, Brown. The information didn't delve into specifics on the services desired. It contained enough information for the investigators and nothing more. She forwarded the one-page document to the private investigation team she kept on retainer. They'd conduct a thorough investigation into databases containing both public and private information, such as criminal records, lawsuits, and the like. Ryan refocused on the contact information. Bluetooth headset in place, she punched in the number.

"Hello?" The voice on the other end was tentative.

"Good evening. Is this Daniella Brown?"

"Speaking."

"Excellent. This is Ryan Lewis, CEO of the Agency. Is this a good time for you to talk?" She smiled at the sound of fast breathing coming over the line.

"Just a minute please."

She scrolled through the intake again and committed a few details to memory. A click announced the client had returned.

"I'm ready when you are."

Ryan cocked a brow. If Ms. Brown knew how ready Ryan always was, she wondered if she'd continue talking with her. "What type of services are you looking for, Ms. Brown?"

"I'm not sure what you mean?"

"Are you looking for a dinner companion? Someone to accompany you to an event? Or a woman to fulfill another type of need, such as a fantasy or sexual encounter?"

"No beating around the bush then. Pardon the expression," Daniella said.

Her words were refreshing. Most first-timers were tentative. "I find small talk a waste of time when we would eventually have to broach the reason for your inquiry. It's important for me to understand your particular needs."

"Dinner would be a nice way to start, but what I'm really looking for is to live out a particular fantasy, if possible."

"Let me assure you," Ryan said. "Anything is possible, if you want it enough." Her imagination stirred. "What's your fantasy?"

Daniella's inhalation traveled over the airwaves. "Having sex with a woman."

"Just sex? That's not really a fantasy," she said. "It's more of a desire."

"Not just sex. Tie me down, fuck me hard, make me scream kind of sex. Can you provide that?"

"Not only can we provide it, we can guarantee it. We'll need to discuss the specifics of your desire at some point. For instance, whether you want a full bondage experience which includes being tied down with elements of sensation exploration, pain, or tied down without anything else."

"Oh." Daniella's voice held surprise. "I guess that would be good to know."

This time the anxious undertone was unmistakable. "I have a two-day mandatory waiting period before I confirm the availability of an escort. During that time there will be a criminal background and extensive personal history check. If you have any objection to our policy, I need to know now."

"Except for a few parking tickets and a disorderly conduct during high school, I've nothing to hide."

"Very good, Ms. Brown. Do you have a date and time in mind?"

"I'm not comfortable bringing a total stranger into my home."

Ryan smiled. Curious, cautious, and witty. The combination was impossible to ignore. "We will provide you with a safe space and I assure you there's nothing to be afraid of aside from your nerves. Are you available on Monday evening at six for dinner and your pleasure?"

"Uh, I…hold on please while I check my work schedule." A few minutes later, Daniella returned. "Yes, that's fine."

"Very good. I'm going to email you a file containing pictures of our escorts. You can ask me questions about whomever you like, except personal or identifying information. Is that clear?"

"Yes."

Ryan opened a new email with her standard greeting, attached her employee photos, and hit send. "I would suggest you view the document on a computer rather than your phone."

"Already logged on." There were several distinctive mouse clicks in the background, followed by a gasp.

"Is everything all right, Ms. Brown?"

"It's Dani. I'm fine. I just…never mind. Can I have a minute, please?"

"Of course. Take whatever time you need." Ryan reviewed the next week's calendar while she waited with the escorts' information on the screen. Hers was still there and she thought about why she hadn't removed it. It had been a while since she'd personally taken a client and that had been for logistical reasons. She didn't like turning away anyone who had a need to be fulfilled.

"Ms. Lewis?"

"Yes?"

"How tall is number four?" Dani asked.

Shit. "Five foot eleven, one hundred seventy pounds," she said as she described herself, although she was closer to one hundred sixty-five at the moment. Her appetite wasn't what it once was, but she continued to work out six days a week.

"And will she provide what I want?"

More than you could ever possibly imagine. "Absolutely. I wouldn't have included her if she couldn't, though you should take your time and review each photo again before you decide."

"I'm already sure."

Ryan silently sighed. "Very well."

"I might want to see other women, too," Dani said confidently.

"I would encourage you to do so. Especially since you may not realize how much variety is available to you." She was relieved to hear she wasn't locked in. There were rare occasions when a client was actually looking for a part-time lover and became somewhat possessive of their escort. In those instances, Ryan stepped in and ended their contract.

"I'll text you her first name as soon as you've cleared our background check. Then we can discuss your kink needs." Ryan didn't believe she'd be ready for everything on the first night, but Dani wasn't the only one curious.

"Ms. Lewis?"

"Yes?"

"I need to know how to pay and how much?"

Wondering what the woman did for a living to make her concerned about the cost, Ryan answered as honestly as possible. "It usually depends on the service provided. I would plan on two thousand. Tips are optional." She thought she heard swearing. "Is that a problem?"

"Jesus. Sorry. That's a lot. I may have to wait to do this." Disappointment creeped into Dani's voice.

For some reason she wasn't willing to examine, Ryan softened. "Don't be too hasty, okay? I'll give you a definite number when I text you." She heard Dani blow out a breath. "Good night, Ms. Brown."

"Good night."

❖

"What do you think you're doing?" Drake's voice rose above her normal calm cadence.

Inside, Ryan was an exposed electric wire in a pool of water that sparked and jumped. "You're the one who asked when was the last time I'd felt anything other than an orgasm."

Drake scoffed. "You haven't even met her. How do you know you will?"

She stood to pace, not understanding any of her actions when it came to Daniella Brown, or how her body reacted to the thought of being the one to fulfill her fantasy. She turned to Drake. "I'll never know if I don't go."

"It's foolhardy and you know it. Send someone else. If she's that important to you, send me. Then you won't have to ignore your rule about dating clients."

Jealousy flared white hot. "It's not a date for Christ's sake. I just said there was something about her that interested me. I'm not asking her to marry me." She had no rational reason to be angry, but she was. "I'm still the CEO. I decide if and when a client is scheduled. And with whom. I'm sure you remember that little detail, Drake."

"Oh, so you're going to pull that card? With me?" Drake's eyes were molten, a mix of fury and disappointment. "Just listen to yourself. What reason could you possibly have for taking on a client after all this time?"

"That's the exact reason. Because for the first time in a long time I actually *want* to."

Drake's face turned impassive. "You're acting like you did with Sarah. The only difference is Dani's a client."

The pain in Drake's eyes couldn't have been clearer if she fell to the floor writhing in agony. Of all the people in the world she might have had a valid reason to be angry with, Drake was the last one she wanted to hurt. Ryan clasped her shoulder, pulled her close. "You know I love you. Trust me when I say this is something I have to do. Trish woke the beast inside, but she's only brought her out of hibernation. I need…" Ryan shook her head. "I want to keep her out for a while." The mix of emotions she saw in Drake's eyes was disconcerting. There was no question why she was so opposed to Ryan taking on Dani as a client, but she never wanted to fuck up the one good thing in her life.

Drake took a step back. "I can't stop you." She let out a bitter laugh. "No one can. I just hope you know what you're doing." She closed the door without looking back.

"So do I," Ryan said to the empty room. Behind the security of her desk, she brought up the file. "Well, Ms. Brown. Let's see if I can make you an offer you can't refuse."

Chapter Five

Dani, can you come here?" Pam, her friend, and coworker, called to her. "What do you think?" Pam was doing a fade on a young man who looked like a movie star.

"A little tighter here with a sharp line there."

Pam executed the cut and the customer smiled in the mirror. "Perfect."

Her pocket vibrated and she excused herself, stepping out to the alley for a breath of something other than bleach, dye, and perming solution. "Hello?"

"Good afternoon, Ms. Brown. This is Ryan Lewis, from the Agency. I hope I'm not disturbing you."

"You aren't." Dani waited. The voice on the phone was the same clear alto, smooth and commanding, that she remembered. She tried to imagine what the woman looked like, but she had little in the way of reference. The CEO of the escort service she'd managed to find her way to would remain a mystery.

"You've cleared our background check and I've scheduled your escort for Monday at six o'clock. She'll be driving a white Audi and will pick you up at your home."

Dani bit her lip. She hated to press the issue, but she needed to know. "You said you'd give me her name and the fee."

"Indeed I did. Your escort is Ryan, and the fee is one thousand dollars. At the end of the evening, she will ask if you were satisfied with the outcome. Depending on your answer, the office will complete the transaction the following morning using the card you provided during the intake."

"All very professional and cold."

"Ms. Brown—"

"Dani. Please."

"Dani, there will be nothing cold about the evening ahead. The level of heat obtained is entirely up to you."

"You're right." She didn't have a reason to be short with the CEO. She was only telling Dani what she needed to know.

"You mentioned you wanted to be tied down and fucked hard, but it would be helpful to have details."

She wasn't sure where the conversation was going. "Like what?"

"Have you thought about the type of bondage you want to engage in? Are you interested in floggers or paddles, or something more intense like crops, breath play, suspension? Other types of stimulation? Other sensations?"

"Jesus." Dani's hand trembled as she wiped her forehead, but the stirring in her belly wasn't fear. It was excitement.

"Have I misunderstood what you wanted?" Ryan asked, her voice empathetic.

Dani blew out a breath. How could she even begin to describe what she didn't know. "No, no. I just…I want to try it all." She laughed nervously. "Well, maybe not all." She groaned at her own ineptitude to describe her wants. "This is a lot harder than I thought."

"You don't have to decide now, but I do want you to think about a safe word. It should be something you wouldn't normally think of, especially during sex. You can tell your escort when she asks."

"Fine," she said in a clipped tone. "I'm sorry. I just…I've never done…" God, she was making a mess of things.

"It's all right, Dani. Nerves are to be expected. I just hope you're relaxed enough to enjoy your evening. In case you were wondering, cocktail attire would be appropriate. If you have any questions, just call the office."

There were at least a million things floating around in her head, but she wasn't about to share them with the woman on the phone. She should say something, though what did you say to a woman asking about your level of kink? *Thanks for whipping me into shape?* She slapped her hand over her mouth to stifle the laugh. "Thank you."

"Good night, Dani."

For fuck's sake. Her hand shook so badly she had a hard time getting her phone into her back pocket. She needed to talk to someone. Mark was the only person she could confide in. The only one who would understand the act of a desperate woman yearning to be taken to places she'd never been by another woman. She closed her eyes and the woman from the bar zoomed into view, looking right at her, knowing each one of her desires.

"Dani?" Pam called out the back door. "Your three o'clock is here."

She took a breath, then another. That talk with Mark would have to wait. "Thanks, Pam. I'll be right in." Smoothing her hands down her pants, she concentrated all her energy on the woman sitting in her chair instead of thinking about the gorgeous woman she'd picked as her escort.

Ryan pulled the Audi to the curb and cut the engine. The apartment complex sat in a modest neighborhood of Ballston Spa and appeared well-tended with large clay pots filled with colorful flowers on the top step of each entryway. This residence wasn't anything like the flamboyant homes of the rich women who frequently used their services, but then Dani wasn't anything like those women either, as far as she could tell from the background report. She mentally pulled up short, then shook her head. Since when had she become so opinionated like a majority of her clientele? Her childhood served to remind her that being an elite snob wasn't who she was…or who she wanted to be.

As she exited, she threw off the persona of an executive and took on the demeanor of escort. She strode purposefully up the walk. Movement at the window caught her attention, and she suppressed her smile. Ryan took a steadying breath, then rang the bell. She didn't know what to expect. Dani had the advantage of having her picture first, but Ryan had done a little recognizance and found a Facebook account. The picture of Dani had been at a distance and blurry, but her posts were bold and playful, like the direct, open conversation they had. Nothing out of the ordinary. Dani might not have been able to give explicit details about the type of interactions she wanted, but that hadn't dissuaded her from expressing herself. Somehow this stranger had reached inside of Ryan and stirred her dormant need to connect. Be that as it may, whether she was personally intrigued by Dani or not played no part in the evening ahead.

The door swung inward, and the sound Dani made was one of surprise. Her hand trembled at her side. The scent of her perfume was light and fresh like a mountain spring in winter. Her makeup was reserved, defining her bone structure. The mascara she wore only highlighted her light brown eyes, as did a fine stroke of eyeliner. It suited her. Her brown hair hung in loose waves over her bare shoulders. Ryan liked seeing her natural beauty shine through. Dani might not be considered a runway model, but she was pretty in an understated way.

"Dani?"

"Yes," she said, her voice low and strained.

"I'm Ryan." When their hands touched Dani paled, and she was afraid she might faint. "Are you all right?"

Dani blinked several times, seeming to refocus. "Your picture doesn't do you justice." She let go of her hand and stepped back. "Is this okay?" Dani smoothed her hands over her sides.

The mid-calf silk dress with embroidered red rose petals hugged her generous curves in all the right places, and Ryan briefly pictured her not wearing anything at all. Ryan wanted to touch her. "You're beautiful."

A flush colored Dani's cheeks. "Thank you, but I'm not sure I agree."

Ryan stepped forward, wrapped her arm around Dani's waist, and pulled her in. "We can skip dinner if you'd like me to show you just how beautiful you are." She brushed her lips against Dani's ear, her breath moving tendrils of hair from her neck, making her shiver.

Dani sucked in a breath before gently putting her hand on her chest, pushing her away.

"I believe dinner was supposed to happen first." Her eyes flashed with determination.

She would have to be careful and keep a tight rein on her control. Attraction she understood, but this hard flare of heat and desire to take Dani where she stood was strong. Dani was a virgin with women, and she had an obligation to remember that. "I believe dinner was *requested*." She offered her arm. "Shall we?"

Dani picked up a matching shawl and small clutch, then slid her hand until she grasped her forearm. The move was possessive, and the contact jolted her as her clit surged.

Once in the car, Ryan attempted to clear her mind, but it refused to settle. How far did Dani's fantasies go, and how could she fulfill them? Excitement coursed through her. Even if she didn't climax, which she rarely allowed when she worked, she'd experience a euphoric state that couldn't be matched in any other situation. She would provide what Dani wanted and show her how different being intimate with another woman was. After all, it was a skill she'd honed since following her attraction for girls in high school. She glanced across the console, the tension from Dani palpable.

"Are you comfortable? I could adjust the temperature."

Dani stared straight ahead. "No. I'm fine." Her eyes squeezed shut and she took a shuddery breath. "That's not true. I'm not fine at all."

"What's wrong?"

"I don't know what's going to happen tonight." Dani was pale and breathing quickly, her voice strained.

Ryan took pity on her and reached across the space between them to touch Dani's hand liking how smooth and small it was. "Nothing you don't want, and everything you do."

Dani laughed nervously. "You make it sound so simple."

"That's because it is."

"I'm glad one of us is so sure." Dani glanced over. "That's why you're employed by the Agency, right?"

"I started the business, Ms. Brown. I'm quite capable of entertaining you for the evening."

Dani sucked in a breath and her eyes grew big. "You're *that* Ryan?"

She tipped her head in acknowledgment. "At your service." Ryan chuckled as Dani stared at her, her mouth open in surprise. "Is that going to be a problem?"

"I…no. I didn't think you'd be having se—" Dani didn't finish.

"I happen to like sex very much, Dani." She pulled the car in front of Siro's. "But first, we're going to have dinner and conversation." Ryan got out when the valet opened her door. She wondered if Drake had been right because for the first time in ages, she wasn't sure what the hell she was doing. Or why.

Dani studied Ryan's strong, handsome features as she exited the car. Her short, dark hair accentuated her slightly almond shaped eyes and high cheekbones. Her lips weren't plump but full, and she wondered what they would feel like pressed to her own.

A valet opened her door, and Ryan's waiting hand appeared. Long, somewhat slender fingers and a wide palm gently closed over hers.

"Have you ever been to Siro's, Dani?" Ryan's intense gaze met hers, and for a brief moment she wanted to know what she was seeing.

"No, I haven't, but I've heard of it. Fine dining is a luxury." She wasn't sure how much she should reveal about herself, but considering she was going to be naked with her in the not-too-distant future, it likely didn't matter.

"You deserve to treat yourself to the finer things in life." Ryan's tone was somber.

"Does tonight count?"

Ryan flashed a smile full of bright-white teeth, her intelligent eyes sparkling. "I hope so."

She stopped before they reached the door and studied her. "You aren't concerned about tonight at all, are you?" The air of confidence that enveloped Ryan spoke volumes, and while she was glad to not have to think about finding someone who knew what they were doing when it came to playing out her fantasies, her own ineptitude remained in question. Would she know how to touch Ryan? How different would it be to feel her climax? What would she see when she looked into Ryan's eyes in the throes of orgasm? They reminded her of deep pools of the clearest blue waters Dani had ever seen.

"No."

"Then I'll try not to be either."

"Ms. Lewis, it's a pleasure to see you again," the hostess said. "Please follow me."

Her pulse pounded in her neck so hard, she worried the vein might burst. Ryan held out her chair and waited until she was seated before sitting across from her. None of her previous dates had ever been as chivalrous. None of her dates had ever taken her to an expensive restaurant either. They settled at their table for two in a secluded niche away from prying eyes and she took the opportunity to consider her good fortune.

Ryan, the owner of the velvet smooth voice she'd heard on the phone, was sitting across from her…and they were going to have sex. Well, not in the restaurant of course, but at some point, it was going to happen. After all, that's what she was paying for. *Oh my God, I'm actually going to do this.* Her heart hammered hard in her chest. She'd been waiting for months, maybe years, to be in the arms of a woman. To be kissed and touched and fucked. She had no idea what sex with Ryan would be like, even after watching a couple of online videos. Then she'd searched the web and was amazed by the plethora of resources. But she wasn't sure how much stock to put in what she'd read or seen. Some of it seemed unrealistic. She almost laughed. How did anyone prepare for the unknown in situations like this? Maybe she should go into it more as an adventure without expectations. Yes. That's how she needed to think about tonight.

"Dani?"

"Hmm," she said. The heat in her face burned hot. She'd been caught daydreaming and desperately wanted to stay in the here and now.

"Would you care for something to drink?" Ryan asked.

"A gallon of anything would be good right about now." She smiled, more from nerves than anything. God, she was a mess.

Ryan's hand took hers. "I know tonight might feel a bit overwhelming, but it's something you wanted enough to contact us, and that took courage. I meant it when I said nothing will happen that you don't want." Ryan's eyes were full of empathy and understanding, yet when they moved from her eyes to her mouth, she also saw desire. The kind of desire she'd longed for in a bed partner.

"I appreciate your kindness, but that doesn't excuse my rude behavior." She slid her hand away, unable to concentrate with the warmth of Ryan's skin against hers. "I'd love some wine."

"Certainly."

She asked about several items on the menu then ordered their selections. Ryan appeared in her element. The lull in conversation gave her an opportunity to pull from what she knew she was capable of. After all, the salon was notorious for hearing a plethora of topics and she pulled something from that to talk about. "Have you done much traveling?" Small talk, but at least it was something.

Ryan sipped her wine. "Not in many years. The business is robust and there's a lot of moving parts to keep track of." She appeared to go elsewhere for a moment. "I'd like to at some point though."

She didn't miss the undercurrent of pensiveness and she wanted to chase away whatever was bothering her. "If I could afford it, I'd go somewhere warm in the winter."

"Tell me more."

Before long she was rambling on about all sorts of things. "My parents are conservative Catholics. Life growing up was fairly rigid. They felt the need to control everything I did."

"Were you a naughty girl, Dani?" Ryan's mouth quirked into a partial smile.

She laughed. "I probably would have been if given the chance." Dani considered what else she wanted to share. "I couldn't wait to get out from under their thumb and start living. If I hadn't, I think I might have gone a bit crazy."

"Is that why you called us? Because now you can explore things that were considered taboo?"

Ryan read her thoughts. She hoped she'd be able to do the same later when Dani might be too nervous to express herself. "Yes, it is."

"Then I'll make sure you have what you want. And what you need."

For some reason she didn't doubt Ryan would do just that. The rest of dinner was filled with enjoyable banter, though underlying it all was the anticipation of what would follow. Ryan was an excellent conversationalist with a wide and varied repertoire of topics, and as the evening progressed she relaxed more than she had on any previous dates. And she laughed. Ryan was charming. Had she ever been with anyone whose charisma seemed as natural? Even when they veered into topics that skirted her bedroom preferences the discussion was easy, and the notion of another boring horizontal night ahead where she would be left feeling unsatisfied vanished. The change was refreshing.

"I hope you can relax and enjoy our time together." Ryan's focused gaze bore into her.

It was time to get down to the details of the Agency's agreement. "How long…" Her voice broke, she glanced around to make sure no one could hear her and tried again. "How much time do we have?"

Ryan sat back, removed the napkin from her lap, then lay it on the table. "As long as it takes."

"For?"

"For you to be satisfied."

Dani watched Ryan's eyes reflect her own desires, hot and intense. There was nothing she could do to stop her body from reacting as her panties dampened. She almost wished she hadn't asked for dinner first.

The minute the words left her mouth, Ryan was more than ready to begin. Dani had requested dinner as part of her services, and from their conversation she guessed Dani had never been treated to a luxurious meal. The idea that people who dated were unwilling to expend a show of appreciation to their companions pissed her off. Women deserved to be treated as the gift they were, and while Ryan was part of the same population, she preferred to do the pampering.

To her surprise, Dani wasn't tentative or shy about being out with another woman. Though a bit reserved during casual conversation, Ryan read the curious glances for what she assumed they were—wide-eyed wonder for whatever secrets she might be prepared to share with her.

"Would you like coffee or dessert?" Ryan asked after Dani set her fork down, leaving a fair portion of her food on the plate. For herself, she'd stuck to a light seafood entree, not wanting to be too full to enjoy the rest of their evening.

Dani evenly met her gaze. "Yes, but not here."

Ryan's sex clenched. Dani was an enigma. Sometimes quiet and reserved, at others forward and forthright. "As you wish." She stood and held out her hand. Dani took it and she led her from the restaurant, exchanging well-wishes with the staff on the way out.

Dani pulled up short. "Aren't you going to pay for dinner?"

"No." She chuckled when Dani blanched. Ryan lifted her chin with her fingertips. "The Agency has a running account here. They'll be well paid for the meal."

"Does money provide privileges not offered to those without?"

It was a fair question. "Doesn't it always?" Still, the idea that she or her company were being judged based on the monetary value of what they did irked her. She wanted to call Dani on it. Tell her she had done much the same by hiring a stranger for what she wanted, but she was above petty arguing. As a hired escort, at least for tonight, she would rein in emotions that wouldn't serve the desired outcome. "Unfortunately, it's how the world assesses value. I do not share that view."

"I didn't mean to sound judgmental. I appreciate your honesty." Dani took her hand. "Shall we get to that dessert you promised?" Dani's tone was playful, but there was fire in her eyes. The kind that sparked the flames in Ryan's core.

"I'd like nothing more." She wrapped her arm around Dani's waist as they waited for the car. Dani trembled beside her. "Don't be afraid."

Dani smiled, though it appeared tight. "I'm not. It's more anticipation than dread."

"I don't know whether that's a compliment or not." Ryan laughed. "I'm not sure if anyone who requested my services has ever used the word dread." She helped Dani in, then went around and slid onto the driver's seat.

"Do you have a lot of requests for your time?" Dani asked as she buckled in. "Personally, I mean."

"Not in a while."

"Oh."

Ryan shifted and the car roared down the road. She was anxious to have Dani naked. Her own cravings would have to wait of course. She wasn't there seeking her own pleasure, though she'd likely come at some point. Dani would never know. "I've stepped back from seeing clients for about a year, unless needed."

"Then why are you here?"

"Our conversation intrigued me. I wanted to be sure you got exactly what you desired." She downshifted as they approached the condo. Their custodian would have been there earlier to make sure everything was clean and sanitized. She would have taken inventory and replaced any missing items and restocked the bar and the refrigerator with the food she requested.

"Isn't there anyone else who would have been able to do that?" Dani asked.

Ryan switched off the ignition and faced her. "Several."

"Why didn't you send one of them?"

She ran her fingertip along Dani's cheek then cupped her chin. "Because I want to watch you come for the first time with a woman." When Dani sucked in a quick breath, she got out, gave herself the stern warning she'd perfected years ago, then led Dani inside.

Chapter Six

The seamless flow of the evening's events boggled Dani's mind. The only interruption so far had been her own thoughts drifting to what Ryan had in store for her. Surely as the owner and CEO of the Agency, she had her pick of women, though she'd claimed to have been content to remain in the background for a while. Of course, her own curiosity demanded satisfaction, and Dani had pictured hundreds of made-up scenes over the last week. Now she was about to act some of them out and her body hummed. Ryan used a keycard to unlock the door.

"Please make yourself at home. The bar is fully stocked. I'll join you in a minute." Ryan set the card on the entry table and headed toward a short hallway.

"Where are you going?" she asked with a squeaky voice, her sudden case of nerves back.

Ryan's easy smile revealed she was more in her element than Dani would ever be. "To make sure everything is as I requested."

"Oh." She wasn't sure what that meant but had a feeling she'd soon find out. Wanting to focus on something other than what Ryan was doing, Dani wandered through the spacious condo. The blue, green, and burnt orange palette was both bold and calming, lending a bit of class and originality to the décor. The forest green leather sofa was soft as a newborn's skin. The art was abstract and modern including a semi-nude portrait depicting a woman on the brink of ecstasy. The skin tone and coloring of the woman's hair closely resembled Dani's. She closed her eyes wanting to exchange places with her. Ryan's soft voice was at her ear, her warm breath on her neck.

"Would you care for a drink?" Ryan's smooth, firm hands slipped over her shoulders and down her arms.

"Are you having one?" She was already so aroused she couldn't think.

"No." Ryan's mouth was teasing the skin beneath her ear with tongue and teeth. "I don't want anything to interfere with my senses," she said as she wrapped her arm around her waist and pulled her against her firm body.

Dani trembled as the sheer exhilaration of finally, finally being alone with a woman coursed through her. She was ready. "Take me to bed."

Ryan took her hand and led the way. When she stepped inside, her world tilted on edge. The stark white linens played off the dark gray walls and the accents of vivid blue lampshades and the thick blue rug covering the center of the room begged for her to run her bare feet through the pile. The trace ceiling lights, which she assumed Ryan had turned on, along with a lit candle on a high dresser made the big space feel intimate. An armoire stood against one wall with the doors slightly ajar, but she couldn't see inside.

Ryan brought her next to the incredible soft looking king bed and she moved her hand under her hair, cupping her neck as she leaned down until their mouths met, sliding her lips over Dani's, and teasing at them with her tongue until she opened to her. The exploration was slow, soft, and passionate, unlike any former kisses she'd ever had. She wasn't prepared for the intensity of sensations coursing through her. Her sex clenched every time Ryan's tongue slid against hers. The heat of the kiss went all the way to her toes. Ryan stole her breath, and she broke the kiss, her chest heaving.

"Are you all right?" Ryan's gaze narrowed and she studied her while she got her breathing under control.

"No." Dani was far from all right. "God, you can kiss." Her body had never responded to anyone the way it was responding now. Her nipples were tight knots of need and her panties had gone from damp with arousal to soaked.

Ryan stepped back. "Do you want to stop?"

She took another breath, shook her head. "No. I want you to undress for me."

Ryan's eyes darkened before she took another step away. Her jacket was the first thing to go and revealed a styled royal blue silk shirt that showed off her wide shoulders and accentuated her eyes. As each piece of clothing came off, Dani took in every detail of Ryan's carved body. Her breasts were small, high, and soft looking compared to the rest of her. In fact, the entire length of her was a study in art. The dark thatch of close-trimmed hair between her thighs made Dani's fingers tingle.

"I'm not sure what you were expecting. I hope you aren't disappointed." Ryan took a step forward, her muscles flexing beneath her bronze skin. "What would you like me to do now?"

Oh, God. Dani couldn't stop looking at her. Her hand shook as she lightly trailed her fingertips from the hollow of her neck, to between her breasts, to her carved abdomen. She wanted everything Ryan had to offer and then some. "Undress me."

"Take a breath. I'd prefer you not pass out before we've started."

Understanding how potent the moment was for her helped calm her a bit even when the mere presence of Ryan's nakedness stirred an untapped well of longing for more. Ryan came closer and stepped behind her, slowly drawing the zipper down and letting her dress flutter to the floor. She hadn't worn a bra and for a fleeting second wished she had, but when she turned to find an appreciative look in Ryan's eyes, the thought quickly vanished.

"Magnificent." Ryan placed a kiss on her chest then went to one knee. Her lips moved downward, and she stopped at the lace waistband of her panties.

The trembling she'd fought to control until this point refused to obey her. "I'm going to fall."

"I won't let that happen. Stand another minute for me." Ryan's voice was firm, but not sharp.

Dani fought the wave of dizziness as Ryan guided her panties from her hips and along her legs. Every few inches, Ryan's lips or teeth or tongue grazed her skin, setting her on fire. Ryan finally finished, and her knees buckled, but she didn't fall. Ryan was there, one arm wrapped around her, the other supporting her head.

"I've got you."

Ryan's mouth found hers again, her tongue slipping inside of her lips. This wasn't anything like she'd conjured in the long nights she lay awake. This was passionate and unhurried. Why had she waited so long to experience it? She felt bereft when Ryan's mouth moved away, and she swayed in her arms. Ryan picked her up as though she were a feather and laid her on the bed before stretching over her.

"Skin to skin," she said.

Ryan's flesh was warm. Her body was hard in places, soft in others. She rested her weight on her forearms and brushed strands of hair from her face. Their centers met, and she pressed upward, greedy for more.

"What do you want?"

Dani bit her lower lip. "I wouldn't know, except I want you to touch me."

Ryan growled low. "Have you been thinking about me touching you? My fingers playing with you. Inside you. Did you imagine the mouth that's been kissing yours against your skin?" She nipped at her collar bone. "You say you don't know, but you've been getting yourself off to what you want, haven't you?"

Her hips rose. "Yes."

Ryan's mouth moved on her, blazing a trail over her fevered skin. The weight of Ryan's body pressing against her made her long to touch her and she scored her short nails along her sides. Ryan groaned and thrust against her.

"Tell me what you want me to do." Ryan pulled the tender skin at her throat with her teeth, gentle but insistent.

"Anything." She gasped when Ryan's teeth nipped harder at her chest. "Everything."

"Everything?"

"Yes." The word might not have been a plea, but it definitely sounded like one. Her body yearned for more. She wanted more of whatever Ryan would give her.

Ryan's strong pulse beat in time with her surging clit. Dani was brazen, fearless in expressing her need even if she didn't really know what she was asking for, and her desire flared. She moved lower as she pressed her thigh into Dani's hot center, before closing her lips over one tight nipple to suck and pull taut as she smoothed her hands over her flushed, yielding body. She brushed over Dani's mound, skimmed inside her soaked flesh. Ryan tapped her fingertip against Dani's clit and she jumped at the contact, eliciting an oath.

"You'll need a safe word. One you will remember. If you say it, I will immediately end whatever I'm doing. If I push you too far or do something you're not comfortable with, it tells me to stop." Ryan moved to one side and massaged Dani's inner thigh, and her body rose to meet her caress.

"What?" Dani's eyes were hazed with lust.

"I don't think you'll need to use it tonight, but I want to know what it is if for any reason I have to stop what I'm doing." She smoothed her hand over Dani's abdomen, along her ribs, and cupped her breast. She had magnificent breasts. Full and firm and tipped with dark brown centers. "My fault. I should have asked before I started touching you." Being lost in Dani's excitement was so unusual she'd had to break contact to slow down and be the person Dani needed.

"Thunder." Dani whispered the word as she pressed against her. "I don't like thunder."

She leaned in for a short kiss and smiled against Dani's cheek. "Thunder." She kissed her again, drawing it out as she played with her. When she pulled away, Dani's desire was so blatant—so vividly written on her face—she had all she could do not to take her hard and fast. And Dani had said that was what she wanted, but Ryan wanted to go slow to start in order to make sure Dani was good with what was happening. Ryan entered her slowly, and Dani sucked in a sharp breath. Dani's mouth sought hers, catching her lip in her teeth, sending her libido higher. Ryan told herself to "stand down." Tonight was not for her personal pleasure.

"You feel so good."

A few strokes later, she added a finger. Dani's nails dug into her, bringing a burst of pain and edging her toward climaxing. She claimed Dani's mouth again, moving her tongue slow and deeply probing. She changed positions and moved Dani's thighs to accommodate her. "Open your eyes. Watch what I'm doing to you." Ryan spread her and closed her lips over the hard bundle of nerves. When Dani's hips rose, she pushed them down. She would steer what happened and how. She'd asked to be pushed in ways she'd never been, but tonight was for pleasure alone. She'd been doing this long enough to know that although Dani might want to experience *everything*, taking it slow was the best way with someone who had no experience with *anything*. She sucked and nipped and pressed, holding Dani off, refusing to let her come. She lost track of time and space until Dani's ardent plea broke through her haze.

"Please, please. I'm going to die. I need to come so bad."

Ryan withdrew her attention and kissed the inside of her trembling thigh. "I promise you won't die." She moved her lips lower, raised her leg, nipped at the back of her knee. "Deep breaths." Ryan needed to kiss her, and the need was much harder to resist that it had ever been. She didn't lose control, never wavered in maintaining an emotional barrier. But watching Dani respond to her and knowing she was Dani's first made her heady. Refusing to give in, she leaned over her and entered her fast and hard. "Is this what you want? Do you want me to fuck you?"

"Yes, God, yes." Dani pushed up, meeting her, and captured her mouth.

Rubbing her thumb over her clitoris as she entered her again and again, Ryan watched Dani's face as her body raced toward the orgasm she'd begged for. She curved her fingers, found the sweet spot inside, and alternately tugged the hard knot under her palm. Dani stilled beneath her then exploded, arching off the bed and crying out. When her muscles finally relaxed, Ryan withdrew and lay alongside her. Her center clenched. She'd had all she could do to keep her orgasm at bay. She massaged Dani's legs, smoothed over her abdomen, cradled her breast. Dani's eyes fluttered open and she couldn't help smiling. "Are you okay?"

"Jesus. Is it always that intense?" Dani asked. "I can't move."

Ryan placed a chaste kiss on her cheek. "In my opinion it *should* be, but not necessarily." A shadow crossed Dani's face. "Is there something wrong?"

"I was thinking about what happens next. Do you drive me home or do I call for Uber?"

The laughter came from somewhere deep and put some distance between her thoughts and her body's longing to climax. "Dani, you paid a large sum of money for tonight. We're just getting started."

Dani's body tingled with the last vestiges of her orgasm. As Ryan's warm hands continued to smooth over her hot skin she tried to gather her thoughts. Not an easy thing to do when sorting out what had happened while being the recipient of Ryan's intense focus. She still wanted to engage in some kink, including bondage, even though the sex itself had been incredible.

"Are you going to tie me up?"

Ryan's smile formed slowly. "I like how curious you are about everything, but for me to engage in that type of intimacy, even for kink, I want to know you better. A good dynamic, in my opinion, takes a certain amount of trust that's built over time. I could tie you up, but I think it would be better for you to immerse yourself in the moment and try new things at different times so you can appreciate them all the more." Her hands were warm, soothing. "Tell me how you're feeling?"

"That's the hardest I've ever come." Ryan's intense gaze told her she wanted more. "I feel like I haven't really been touched before." She laughed, though it wasn't from anything funny. "I've always felt like a blow-up doll, used and left deflated."

Ryan's body stiffened. "I hope you never feel that way again. Women are to be worshipped and cared for." Ryan rubbed her thumb gently over her lower lip. "The things we do together are for your pleasure. Choosing to share your first experience with me is a gift. Tonight is for you to see that, and feel it, and know it's true." Ryan kissed her. "Will you let me show you?"

Her mouth was as gentle as her touch, and it stirred something deep in Dani she didn't know existed. And now there was to be more? Ryan's mouth was an implement of pleasure that Dani had no one to compare to. *How could that be?* She wasn't a virgin. It wasn't like she'd never been with boys as a teenager, or men when she'd gotten older. But none had kissed her with care, slowly and carefully building in intensity. She'd *felt* Ryan's passion rise, along with her own.

"Oh yes." The pressure from her thigh pressed to her and the insistent slide against her slick center inflamed the smoldering fire already ignited in her. Her gaze met Ryan's as she lay next to her. The blue of her eyes darkened. When she looked along her body and stopped at her breasts, Ryan's nipples visibly tightened, and she molded her hand around it. Dani's excitement renewed as she gently squeezed and Ryan's nipple hardened into a diamond point beneath her palm. "Do you like that?" she asked.

Ryan's eyes fluttered for an instant before clearing. "Yes, but I'd like to give you more pleasure."

She shivered at the thought of Ryan's insistent touch demanding more from her. Dani wanted that, too. How much satisfaction could she expect in one night without appearing greedy? "Don't you want to come?"

"My pleasure is in pleasing you." Ryan caressed her cheek, then her mouth pressed to hers. Ryan's tongue traced her lips before she slowly moved away. "Can I, Dani?" Her irises contracted and darkened, like a midnight sky illuminated only by the moon.

A fist of desire punched her, leaving her breathless. Dani gasped as she guided Ryan's hand lower.

"Do you trust me?" Ryan asked, her palm moving over her side and stopping at her throbbing center while her eyes held Dani's.

"Yes."

Ryan growled low and turned her onto her side facing away, then wrapped her arms around her. She kissed her neck. "Relax against me." Ryan's tone was deep and lusty. She rolled them both until she lay on top of her with her ass nestled in the curve of Ryan's pelvis. Her lips grazed the side of her neck as her hands cupped her breast and thumbs brushed her tight, aching nipples.

Dani's pulse beat in her pussy. She sank into the nurturing feeling of Ryan wanting to protect her, care for her. She didn't miss the tight trembling beneath her.

"I want you, Dani. I want you to come on me." Ryan pulled and squeezed her tender nipples before moving over her heaving stomach, brushing her fingertips through her curls, but avoiding her aching clit. Ryan's other hand moved to join the first.

"Spread your legs, baby, and let them rest on the bed."

Dani opened her legs wider until they were wrapped around Ryan's hips. She was wet and swollen. More than anything she was impatient for whatever Ryan had in store for her as her hot hands massaged the inside of her thighs, working their way to where Dani wanted them most. Her thumbs slicked inside before she slipped in her fingers, filling her. Between the deep strokes and light rubs to her clit, Dani soared higher. Ryan added a third finger, filling her, and she clenched.

"What can I do to please you, Dani?" Ryan asked, her voice deep and her breath searing her skin.

What *did* she want? After their conversation when Ryan had asked her to think about it, she'd done extensive reading, all the while picturing herself in a myriad of scenarios. She landed on one that made her belly stir. "Don't let me come. Make me beg." Ryan growled and stopped touching her, making her whimper. "I…" she began, so turned on and ready to explode she could barely breathe. "Is that okay?"

Ryan slid from beneath her. "Everything you desire is okay," she said. Her eyes were heavy-lidded. She leaned over, closed her mouth on her breast and traced her tongue over her nipple, then bit with her teeth.

Lost in the moment, the sharp sensation of pain made her gasp before Ryan followed with a soothing swipe of her tongue.

"Are you okay?"

How could she be when her fantasy woman was playing with her? "Are you going to hurt me?"

Ryan's eyes stormed. "No. We aren't in a scene, Dani. We haven't discussed boundaries or hard limits. Even if we had, there are certain things I won't do. I'm not going to hurt you but denying orgasm *can* become painful in a different way. It's called edging and that *is* something I enjoy." Ryan slipped her hand between her thighs. "Mmm. So wet and hard. So ready to come for me."

As Ryan stroked her clit a tingle began and the knot in her belly shot outward. "I'm going to come." She struggled to hold on against the insistent touch of Ryan's talented fingers.

"Not yet." Ryan squeezed her clit hard enough to bring tears to her eyes and she struggled. "Breathe, Dani. You're going to be okay. I promise." The low tone was surprisingly reassuring. "This is what you asked for. I will tell you when you can come."

Even as she whimpered, Dani soared at the idea of her ultimate pleasure being at Ryan's discretion. When Ryan released her clit, the rush of blood made her cry out.

"Do you want to come?"

"No."

Although her body screamed for release, her imagination took her in the direction Ryan led her. She wasn't even sure anymore how long she'd been on the brink. Ryan's fingers moved inside, outside, everywhere, and nowhere. Bereft of any sensation except her white-hot need, she began to beg and plead, unable to control the tremors coursing through her.

"Needy baby, you may come now."

Ryan filled her with her long, strong strokes and her pussy sucked her fingers in greedily. The tsunami of ecstasy broke over her, bringing a scream from her depths as she writhed and bucked under Ryan's onslaught to her over-sensitized flesh until she had nothing more to give. She'd never felt so totally taken or so fully satisfied.

"Watching you give yourself to me is so beautiful," Ryan said as she gathered her limp body against her. "You're amazing, Dani."

She drifted on calm waters that held her aloft and she was blanketed by the warmth of Ryan's skin, like the sun on a summer day. A little while later, she roused. Ryan lay on her side watching her.

"Hi." Dani struggled to sit up and Ryan helped her.

"Are you okay?" Ryan asked. "Do you want to talk about anything?"

Dani took a minute to take stock. Her body was a little sore, not because of anything Ryan did, she just wasn't used to multiple orgasms. Emotionally, she was confident she'd made the right decision in seeking out what she'd been thinking about. "I still want to try other things and explore."

Ryan nodded. "How about we get up and have something to drink and we'll talk more?" She took two thick robes out of the closet and held one open for her before putting the other on. They held hands all the way to the kitchen, then sat at the small table. Ryan pulled a tray of cheese and fruit from the refrigerator, along with a couple of bottles of water, then settled across from her. "How much do you know about BDSM?"

Heat suffused her face. "Not much really. Some that I've read and seen on Reddit."

"Don't be embarrassed, Dani. Kink can be misunderstood and the mystique about it keeps people from exploring deeper, even if they are curious."

"How much experience do you have?"

"About sixteen years."

"Wow."

Ryan laughed. "I may be older than you think. But it's definitely important to have someone with experience introduce you if that's what you want."

"I promise to do my homework."

They talked a little about the options available, and Dani was pleased with Ryan's simple, nonjudgmental descriptions and explanations. The option for Ryan to spend the night with her was available, but that felt too intimate, too real, and she didn't want to have any illusions that this was more than an arrangement. Ryan brought her home a little while later. The good night kiss had been gentle, and the tenderness told her so much more than words ever could.

CHAPTER SEVEN

Ryan threw back a finger of scotch and poured another. She'd been so into Dani she'd almost lost it. "Fuck." Out of practice and nearly out of control, she had no business seeing clients. Doubting Dani would call again, based on her obvious money issues, she didn't think she needed to worry. She'd also done something she'd never done before. When Dani asked if she could touch her, could make her come, she'd told her since this was her first experience, the focus should remain on her own pleasure. Dani had accepted the lame excuse. If Dani had touched her, pulled on her clit the way she liked, she would have come and wouldn't have been able to hide it. She hadn't allowed herself to truly let go with a woman professionally since her ex-lover, Sarah, had accused her of being "more into clients than she was with her." And she didn't want those thoughts invading her night with Dani.

Sarah had never really taken the time to know her. Ryan knew the difference between work and a commitment, but unconsciously, at least at first, she started denying herself the pleasure of climaxing when she worked, and after a time her body fought against the natural reaction altogether. When their relationship fell apart and Sarah left, she would occasionally allow herself to climax, but she'd mastered the ability to keep her partners from witnessing her release.

The mantel clock glared at her from across the room. She'd brought Dani home a little over an hour ago. At two thirty in the morning, she should be in bed, but nervous energy and the orgasm that hung heavy in her center wouldn't let her sleep. A hot shower and her own hand were her only options. The last thing she remembered as she drifted to sleep was the vision of a very satiated and exhausted Dani.

She slapped at the insistent noise next to her head before realizing it was her phone. "Hello?" Her voice was raspy, heavy with sleep.

"You still joining me this morning?" Drake asked.

Ryan opened one eye and tried to focus on the clock across the room. "What time is it?"

Drake chuckled. "Six. Did you have a late night?"

Sitting up in bed, she rubbed her face. "Something like that."

"Oh, do tell."

"Later," she grumbled. "Give me thirty minutes and I'll meet you downstairs."

"You got it."

Drake was way too chipper this morning and she was going to be full of energy and questions Ryan wasn't sure she wanted to answer. Drake had given her a hard time for taking on a client after all this time. Hell, she wasn't even sure why she'd done it, and though she knew it was a mistake, she was glad she had. Dani had been a nice change of pace from the disconnected, unemotional sex she was used to, and watching her body come alive had been a rhapsody to behold.

Hetero sex was fine if you liked that kind of thing. In her opinion, no man could truly satisfy a woman. Only another woman could do that. She was certain she had satisfied Dani. They could have spent the night together, but Dani had declined, likely needing some head space to deal with what had happened.

After hours of exploration, Dani had been doe-eyed and limp in her arms. Ryan had been cognizant of the emotional state Dani may have been in even though they hadn't been in an actual scene. She'd been young when she'd had her first BDSM encounter with an older, skilled woman. The connection had been profound, moving her far beyond physical gratification. She'd been emersed in sensations not even the most enjoyable sex could obtain, though tonight had come close.

When she got downstairs, Drake was leaning against the sandstone wall that surrounded her home, scrolling through her phone, earbuds in place. As she approached, Drake glanced up and smiled at her, and she wondered for the thousandth time why her handsome friend had never found a partner. Of course, finding a partner who wasn't put off by their profession wasn't easy to do and led to complications that sooner or later destroyed the relationship. She should know.

"Good morning," Drake said before stretching her legs and doing that little hop-jump thing she did before a hard run.

"Morning. Sorry to keep you waiting."

"I've only been here a few minutes." She waved her off, then scrutinized her. "You okay?"

With a sigh, she shook her head. "Not sure, but a run with you will help." Ryan slung her arm around Drake's shoulder.

"Okay, but you know I'm going to ask, right?"

Laughing, she smiled as she finished her hamstring stretches. "Oh, I know you won't be able to help yourself." She glanced up at the stark blue, near cloudless sky. "So, where are we off to today?" Drake had already run the two miles that separated them, evidenced by her damp shirt, but she was a fastidious planner and would have plotted their run before ever leaving her apartment.

Drake mischievously smiled. "Woods Hollow." Ryan groaned. "I figured with all that pent-up energy of yours you could use a hard run."

Woods Hollow was a nice, semi-flat six-mile run. Getting there, however, would entail a number of hills and steep inclines. "Great," she said without enthusiasm. "Last one back buys breakfast." Drake was a great runner with an easy stride, but Ryan was taller and a bit leaner. What she lacked in durability she made up for in speed.

Drake slapped her on the back. "Hope you brought your wallet." She took off and Ryan swore before falling in beside her, glad to have a diversion from thoughts of Dani.

❖

"So, you went through with it?" Drake asked around a mouthful of omelet.

Ryan hesitated, already knowing what Drake would say about the subject, but there was no point lying. They'd been friends too long and had no secrets between them. "Yes," she said nonchalantly as she poked a forkful of her eggs Benedict into her mouth.

Drake set down her juice. "Christ."

She shrugged. "I already know you don't approve."

Drake had borne witness to the devastation Sarah's abrupt departure had caused her. Ryan had been convinced she'd found her life-mate, someone who understood who she was and that what she did for a living was just that...a job. At least, that's how their relationship started. They'd met at a party and hit it off immediately. When they started dating, they'd been good together. A few months later, Sarah began to verbally assault her, calling her hurtful names like "slut" and "whore."

She'd tried to explain that the clients she slept with meant nothing to her, it was just sex. That's when she started denying herself orgasms to prove the point. In the end, it hadn't been enough, and the breakup was ugly for them both. She swore off even thinking about another relationship, but by that time, she'd trained her body so well Ryan rarely ever wanted to come. When she did, she wore a mask of indifference. Drake continued to stare at her.

"You're the one who asked why I didn't connect with the women I slept with. How can I do that if I'm on the sidelines?" She blew out a frustrated breath.

"I wasn't talking about clients, and don't try to put this on me. You said it yourself, that there's something different about this woman. I remember you saying damn near the same thing about Sarah." Drake's tone relayed her displeasure at being used as a scapegoat.

Ryan ignored her response, forging ahead in her headstrong way. "Why is it an issue that I helped one woman live out a fantasy? You do it all the time."

"We aren't talking about me."

"Do we ever?"

Drake sat back. "Ryan..." she began, but her gaze moved away, then returned. "And what happens when she calls again?" Drake studied her.

She'd hurt her feelings before and didn't want to do so again. "I doubt she will."

"What? The great master seducer fell down on the job?" Drake's words held a biting edge, obviously meant to drive home her point.

Her words stung. "She was satisfied at the end of the night, but I don't think she's financially in a position to indulge beyond the one time." She'd already given Dani a reduced rate. Money should never stand in the way of fulfilling one's fantasies. Dani didn't need to know that Ryan would have charged three times as much for anyone else. She didn't need the money and she'd paid the difference from her personal account. She definitely wouldn't be telling Drake *that*.

"And that makes this whole thing better somehow?" Drake's hand dramatically waved in the air. She took a deep breath before continuing, "I don't want to argue with you, but I still don't understand why you had to be with *this* client when there are plenty of women outside of the business who'd jump at the chance to sleep with you."

Ryan studied her. True, she'd taken a break from being an escort, but that didn't mean she couldn't or didn't want to see women both professionally and personally. The demons of her past might always be lurking in the background, but she still enjoyed sex, even when she didn't let herself fully let go. The inertia of not putting herself out there and tempting fate had taken a back step with Dani, and it felt good.

"I know that you're looking out for me. That you think there's some nefarious reason why I'm back in the saddle again. There isn't. I just...I needed a change and it presented itself. Itch scratched. Can we let it go at that? Please?" Drake's gaze didn't vacillate. Of the "Dynamic Duo" as they'd called themselves in their younger days, Drake had always been the more sensible one, always considering all sides of a situation and the possible outcomes. It was hard to believe Ryan turned out to be the one who had to maintain strict control, over the business, herself, and her employees, though that had happened by default since her family had lent her the start-up money.

"Yes, okay." Drake stared into her cold coffee. "Just be careful. If you get another itch, will you come to me for advice?" The waitress began to clear their plates. "You want anything else?"

"No." The word was hollow. Did she want something else? Was she looking for something that wasn't there? Something that had never been in her life because of her business and the independence she needed to run it the way it needed to be? She looked at Drake. "You?"

"I'm good."

Ryan wasn't so sure. "Just the check then."

"Hey, I'm supposed to be paying."

She grasped Drake's hand. "And I'm supposed to remember why you're my best friend. I'm sorry I sometimes forget."

Drake's eyes shone with emotion she'd never let anyone see except Ryan. She squeezed back. "Double or nothing next weekend?"

"Ugh. You're trying to kill me." She laughed. "Why not."

Outside the diner, she gave Drake a bone-crushing hug. There'd been times when she wouldn't have survived if it weren't for Drake at her side. She never wanted to forget the moments she'd almost wished she hadn't, but that was before her life turned the corner and she became the steadfast woman she was today. "I'll see you at the office tomorrow."

"I might be a little late." A knowing grin lifted the corners of her mouth into a full-blown smile.

"Anyone I know?"

Drake looked sheepish. "Trish."

"You may be a bit more than a little late, depending on her mood." It wouldn't be the first time they'd slept with the same woman and neither of them cared. Ownership of anyone they saw didn't have a place in their lives, nor was there room for long-term.

Who would want to be permanently partnered with a woman who slept with other women, even if it was their job?

"I'll be there for our meeting at eleven. Have a good day." Drake started to back away, already in run mode. "Don't do anything I would."

Ryan laughed. Since Drake would do just about anything, that was her attempt at hamstringing her, something no woman had ever been able to do.

Chapter Eight

Well, was it worth it?" Pam asked as they sat at the small picnic table behind the salon on a narrow strip of grass under a small shade tree.

Aside from Mark, Pam was the only one who knew she'd gone on a date with a woman. One of the few who had warned her to not pick up a random person to fulfill her fantasies, stating she'd likely be disappointed. She squirmed. Dani still felt Ryan's touch, her hot mouth driving her to the brink of orgasm over and over. She might have hoped the experience would satisfy her curiosity, but it had only stoked the fire for more—of what Ryan, or another woman, could give her. The feeling she'd been holding back, not wanting to overwhelm Dani, had been clear, and Dani still longed to know what it would feel like to touch Ryan and see her climax. She squeezed her thighs tighter. "Every damn penny."

"Shit," Pam said. "I need a second job."

They laughed. Pam had asked for details, but part of the contract she'd signed stated she was free to share general information only. Particular details of sexual acts were not to be discussed because what one woman found exciting another might find offensive, and since each escort had skills in different areas, it would be unfair to both parties to have preconceived notions.

"So, are you going to have another date?"

"I'd like to."

"What's stopping you?" Pam pulled out another cigarette, looked at her watch, then shoved it back. They only had a couple of minutes left.

"Money, for one thing."

"What else?"

"I don't know if I want the same woman, but I'd like to see what else she can do." Ryan's explanation of the trust issue made sense, but that didn't mean she didn't want to explore more with her.

Pam stood and stretched out her back. "I'm sure if you request her or someone else, they'd be willing to oblige. After all, if the client isn't happy, word gets around."

Dani held the door open. "Maybe. I should look for a second job myself. I think I'm hooked." Pam laughed at her. The idea she was only getting started experiencing what the Agency had to offer excited her in ways she was only beginning to understand. She'd been thinking along those lines since she hadn't been able to stop the continuous loop of what Ryan's touch had awakened in her. The more she pushed the images away, the more obsessed she became. One time definitely wasn't going to be enough, and she wondered how many *would* calm the insistent urges. Dani bit her lip, knowing what she had to do. When George came in, she would ask for additional hours. They were short-staffed as it was, and with the track season opening soon, the influx of wealthy women would keep them plenty busy.

Maybe her friend who worked at one of the upscale restaurants could put in a good word for her. She'd recently had a nasty fall and broken her leg and would be out of commission for three months. Ellen often bragged about her tips ranging from two to four hundred a night, depending on the crowd. That would certainly add to her pleasure fund.

While she waited for her next customer to be shampooed, the idea of a threesome made her entire body twitch. Oh yeah, she had it bad and knew it was only going to intensify.

Ryan leaned close so the others couldn't hear. "So, how was your night with Trish?" Drake had slid into her chair two minutes before the last person joined them.

Drake quietly moaned. "I'm not going to be able to walk for a week."

She raised a brow. "You have an appointment tomorrow. If your extracurricular activities interfere with work the boss won't be happy."

"I'll be ready, don't worry. In the meantime, I was hoping my BF would be cheering me on."

"She is." Ryan smiled and turned to the others gathered around the conference table. "All right, everyone. We'll go around the room for reports and updates. Anna, would you please begin?"

"Certainly, Ms. Lewis. During the last quarter, we had a total of ninety-two new client inquiries. Of those, seventy-three have either had an initial encounter or have one scheduled. Of those seventy-three, fifty-two have already scheduled a second appointment." Anna turned to her. "The calendar of availability is getting really tight. We're going to need to either hire more escorts or start declining new inquiries."

Because of the way the Agency scheduled escorts, there were only two appointments per day, per employee, depending on availability. Of the fifteen people working in that capacity, not counting herself or Drake, that left little wiggle room for time off, illness, emergencies, etc.

"Turning away clients isn't an option. Solutions?" Ryan glanced around the table. After a few minutes for reflection, the staff began to throw out ideas. Some plausible, some not. At an average of three thousand dollars per time slot, money wasn't an issue. Lane confirmed the actual numbers regarding income vs. expenses for a given week. Financially, they were in great shape. She jotted notes during idea lulls, but still gave the staff her undivided attention.

"I'll take all of your suggestions into consideration and let you know my final decision. We've got some work ahead of us, but you've never let me down and I assume you won't this time either. If you think of anything else, email or call. Have a great week." With the meeting officially adjourned, Ryan strode to her office, desperate for an espresso, a bad habit she hadn't been able to shake and had no intention of doing so. Drake strode in after her and shut the door.

"Want one?" she asked as she glanced over her shoulder.

"I can use all the caffeine I can get." Drake dropped onto the sofa and slouched.

She busied herself with the task. "My, my. Did you pay her for your punishment, or did she willingly provide it?"

"Don't burst my ego. It was purely pleasure." Drake took the petite cup from her. "Thanks."

"I'm serious. She's talented. Maybe we should interview her." Ryan hung her suit coat on the back of the chair before rolling up her sleeves and settling next to Drake in the leather club chair. "We could use a few more women like her. We seem to be getting more requests for toppy femmes, and there's currently only three."

"Not a horrible idea." Drake sipped, a look of concentration on her face.

"What?"

Drake shook her head, a tiny smile lifting her generous lips. "Reminiscing. When you started this business did you ever think it would be like this?"

Ryan grew quiet, saddened by reality. The reasons she'd started the Agency lingered. She'd done it for the sheer thrill of owning a business she could call her own, and for proving she'd risen above her troubled past. And why wouldn't a young, sexually active woman want all the sex and none of the complications…until there had been the one that had been a mistake. The same reason she'd learned to control her emotions and the mistake that had stopped her from looking for more than just the physical connection she enjoyed.

She couldn't ever see closing the Agency. A lot of women depended on their services for a variety of reasons, not all of them sexual. Some women didn't like attending social events alone and having to keep the wolves at bay. There were several of her employees who had been hired for their intimidating presence as well as their sexual prowess. But she'd never imagined becoming wealthy because of it, and considering her childhood, she was grateful for every dollar she earned. Her home was modest by today's standards. Her most extravagant purchase had been her car. She wasn't about to give that up either. "I didn't know there were so many women in situations that would want what we offer, that's for sure."

"But you did a good thing too," Drake said earnestly. "Who knows how much danger those same women might have put themselves in to experience what we safely provide."

It was true. Today's society held all types of deranged individuals, intent on taking advantage of others at vulnerable times in their lives, not to mention the horror stories in the news where women were abducted and never found. She caught Drake's gaze and held it. "I wouldn't have been able to do it without you." Drake waved her off. She set her cup down and went to her. "I mean it, Drake. This wasn't just my dream. It might have started out as my idea, but you're the one who convinced me it could be done. That it would be a sophisticated service that would draw the type of clients we wouldn't have to worry about taking advantage of us." She placed her hand on Drake's leg. "I'm not sure I've ever thanked you for having the courage to see it through. Thank you." Ryan sucked in a breath when Drake's gaze fell to Ryan's lips. Then Drake pulled away and shared a knowing smile.

"You're welcome. We may have started the adventure together, but this baby is all yours. I know it's not as glamorous as people think." She stood. Ryan didn't miss the tremor in Drake's hand as she picked up her cup and set it on the credenza. With her back to her, Ryan watched Drake take a deep breath, then she rapped the surface with her knuckles before spinning around. "Let me know if you want to talk about the meeting. I've got a few things to do in my office."

She almost stopped her to ask what was going on, but if Drake wasn't ready to share, she must have a good reason. They'd been through enough together that she knew when to let something go, at least where Drake was concerned. As for Dani, she wasn't sure she wanted to.

Chapter Nine

Lane reviewed the list Ryan had handed her. "Five more apartments or condos and six more employees. You want them on board as soon as possible with the rentals to coincide."

"Correct. Try to keep the condos within a twenty-mile radius, but if you have to go farther away to find them, let me know first. I'll put out the word about employment opportunities today. I just want to be sure we can handle the increase in expenses as well as the influx of income."

"I'll run some hard numbers right away, but I've already told you it won't be a problem. I don't think anyone will complain about a day off now and then, either. A few of the escorts have actual lives they'd like to enjoy." Lane left with the pages Ryan had meticulously outlined with her expansion plans. They included the things only her staff paid attention to, like cleaning services, health insurance, and the vehicles and wardrobes each person she hired was allotted. They charged high fees so expenses were covered and the employees well compensated.

Her phone buzzed. "Yes, Anna?"

"Ms. Daniella Brown for you on line one. I can take a message if you're busy."

Ryan's pulse quickened. It had been two weeks since their night together. She honestly didn't think Dani was going to call for a long time, if at all. Of course, Dani hadn't gotten everything she'd wanted, and although Ryan believed she'd been physically satisfied, she wasn't sure why she'd not given in to Dani's request. Normally, she gave a client what they asked for, only putting limits on it if there was a safety issue. Unless, subconsciously, she wanted to see her again. Perhaps Dani was calling to ask for someone who would give her exactly what she asked for. Ryan's gut twisted. "Put her through."

"One minute please."

The phone rang twice before she picked it up. "Good afternoon, Dani. I trust you're well." Normally, she insisted on formality whenever dealing with clients, but the stilted conversation wasn't how she wanted to communicate with Dani.

"I'm fine." The clipped response made her sound anything but.

"What can I do for you?"

"I'd like to make another appointment."

Ryan's center grew heavy and her clit surged. "I take it you were satisfied with the outcome of the last one?" She was pushing in a way she never did. If a client wanted an escort she booked it after finding out what type of an engagement they were looking for, keeping interactions brief. Simple.

"Yes and no."

Ryan sat up, all business now. She'd never had a disappointed client and the idea she'd left Dani unsatisfied upset her for a handful of reasons. "Would you please explain?"

Dani laughed. "You did your part and I enjoyed it, but I want to explore my own capabilities in satisfying a woman. That was something I didn't have the opportunity to do."

"I see." Ryan tapped her notepad with her sterling and pearl ballpoint pen. "Are you requesting a refund?"

"No. I want another appointment with you," Dani said.

As much as the idea excited her, Drake's words of caution played in her head. "I don't know if that's a good idea since I apparently didn't give you everything you wanted." Dani would be better off with someone else, and she'd already expressed wanting variety, so it made sense. Even as she thought it, her insides tightened in an unpleasant way.

"What I want," Dani said, "is to have the best instruct me in how to be the best. Unless that isn't you, of course."

Dani's tone was teasing, and Ryan was aware that she was testing her, calling her bluff in a way no woman did. She shouldn't take the bait. She should insist Dani try another escort.

"What services are you requesting?" Ryan opened the spreadsheet tab on her forty-inch monitor. It contained a brief description of each employee's particular skills as well as the number of clients they saw each month, what their services were, and the fee charged.

"Sex where I get to do the touching."

"No dinner then?" Maybe Dani's silence meant she was changing her mind.

"Would we be going back to that apartment?"

"Or one similar."

"Maybe just some light food available for stamina's sake."

Her rock-hard clit surged against the seam of her pants. "That can be arranged." Ryan's availability wasn't on the screen. She was always free. There were perks to being the boss. "When would you like to schedule?"

"Is tomorrow night good for you?" Dani's voice had dropped an octave into a warm and seductive tone.

Her nipples rubbed against the crisp fabric of her pressed shirt. "What time shall I come for you?"

"I hope you'll come for me more than once, but you can pick me up at seven. Good-bye, Ms. Lewis."

"Christ." She pulled up her calendar and booked herself out at five o'clock the next day. The only person who had access was Anna and she never shared the information unless absolutely necessary. Drake would give her shit when she found out, but it wouldn't stop her from seeing Dani again. After all, a client had requested her, and Drake knew the Agency's unwavering policy of always providing what a client wanted. The only place she drew the line was permanent physical damage or psychological harm. She didn't allow abuse in any form by or to her employees.

"Anna, please hold my calls and visitors."

"Of course."

She pushed back her chair and stood. She was desperate to come. She hadn't needed to relieve herself at work in ages. Talking to Dani should have been a simple phone call with a client, but nothing was simple when it came to Dani. The pent-up energy she'd been ignoring since being with her had coalesced into a seething thing that didn't go away even after immersing herself in work. Try as she might to ignore the conflicting feelings of unwanted arousal and longing for more, nothing calmed her inner turmoil. Knowing she was going to see Dani again, and that Dani wanted to see *her* left no choice.

After locking her office door, Ryan pulled a hand towel from the credenza drawer and settled on the couch with her pants around her ankles. Slicking her finger along the sides of her clit only made the need harder. She circled and stroked and pulled as her vision filled with snapshots of Dani's naked body responding to her touch. Just before Ryan came, the scene changed. *She* was the one writhing beneath Dani as her fingers and mouth played at her center in slow motion until all she could feel was the pounding of her heart as she came and softly cried out.

Once her body settled, she used the towel to clean herself and deposited it in the laundry basket in her en suite bathroom. She washed her hands and face before getting herself back together. The reflection in the mirror revealed a confused woman. *What the hell has gotten into me?*

Her reason for today's behavior did little to improve her mood. She dropped into her leather chair and let her mind drift as she rubbed her hand over the smooth surface of the oversized mahogany desk. The wood warmed beneath her touch like a woman's flesh. What was wrong with her? She hadn't been this fixated or unable to control her desires since—no. She wouldn't go there. *Couldn't* go there.

Thirty minutes later and more focused, Ryan picked up the phone. "Drake, could you come to my office? There's something I want you to look at." Ryan glanced at the report in the center of her orderly desk. At least something in her life was in order.

"Be there in five."

While she waited, Ryan went to her bathroom and splashed cold water on her face again. *Maybe I'm coming down with something.* She laughed. If only it were that simple. The rapid knock in Drake's telltale pattern made her laugh.

"Come in."

"Hey, boss.

Drake sauntered in and her bright smile helped put her at ease. She had that effect on Ryan. Maybe they should go for a drink... or two...and get to the bottom of her preoccupation. Of course, her upcoming appointment with Dani had nothing to do with it. "Drake, to what do I owe the pleasure?"

Drake stared at her. "You must be getting old." She shook her head. "You wanted to see me. Remember?" Her focus changed from amused to concerned.

She took a breath. "Right." Ryan pushed the report across the desk. "These are the projections of the expansion proposal. It looks fairly straightforward to me, but I want your opinion."

"I'll review it and give you my take on it tomorrow." Drake studied her. "Are you okay?"

The idea she was so easy to read irked her, though it shouldn't have. Not with Drake. "I'm not sure." Ryan looked around at the expensive finishes and the high-end furnishings. In her current mood, they didn't mean much. She turned her gaze to Drake. "Do you have time for a drink after work? Maybe more than one?" For a minute, she thought Drake was going to decline.

"Let's go to Indigo, then neither of us have to worry about driving."

The tightness in her chest loosened. "Six?"

Drake stood with the report. "Meet you there."

The door closed softly, and Ryan was once more left alone with her thoughts.

"Glenlivet Fifteen on the rocks," Ryan said matter-of-factly.

"Oh, this should be good." Drake sipped her dirty martini.

"What should?"

Drake quirked her eyebrow. "You only go for the really good stuff when you're uncertain about something. I mean, I know it happens, but rarely, and it's been a while."

The alcohol burn wasn't unwelcome and, oddly enough, neither was the probing question. "Unrest, uneasy. Hell, I don't know." She grasped Drake's forearm as an anchor. The muscle flexed beneath her fingers. Ryan eased her hand away. "That's why we're here. You've always been good at figuring me out when I couldn't."

Drake's gaze drifted over her. "If I didn't know better, I'd say a woman was responsible, but you haven't allowed anyone close in ages, so it can't be that."

She motioned to the bartender for another round while contemplating how to answer Drake. The encounter with Trish had awakened her sleeping dragon, but all she'd felt when they parted was relief. The same had not been true with Dani, and the usual detachment was missing. Sure, Dani had been a refreshing change from previous clientele, but there was more to it than that. She'd actually *wanted* a connection. Wanted to feel like she'd been more than bought and paid for, but wasn't that what they were all doing? Providing a service lacking the pitfalls of random hookups? Ryan nodded her thanks, took a smaller sip, and locked on to Drake's questioning gaze.

"You know, at first I thought it was the idea of expanding," Ryan began. "There's so many pieces that have to fall into place to make it work, but it's not like we haven't done it before. And, really, with you, Lane, and Anna I know it will be a smooth transition."

"And now?" Drake swirled her olive before sipping.

"Maybe old memories are creeping in." She shook her head. "Fuck. I don't know." She finished her drink and thought about another. "Do you regret doing what you're doing, being employed by the Agency?"

"Ryan," Drake said as she slid her hand up her arm to her shoulder and squeezed. "I've never felt like an employee, you've made sure of that."

She nodded. Taking a bit of comfort from Drake's words. The mix of emotions was confusing, and she didn't like not knowing which way was up...or forward.

"I've never regretted being on this adventure. In many ways, I've lived a charmed life and it's far from over." Drake's smile was tentative but infectious. "There was a time you thought so, too."

Ryan sighed. "I know. I still do. I'm not sure why I'm questioning everything now."

"It's time you removed yourself from the selection of escorts. Maybe being back in action has you asking questions there aren't answers for. Besides, it's not like you need the cash."

She laughed. "True. You did warn me not to do it."

"Clearly, I had reason."

"Yes, but it's not for the reasons you thought."

Drake pushed her empty glass away and motioned for another. Ryan couldn't tell if she was annoyed or disappointed, or something else entirely. "You mean it isn't because of the sex?"

"No. Yes. Jesus." The bartender pointed to her empty tumbler. "Neat."

"I can't wait to hear your explanation."

"Okay." She took a breath, settling her thoughts. "Being CEO of a thriving company is great. I love what I do." She thought about being with Trish and the lack of intimacy and passion. "I think I'm missing the thrill of the moment. The passion I used to feel when the woman I was with trusted me to take care of her, and sometimes I did the same." She hadn't allowed anyone that close in a very long time. "Remember those days in the beginning when all we did was enjoy the moment, build a temporary rapport with the women we bedded, and had fun?"

Drake's warm gaze held hers. There were emotions she couldn't read even though Drake didn't look away, but her eyes were storm clouds. "I still have fun. I *still* connect with women."

"Then what the hell is wrong with me?" She swallowed down half her drink, and the burn reminded her of the fire she used to feel when she slept with a woman, even if she was being paid to do so.

"I'm not sure there's anything *wrong* with you. Changing priorities, maybe." Drake looked behind her and smiled. "Which is why I've asked a couple of women to join us."

Ryan turned to find Trish and a woman she didn't know standing a few feet away. Trish smiled at her, fire burning in her eyes, and Ryan's body stirred. The woman next to her was handsome and definitely MOC, and the contrast between the two made her clit rise. Maybe it was time she stopped trying to control everything that happened in her life, especially when it came to what went on in the bedroom. She turned to Drake. "Do you think sex is always the answer?"

Drake clapped her on the back and smiled. "No. I think it's the cure for whatever's ailing you." Ryan laughed. "Come on. We've got the penthouse. You can take your pick once we get there."

She cocked a brow, wondering what Drake was trying to prove. Or maybe it was time *she* stopped trying to prove something to herself and just let things proceed on their own.

"I'm sure you remember Trish," Drake said.

"Of course. It's good to see you."

"Likewise," Trish said.

"And this is Jay."

She stuck out her hand. "Ryan." Jay's handshake was firm but not overly so.

"Shall we?" Drake motioned toward the elevator and they moved forward. Trish fell in beside Drake, and Jay walked next to her. It seemed the choice had been made for her and all she felt was relief at not having to bear the weight of another decision.

CHAPTER TEN

Dani stood outside on the top step, a tiny overnight bag at her feet. She hadn't remembered asking Ryan if they could, or would, spend the night together. Not just for sex, but to discuss all the other intricacies she'd read about that were common in BDSM relationships. She tapped her foot. There would be no relationships forming with the women she was having sex with. Maybe it was an unspoken rule, though she doubted it since Ryan had been up front with her about everything else.

Her legs and arms tingled. For the last twenty-four hours all she'd thought about was what she wanted to do to Ryan. She wanted to see her naked with need. Yes, she definitely wanted to see her naked again. Even the thought of her small breasts with the dark centers that became so hard, made her mouth water. At the end of the block, an engine growled low and the Audi appeared, whipping to a whisper quiet stop.

Ryan rounded the car and met her on the walkway. "Am I late?"

"No. You're right on time."

She pointed to the bag. "Would you like me to take that?"

"Not until I know it's okay if we don't leave until morning." Dani bit her lip, certain there were protocols and a list of dos and don'ts she might not be aware of. She had no clue if she'd crossed a line but was certain she'd find out.

Ryan slid the bag from her fingers. "It's not forbidden, though the request isn't common. But like I told you last time, it takes as long as it takes for you to be fully satisfied."

Dani got into the car while Ryan stowed her bag in the trunk before taking her place in the driver's seat.

Using her thumb on the steering wheel control, Ryan gave a command. Three rings later, a woman picked up.

"Yes, Ms. Lewis?"

"Please reschedule the cleaners for condo forty-eight for nine in the morning." The engine purred to life and Ryan drove the car toward the west side, where the posh and polished lived.

"Right away. Will that be all?"

"Have a good evening, Anna." After Anna hung up, Ryan glanced at her. "You do realize there's an extra fee for extended engagements."

"I figured as much." She dragged a freshly manicured nail along the sharp crease of Ryan's slacks. "I'll be sure every cent is well spent."

Heat traveled rapidly up Ryan's leg. This was the Dani she'd been intrigued by. The bold, demanding woman who knew, perhaps not *exactly* what she wanted but how she wanted it. And Ryan's body was responding in ways it hadn't since she'd learned how to rein in all that pent-up, volatile energy. Like a volcano dormant for years, under the surface she was on fire, her blood molten. She needed to move the topic in a different direction.

"Have you given any more thought to kink or bondage?" Dani was quiet, though her hand remained on Ryan's thigh, it too stilled.

"I still want to explore it, but I thought I ought to know how to please a woman before I could figure out what else might be exciting to me. For me." Dani groaned in frustration. "Am I making any sense at all?"

She downshifted as they entered the underground parking area. "It's not uncommon for a woman to not know all the things that excite or please or make her climax until she's had a chance to explore and discover." Ryan pulled into a space with the number forty-eight stenciled on the wall. For the dozenth time, she told herself to get a grip on her libido and remember whatever Dani wanted was the only thing she needed to pay attention to. "Let's go explore, shall we?"

❖

"How many of these luxury apartments does the Agency have?" Dani asked as she clutched her bag to her when they stepped off the elevator on the fourth floor.

"We have fifteen, but we're expanding." Ryan stopped and pressed her thumb to the small scanner next to the door, a mechanical click sounded before the door swung inward and she held it open for her to step through.

Like the last apartment, it was beautifully appointed, though she sensed something different. Almost as though there were items of a more personal nature. Small pieces of art decorated shelves in the bookcase. A cheval mirror framed in black stood in a corner. The fireplace mantel was thick and hand-hewn, stained a deep, rich brown and covered with what looked like vacation photos, although none showed Ryan or any other person. Dani imagined that much like Ryan's life, most of it was hidden from view.

"This one feels different."

Ryan studied her. "Different how?"

She glanced around again. "I'm not sure. The other one was nice, but this one is more intimate, like someone actually lives here."

"Would you like a drink?" Ryan asked, ignoring the observation from where she stood behind the high polished bar, the statement hanging between them.

Her attire was slightly less formal than the night they'd gone to dinner. The pressed dress shirt of pale gray with white cuffs and collar played well off of the charcoal slacks she wore. Her body appeared slender, the well-developed muscles hidden beneath the smooth fabric. As were her high, small breasts, the tips pressing against the shirt while she stared. "Wine. Red if you have it."

"Merlot, Tempranillo, Syrah, or Cabernet?"

She laughed. "Do you always know what's available?"

"Always."

Something in Ryan's eyes spoke of danger, but she was so charming Dani didn't hesitate to play along. "Tempranillo, please."

Ryan opened a bottle and poured into two goblets. "We should let this breathe a bit. Here or in the bedroom?"

"Are you in a hurry?" She smiled behind her glass, inhaling the bold, fruity scent of blackberry and currant.

"Ms. Brown, I never hurry when it comes to pleasing a woman, unless that's what she wants. Fast and hard." Ryan stepped closer and pressed her thigh against her center. Heat penetrated her clothing and the hard muscle of her leg made Dani gasp.

As much as she wanted Ryan, she also wanted to slow down, afraid if she didn't, she'd be past the point of no return too soon, and she had plans. The memory of her total satisfaction and exhaustion after their first encounter rushed to the forefront. Nothing was going to derail her focus. Ryan had taken what she wanted, now it was her turn. She stepped back. "I'm not interested in fast or hard tonight," she said while she ran her finger over Ryan's chin, down her throat, between her breasts. "Unless that's how *you* get off."

Ryan's eyes dilated. She took a drink, then her hand.

"Then we should get started," Ryan said as she pulled her to the couch, guiding her until she straddled her lap.

Little did Ryan know, Dani had started this fantasy a long time ago, and now she would carry out the parts she longed for most.

Ryan concentrated on slowing her racing heart. Dani was so close and warm, her eyes shining bright with curiosity on the heels of desire.

"I'm not sure where to start," Dani said breathily.

She moved her hand to follow the curve of Dani's neck, her fingers threading through the silky strands. "I've always found the mouth a good place to begin." She pulled Dani toward her until the barest space separated them and she held Dani's gaze in hers. Dani's chest rose and fell quickly. Ryan wanted to press her mouth against the plump lips. She could already taste them.

"Is that what you want?" Dani whispered between quick breaths while her hips moved, seeking contact.

"It isn't what I want that matters." Ryan tugged a handful of hair, making Dani gasp. "Tonight is all about you."

"Wasn't it all about me last time?"

"As it will be every time." Ryan had a hard rein on her desire tonight, determined to be the woman Dani had asked for. Dani's eye flicked to her lips before she moved in. The kiss began slowly, tentatively, before her tongue slipped inside. Ryan let her take her time and kept her hands on her hips. Dani's nipples hardened and rubbed against her chest. She pushed away the rising lust as her body reacted. This was what she was good at, how she handled professional sex, and she wouldn't forget.

Breaking away, Dani slowly smiled. "How many women have you kissed?"

Ryan laughed at Dani's inquisitiveness. "More than I can count."

"I believe that." Dani's nimble fingers began to work the buttons of her shirt. "I like your breasts much better than mine," she said as she took her nipple into her mouth and sucked hard.

The point tightened into a stiff knot before Dani bit down with just enough force to make her hips rise and she forced them back down. *Dani's pleasure.* She'd remind herself as often as necessary to maintain control. A few nights ago, Jay had also taken pleasure in Ryan, but it had been with her consent and for *her* pleasure. She'd been on a date then, not conducting business, two vastly different scenarios. But even with Jay, she'd not emotionally connected, nor had she wanted to. Not that Jay wasn't attractive or capable or easy to be with. The problem had been with her. Dani's hands at her pants brought her back to the here and now, where she needed to be.

"I want you." Dani bit her lip. "Can I touch you?"

"Yes."

Dani looked over her shoulder toward the bedroom and Ryan wrapped her arms around her, then stood before gently lowering her to her feet. She waited for Dani to take the lead, confident she was capable of more than she could imagine. The idea that Dani might ask for someone different in order to explore her kinky side crossed Ryan's mind, and it would be best if she did. She didn't want to encourage Dani to develop a deeper relationship with her, the kind Ryan required for the type of sex Dani had hinted at. She'd be content with being the first woman to share her bed with her. She didn't need or want more.

❖

Standing next to the bed with Ryan's warm gaze on her while she patiently waited, Dani wasn't at all sure she could rely on her earlier confidence to see this through.

"Dani," Ryan said, her lips at her ear. "I'm here to serve you. Whatever you want, all you have to do is ask."

A shiver ran down her spine. She was more than turned on, and Ryan offering herself without question for what Dani would do to her only heightened her awareness of everything around her. The pristine, soft looking bedding. The ambient lighting that helped set the mood. The warmth of Ryan's body so close to hers. Closing her eyes, Dani let the now familiar fantasy play in her head until she was ready and gazed up at Ryan.

"Is there music?"

From the drawer of the nightstand, Ryan produced a small remote. "What would you like to hear?" Ryan's words caressed her.

"Something seductive." She bit her lip as Ryan pushed several buttons. The room filled with instrumental music, the beat steady and strong. Underneath the current, an intimacy built with the sound of violins among other instruments, which struck her with so much force her knees shook and she swayed slightly. Ryan caught her.

"Do you want to sit down?" Concern creased her forehead on her otherwise unlined face.

Dani swallowed her natural instinct to let Ryan take over, remembering how much she'd thought about the first time she would brush her fingers through Ryan's wet heat, and she craved that moment more than she wanted to be touched. Dani had to know the first time hadn't been just a whim she'd indulged in. That her attraction to women wasn't just out of curiosity. "No. I want to undress you."

Ryan said nothing and nodded her assent. Something flared in her gaze, but it disappeared so quickly it might have been her mind playing tricks. When she lifted her trembling hand and reached for the leather belt Ryan wore, she froze. Ryan's finger touched her chin, raising her gaze.

"You want this, right?"

She swallowed her insecurity. She'd trusted Ryan to guide her before and she relied on that trust again. "Yes. More than want, though. I *need* to touch you."

"Then there's no reason to doubt yourself." Ryan's smile said she understood. "There's no rush. I'm not going anywhere."

The reassurance was all the encouragement it took to get her moving. She unbuckled the belt as she watched Ryan, looking for signs of regret or wishing she were somewhere else, but her gaze was singularly focused on Dani and buoyed her desire. The hook and bar of her slacks slipped apart easily, but when she drew down the zipper, her head swam, and she paused for an instant before regaining her equilibrium.

"Slip your shoes off." Her voice was stronger than she would have guessed it could be. Ryan toed them off and she dropped the material in a pool around her feet. The black TomboyX boxer briefs hugged Ryan's firm, muscled thighs and she stifled a groan. She'd been so wrapped up in the sensations that assaulted her, Dani had missed details about Ryan that first night, but she was going to make up for it tonight. Dani went to her knees, then removed her socks and laid her clothes on the chair, having a sense that Ryan's world was orderly and neat. With steadier fingers, she finished unbuttoning her shirt until it hung open and loose from her shoulders. Ryan stood still, her breathing even and unlabored and Dani wondered if her blood raced as frantically through her veins as her own pulse did.

She would have liked for Ryan to undress her, but the minute those warm, strong fingers came in contact with her skin she'd want more. "Lie down and watch." Ryan's obedience gave her power beyond her wildest dreams, and she slid the outer layers slowly from her body, then crawled up the bed until she settled over Ryan's thighs. Ryan's eyes were warm, tropical pools, trusting and patient. "You'll help me, right? Tell me what feels good and what doesn't." She bit her lower lip. God, she wanted to touch Ryan everywhere. See and feel her reaction.

Ryan pushed up on her elbows. "Do you remember my fingers, my mouth, and how they felt?"

Dani sucked in a breath as a streak of electricity shot through her. "All of it."

"I knew what you liked and what turned you on by watching and listening. It's the same for most women. I think you'll know what arouses me."

She leaned down for a kiss as confirmation that Ryan wanted what *she* wanted, and when she slipped her tongue into Ryan's mouth, Ryan moaned. A gush of excitement soaked her panties. Dani pushed on her shoulders until she was prone and opened her shirt to reveal her small perfect ovals tipped in a dusky rose, the nipples prominent and tight. Closing her hands over them, Dani massaged the soft flesh and Ryan pressed against her firmly as if inviting her to take more. "You like that," she said out loud more to herself than for Ryan.

"I do. Some women like their nipples squeezed."

Dani rolled and squeezed both nipples and studied her reactions. "Why don't you make any noise if you like that?" Ryan's lack of reaction was disheartening, and Dani wondered if it had to do with some unspoken Agency rule or if it was Ryan's rule to keep what pleased her hidden in order to remain distant.

"Schooling my reaction is meant to focus on a client's pleasure."

"I'd prefer if you didn't." She squeezed again but there was little in the way of pleasure or emotion from Ryan. "You said I'd be able to tell if you liked what I was doing. How am I going to know if you don't show me?" From Ryan's standpoint it probably made perfect sense of course, but if she were there to learn Ryan would have to give some indication she was doing okay in pleasing her, even if it was only a little.

"I'll try to remember that." Ryan quirked a smile and she rewarded her with a searing kiss.

Dani scooted lower, determined to give Ryan something unexpected. She pressed her lips to Ryan's abdomen and the muscles tightened. Peeling her boxers down one inch at a time, Dani kissed the junction of her thigh, then crossed to the trim mound revealed as she worked the boxers all the way off. She took her time taking in all of Ryan, her long body, her expressive eyes, her glistening clit rising from her center. She moved her hand forward and ran a finger along her slit. "Oh, you're so wet."

Ryan laughed softly. "I hope so, otherwise there'd be something seriously wrong with me."

"Because you aren't normally touched by…clients?" She circled the hard knot several times, then slowly slid up and down the length of soft, silk-coated slit.

"Sometimes, but at the moment it has more to do with a beautiful woman teasing me than anything else."

Dani moved her gaze from what she was doing to Ryan's eyes. Her lids were heavy, her fingers digging into the bedding. "I want to be inside you." She wasn't asking for permission. Ryan had already given her that. But she wasn't about to plunge into her without letting her know. Paid or not, she didn't want to be *that* kind of lover. When she slipped her finger inside Ryan tightened, and she stopped. Maybe she'd hurt her. After several long, drawn out kisses that left her breathless, and a few strokes later, she added a finger and Ryan rose to meet her. "Feel good?"

"Very," Ryan said.

She sighed. "I get the whole schooled response and letting me take control thing, but I'm not getting the vibe you're enjoying what's happening, so what's the sense of continuing?" Dani stilled completely—her breathing, her movements, her thoughts—and focused all of her attention on Ryan. If Ryan didn't interact with her soon, she was going to have to rethink this whole scenario between them.

Chapter Eleven

Ryan hadn't really thought this through. Dani was buried inside her, waiting for signs that she was engaged in what was happening. The idea that she was removed from the scene playing out couldn't have been further from the truth, but she recognized her own shortcomings by appearing outwardly detached.

"Dani?"

With an intense gaze, Dani responded. "Yes?"

"Curl your fingers a little and go slow." When she felt the change in position and the sweep of Dani's fingertips against her G-spot, Ryan grabbed Dani's hip. "Oh, yeah. Will you come with me? Please?"

Heat flashed in Dani's eyes. "Tell me what to do."

She guided Dani's leg over her thigh, instantly feeling how wet Dani was. "Slide back and forth while you're fucking me." It didn't take long for Dani's breathing to become erratic, with her own orgasm approaching as Dani's fingers teased her closer. If she wasn't careful, she was going to come. "That's it, baby. Can you feel how tight I'm becoming? Slip out and touch my clit. I'm so hard for your touch."

"Oh, God." Dani's other hand gripped her breast. She squeezed and tugged her nipple as she pressed inside again, sending a lightning streak of pleasure to her core.

Her legs tensed. "I'm going to come." She cupped Dani's neck and pulled her down for a demanding kiss, but Dani fought for dominance. Ryan pressed her leg tighter into Dani. When she jerked against her and pulled her mouth away gasping, she climaxed, and Ryan followed her over the edge, groaning loudly. The weight of Dani's supple body trembling against her was beyond erotic. A few long minutes later, Dani's fingers moved away.

"Jesus," Dani mumbled against her chest, her hands clutching her forearms. She pushed up and focused on her. "I felt you come. It was hot, and..." She limply waved a hand. "How do you describe something you've no words for?"

She brushed a stray curl from Dani's forehead. "Do you need to describe what happened? Isn't it enough that it did?" Ryan ran her hand over her shoulder to the small of her back.

Dani's passion-scented fingertips traced her jaw, trailed her throat. "You're right." The kiss that followed wasn't timid. If she were interpreting the meaning right, they weren't done. "I need a drink. And food." Dani sat up, her hot center against her stomach. "Please tell me there's food."

Ryan chuckled. "You requested it, so I'm sure it's here."

Tipping her head, Dani looked at her. "How can you be so sure?"

She rolled Dani onto her back, then smoothed her hand over Dani's body, liking how it pressed into her touch. "Because I only hire the best. They've never disappointed me yet."

"Like your business, guaranteed to satisfy?"

For some reason, the teasing lilt grated her nerves, as though it were a dig. "There's been no complaint...until now." Ryan studied Dani's face, trying to read what might be hidden behind the casual banter.

"Ryan, I'm not complaining." She scooted off the bed and went to the closet for a robe. "In fact," she began before turning to face her. "After I regain some energy, I want you to teach me how to lick your pussy."

Fuck. She was in deeper trouble. Dani's honest curiosity wasn't only refreshing, it was a total turn-on. She'd have to pull tight on the reins again. "And you want to see my reaction when you do," she said as she pulled on her robe and met Dani in the kitchen.

"Oh yeah. I want you to totally lose control." Dani's smile was anything but sweet.

"Then I'd better help you here, so we can get back there." She lifted her chin toward the bedroom. If a show was what Dani wanted, she'd give her best performance. And like any actor, she'd make sure it didn't bleed into her personal life any more than it already had.

❖

Dani clutched her purse as the Audi pulled up to her apartment. She hadn't gotten much sleep, but oddly she wasn't tired. Exhilarated was a more accurate description. Still, there were a few things left undone and she needed to face Ryan rather than discuss them over the phone.

"Can we talk for a minute?"

Ryan shut the car off and turned to her. "Of course." Ryan's eyes narrowed. "Is something wrong?"

Shaking her head, she laughed out of sudden nerves. "Thank you for indulging me last night…this morning, too."

"It was my pleasure, I assure you." Ryan squeezed her hand.

"The next time, I'd…God, this will sound horrible."

Ryan grinned. "It can't be that bad. Besides, I've been doing this a while and I doubt there's much I haven't heard by now."

She took a steadying breath. "I still want to be with other women." Dani rushed on. "It's not that I didn't enjoy our times… honestly, I just want to have different experiences." Ryan's face was hard to read. She wasn't sure if she was angry, sad, or unmoved by her request.

"Dani, you said so at the beginning. There's no reason you shouldn't explore more. I'm only one woman, and I only offer my own brand of pleasure. How can you know if there's something else you'd enjoy if you don't open yourself to experiencing more?"

The reasonable tone helped reassure her she hadn't offended Ryan because she had another request. "That's good to hear. Thank you." Ryan must have thought she was done because she moved to open her door and she stopped her. "About the…uh…kink. I still want that, too."

Ryan's gaze softened. "That won't be a problem at all. There are a number of escorts who would—"

"No." She flicked her gaze away for an instant before returning to a look of confusion in Ryan's eyes. "If it's okay, I want you to introduce me to that aspect of sex. I'm not sure I could relax with anyone else, and I think that's important. For me to feel safe, to trust the person to take control. Right?"

After studying her for several long beats, Ryan cupped her chin and rubbed her thumb lightly over her lower lip. "Trust is key in those situations, but I don't want you to rush your decision. Take your time. We'll make appointments with one or more of the other escorts just to give you some more experience. Enjoy your time with as many as you want. After that, if you still want me to initiate you to another side of sexual pleasure, I will."

She may not be big on talking in the bedroom, but Ryan's gaze and touch spoke volumes. "That sounds perfect." Dani smiled, feeling more centered than she had in months.

Ryan opened her door but stopped midway to getting out. "Is it okay if I get out now?"

Laughing, she gave a little shove to Ryan's solid shoulder. "Can't wait to be done with me?" she called as Ryan rounded the car to her side.

"Hardly," she said as she reached to help her out. "But at some point the office will expect me to show and I'm already later than usual."

"Oh, I didn't mean to keep you so long." Dani rummaged for her keys as Ryan retrieved her bag and met her on the sidewalk.

"Dani?"

"Yes?"

"I own the company." Ryan shrugged. "I'll get there when I get there, but I do have to tend to business."

"Right." Heat suffused her cheeks. For a short time, she had forgotten Ryan was more than someone in her bed. She'd been lost in fantasyland for the last twelve hours and now it was over. Ryan set her bag at her feet as she shoved the key in the lock.

"I had a wonderful time." Ryan pressed her lips to Dani's palm. "Have a great day."

Her gaze followed Ryan's retreating figure, the long powerful strides so much like the power she exuded in bed. Ryan waved as she drove off, and Dani was left to relive the hours they'd shared.

"Details, girl, and don't leave anything out." Mark took a bite of his burger and made satisfied sounds.

She wondered if he enjoyed sex as much as he seemed to enjoy food. "Okay, but you promise me you won't repeat a word of this to anyone." Dani swirled a French fry in the mound of mayo sitting beside her grilled cheese.

"You know me," Mark said as he made a zipping motion across his mouth. "Now spill."

Dani went on to tell him about her overnight with Ryan. How reserved Ryan had been until she asked for more and she hadn't been disappointed. "I didn't know sex could be so intense. I felt powerful when I made her come." She kept her voice low. Not because she didn't want anyone to overhear her, but because the act itself felt too intimate to share, even though she was sharing it.

Mark made little clapping motions. "See. You didn't know what you were missing until you tried the dark side." He grinned.

She giggled. "It's far from the dark side." Dani hesitated. "I asked her about being with a different woman."

"Was she upset?" Mark leaned forward conspiratorially. "I mean, did she feel like you'd had enough of her?"

"No, no. It was nothing like that. I'd told her from the beginning I wanted other escorts." She managed to make eye contact. "Then I told her I wanted to try some kink, too, and that I wanted her for that."

Mark's eyes got big. "Like tie me down, fuck me senseless kink? Or something more intense, like whips and shit?"

Dani couldn't tell if he was shocked or excited. "I think…I want someone to wield that kind of sexual power over me. Take me to limits I haven't ever been."

"Just be careful. You don't know these women, and you could end up in some heavy shit you don't want to be in." Mark seemed to be talking about his own experience, but since he hadn't shared, she didn't feel right asking him. He'd tell her when he was ready.

"That's just it. I'm going to see other escorts, but I trust Ryan to not lose control because she's *always* in control, of herself and of the situation. I'm not sure I'd feel that way with anyone else." Having to ask her to let go and outwardly show Dani her own pleasure and excitement had solidified the idea of choosing Ryan to bring her through other expressions of sexuality. Even the thought of acting out a scene with Ryan was enough to get her hot.

Mark snapped his fingers in front of her. "You just totally went there, didn't you?" He grinned knowingly.

"Yeah, I did." She returned his smile. "I'm curious. I mean, it's different than being attracted to men. That's a no-brainer now. I'm a woman who likes women. Maybe I'm bi." Dani shrugged. It didn't matter. She liked men, but she'd never been really into them. Physically or emotionally. She'd have to think more on what that meant in the long-term. "The thing with giving up total control and not knowing what's going to happen…it's exciting and I want to try as much as I can." She took a final bite then pushed her plate away. "I want the tied down part, for sure, but I've also thought about sensory deprivation like blindfolds." She laughed. "It's mind-blowing and a turn-on." She shrugged. "Or I think it would be, anyway. I could hate it, I guess, but I don't think I would."

After a few intense minutes of Mark studying her, he took her hand. "Then you go for it. Just...will you text me and let me know where and when? Let me know it went okay and you're safe?"

His genuine concern spoke volumes of their relationship and she loved him even more if that were possible. "I never know where we're going. Everything's pretty cautious, for everyone's sake. I promise I'll let you know when, and I'll tell Ryan I have to send a non-SOS to my best friend." She was confident Ryan would understand. If she didn't, Dani had been wrong about how much she could trust her.

CHAPTER TWELVE

You wanted to see me, Ms. Lewis?" Beck stood in the doorway.

Ryan looked up from the expense spreadsheet she was reviewing. "Come in and close the door, Beck."

A quick flash of the wariness she remembered from her interview crossed Beck's face and she inwardly smiled. "Have a seat. You've been here a couple of months now and I wanted to give you some feedback, as well as to check in about your satisfaction with your position in the company."

Beck's shoulders visibly relaxed. "I didn't know what to expect really, but everyone is very professional and easy to talk to. I've never been paid so well for doing what I enjoy."

"It's a shame not every job sees the value in their employees."

"I agree." Beck's smile faltered. "I hope my clients have been as satisfied with me."

It was Ryan's turn to be a bit serious. "There's been no formal complaints, however I did want to remind you that gossip, even among the staff, regarding clients, won't be tolerated."

To her credit, Beck looked chagrined. "I apologize, Ms. Lewis. The first couple of weeks were a bit stressful while I settled in. I won't let it happen again."

"I trust that it won't." She stood, signaling she had nothing more to add. Ryan didn't believe in browbeating anyone. They would either take the warning or not. If not, dismissal would be in their future, but she didn't think she'd have to worry. Beck had garnered a solid place among the escorts, and learning the rules could be daunting.

"Thank you, Ms. Lewis. You can count on me."

"If I didn't think that were true, you wouldn't be here." Once she was alone, she made a quick note of their conversation and moved on to her next task. Some days she dreaded the number of emails in her inbox, but when her gaze traveled down the list and she saw Dani's name, she froze. Her heart sped up as she clicked it open.

Dear Ms. Lewis,

I'm ready to discuss kink whenever you are. I trust that we can come to an agreement in terms of expectations and I'm sure a phone call is in order to do so. Email isn't practical for conversations.

Fondly,

Dani Brown

She shouldn't have been surprised. Dani wasn't the type to be put off once she made a decision, evident by her pursuit of what she wanted to experience since she'd contacted the Agency. Ryan glanced at the time stamp on the message. It had been sent less than an hour ago. Maybe she could still catch her at home. She pulled up Dani's file and dialed. After the third ring, she prepared to leave a message.

"Hello," Dani said breathlessly just before Ryan heard a loud clatter and a muffled, "Shit." A few seconds later she was back on the line. "You still there?"

"I'm here, Dani."

"Oh, Ryan. I mean…Ms. Lewis. I wasn't expecting your call so soon."

Ryan couldn't help smiling. "It's okay to call me Ryan, and if this is a bad time, I can call you another time."

"No!" Dani said. "I mean, now is good, I was just taking…oh, never mind." Dani sighed.

She couldn't help laughing in spite of trying to remain professional, as much as she could anyway. "You wanted to discuss exploring kink and the BDSM world. Are you interested in discovering your pleasure/pain threshold?"

"Like how much pain?"

"There are levels. Some people just like a bit of sting, a bit of something extra. Some people like being marked or made to bleed, or breath play. Others are into heavy punishment or torture, like bull whips, although some of those same women are driven to similar extremes as a form of self-punishment."

"Definitely not that. I wouldn't mind my ass slapped, being restrained, that kind of thing."

"Okay. That helps. Because I'm not the woman who would provide the intense type of punishment if that's what you wanted. There are several other women who are capable of providing that particular service." Ryan had never been one who engaged in the far fringe of interplay, though a lot of scenes excited her. "On the other hand, spanking bare-handed or with certain implements, edging, sensory deprivation, and some forms of bondage are all things I'm capable of providing. I can explain any of them now or before we start. If you like, I can send you a list of the things I provide, along with a link to a great directory of fetish/kink terms."

She'd used a cat or cane enough times to know she didn't get any pleasure from inflicting that level of pain and wasn't into that kind of play. She never had to worry about losing herself in the moment like others who were inexperienced, or the way true sadists could.

"I had no idea there was so much. I've read some articles, but they only touched basics."

"A lot of what is kink some call fetishes, and it all ties in with power play and scenes. Confidence in a submissive's ability to recognize their own limits is important, and allowing those limits to be pushed is a shared responsibility. Everyone's level of tolerance is different, Dani. If you want light exploration, I think that would be the best place to start."

"I want to learn as much as I can. I'm just not sure about everything yet."

"It's okay to take your time. See what you're comfortable with while trying to remember that just because you've never done something doesn't mean you can't."

"Uh-huh." Dani didn't sound like she was okay about it, but this was her learning curve.

"I need to know if there are implements you're curious about and would like to try. If you're not sure, the condo will have them available. You can pick whatever you like or leave it up to me."

"Is it okay if I let you decide, based on what I've told you?" Dani asked, her voice solid again.

Ryan wasn't sure if Dani would like her decisions, but she trusted in her experience. "Thank you for trusting me, Dani. I'll see you soon." She put just enough huskiness in her voice to make Dani's breath catch, and she hung up smiling.

Three weeks later, Ryan typed out Dani's name and address, then sent the confirmation off to Drake. She wasn't sure what she was feeling about Dani picking Drake for her next encounter, but they'd also made another appointment for her to explore her boundaries with kink and bondage. Ryan's center stirred. She hadn't played out a scene since her night with Trish, and she'd let Trish lead out of curiosity rather than from any deep desire to sub. Switching was fun occasionally, but it was in her nature to be the one calling the shots. Although it had been well over a year since she'd been a dominant in the bedroom professionally, she was looking forward to it. She pushed away the low thrum of arousal. There was work that needed to be done.

Her email account held twelve new client inquiries. They all required screening, background checks, and if cleared, scheduling for encounters. Ryan sighed. Maybe she should hire a different kind of screener to do the preliminary work, then she quickly pushed the thought away. If something bad ever happened to one of her employees because she'd entrusted their safety to someone less diligent, she'd never forgive herself. Her head jerked up at the telltale rap on her door.

"Come in."

Drake strode in, her long, straight blond hair flowing over her shoulders, and the crisply ironed black shirt lent to her androgynous presence.

"Ryan," Drake said, before taking a seat in front of her desk. "I just opened the email with Daniella's information."

She sat back and maintained her neutral expression. Drake rarely questioned her on business matters, even if she did harp on her incessantly on her wayward personal life. "Go on."

"Are you sure you want me to escort her?" For the first time in years, Drake looked uncomfortable.

"She picked you from the group. It's not about what I want. This is all about what Dani wants. But you already know that." Ryan smiled. Drake broke eye contact, another thing she rarely did. "What's bothering you?"

Drake sat back and studied her for a long beat. The silence between them grew uncomfortable. "You've been with her."

"And she's not the first client more than one of us has shared. What about this time is different?" She could tell Drake was trying to formulate her words so as not to offend, not that she could. They'd been friends too long to let business ruin their connection. She went to the credenza and poured a few inches of scotch in tumblers, handed one to her, and leaned against the front of her desk.

"Because you came out of retirement for her, and I don't want to have to try to live up to your reputation." Drake threw back half of her drink and waited, her smoky eyes full of emotion.

Ryan leaned forward. "You don't have to *try* anything. Just be your usual charming, sexy, self." The statement garnered a smile from Drake. "If I was all that, why would she want to expand her experiences? It appears Ms. Brown has grown tired of me already." She sighed dramatically before laughing, even though it actually hurt a little in a way that surprised her. After finishing the scotch, she tapped Drake's knee with the glass. "Is that what's really got you in a knot?"

Drake ran a hand over her face, swallowed the remainder, and sat forward. "You and I are quite different in bed. What if she doesn't like my style?"

She wasn't sure where the sudden case of insecurity was coming from, but friend or not, Drake was an employee, and she was expected to perform her duty the same as everyone else. "I suggest you make sure Dani has a good time. You've never had a complaint from the hundreds of women you've bedded for the business, including the one's I've been with prior to you. I don't expect there to be any reason for your performance streak to change." Ryan moved behind her desk to take her rightful seat. Drake stood to inherit a small fortune when Ryan stepped down as CEO if she didn't die first, and she trusted Drake to continue to give her absolute best for the sake of the Agency. "I know you were worried that I would make the Sarah mistake again, but as you can see, it's not an issue. So enjoy yourself and show her your way to have a good time."

Drake's eyes sparkled with the familiar light that meant she'd accepted the challenge. "I'll not let you down, Ms. Lewis." The door closed and the soft footfalls of her retreat was a centering sound.

Ryan didn't have an explanation for not telling Drake she'd be seeing Dani again at the month's end when Dani's fascination with kink and BDSM play would come into the picture. She was looking forward to seeing how far Dani was willing to be pushed in her physical and mental limits of pleasure. Now that they've had a discussion, Ryan was certain Dani would enjoy her adventure into the unknown.

One thing was certain, she didn't have to worry about Dani wanting to top her. She probably didn't know what it meant, even though some people were very adept at topping from the bottom. In a way, Dani had done that to some degree by giving orders the other night. As she smiled, Ryan got back to the work waiting for her. There were still a number of women to vet, and it wasn't going to get done if she got lost in her own fantasy world. The one where Dani was tied down and begging for relief.

Dani hurried across the street, dodging traffic, and ignoring the blast of a horn. If she didn't get the deposit in before the bank closed, her boss would have a fit. She was just reaching for the door when it opened, nearly knocking her to the ground.

"Oh my God, I'm so sorry..." Ryan's firm grip steadied her. "Dani?"

She smiled shyly. For some reason seeing Ryan outside of their arranged times made her feel a bit off. "Hi." She clutched the deposit bag to her chest like she was afraid to let go. "I'm the one who's sorry. I was in too much of a rush."

"You're okay then?" Ryan's fingertips moved down her arm.

Nodding, she took a step back. Ryan was too close and it was discombobulating. "Fine. I need to get inside before they close."

Ryan's brows drew together. "You came alone with that?" She pointed to the bag.

"Yeah. It was my turn and..." She glanced at her watch. "I really have to go."

"Okay." Ryan stepped back and opened the door for her.

"It was great to see you outside of..." She shook her head and hustled inside. Ryan must think she was a total moron. She got to the window a few seconds before the guard locked the door and dimmed the lights. Dani was the last person inside. Five minutes later, with the deposit ticket and empty bag stuffed in her purse, the guard let her out. "Good night." No longer in a rush, she took a breath and glanced up at the deep blue sky where pillowy clouds moved slowly to the east. With the rest of the evening off and nowhere to be, she decided to take a stroll along the storefronts. From the corner of her eye, a tall figure approached and for a brief instant, she tensed.

"Would you care to have coffee with me? Or a drink?" Ryan asked, though she seemed tentative.

Dani would have never pictured her as uncertain. She narrowed her eyes. "Are you stalking me?" When Ryan blanched, she laughed. "I'm kidding." Relief showed on Ryan's face as she shared a tight smile. "Do I have to pay for this impromptu rendezvous?"

Light danced in Ryan's eyes. "CEO privilege. This one's on me."

"Well, in that case, I accept." Her heart hammered in her chest. She still couldn't believe she'd slept with the gorgeous woman who had taken her hand and was guiding her to an outrageously expensive looking car. "Is this yours, too?"

Ryan clicked the remote and opened the passenger door for her. "All employees have Agency supplied cars. The Audis are part of our fleet. This one is actually mine."

Dani slid onto the rich leather before Ryan rounded the car and got in, folding her long legs inside gracefully. "No wonder the fees are so high."

There was a moment's hesitation before Ryan pressed the button and the engine roared to life. "I admit they're high to some, but we provide everything and with meticulous detail. It has to be that way. Being an escort isn't a lifetime career. No one wants to sleep with an old person unless they're married to them." Ryan's tone was sharp.

She'd never heard her speak in such a clipped manner. "I didn't mean anything, really. I didn't know the cars were part of employee benefits." Ryan straightened, put the car in gear, and whipped out into traffic with such confidence, Dani wondered if she'd ever driven professionally.

"I'm sorry." Ryan glanced over, then shifted. "I don't like the idea of you becoming a robbery target."

"We all take turns and we've never had a problem." She touched Ryan's forearm. "Thanks for being concerned." Not many people worried about her, or even gave what she did a second thought.

Ryan's face relaxed. "You're welcome, though it's really none of my business. I'm sure you're careful and aware of your surroundings."

Usually she was in a hurry, like today, and barely thought about anything but getting to the bank and then home. That was going to change. Ryan was right. She needed to pay attention. "So, do you live in the neighborhood?"

"Clifton Park. Though this area's been my playground for a while." Ryan gunned through the next intersection and pulled into a parking lot behind Broadway. "Did you grow up around here?"

"Syracuse. Once I got my cosmetology license, I was ready to escape my parents' house. Now I live in Middle Grove. It's a little town—"

"West of Saratoga." Ryan smiled and turned off the car. "I've been there. Remember?"

"Right." What was wrong with her?

Ryan opened her door. "Shall we?"

She hesitated for a minute before stepping out and meeting Ryan on the sidewalk. Being with her like this had her at odds, but she was used to conversing with her clients. "Have you always lived in the area?"

A shadow darkened Ryan's gaze. "No. I'm not originally from this part of the state."

The topic sounded off limits and she decided to let the moment play out in silence. A block later, Ryan opened the door to a quaint bistro on a side street she'd never been down.

"Here we are."

She stepped inside and let her eyes adjust from the bright outdoors. The atmosphere was charming. Small white lights were strung along the ceiling and candles flickered on each dark wooden table. More were evenly spaced on the long, polished bar. Thriving plants hung from the walls in flat, colorful containers, and others sat in huge pots in strategic corners, lending to the warmth. "This is beautiful."

Ryan placed her hand at the small of her back. "I'm glad you like it. Table or bar?"

There was an open table near the big front window, intimate and away from other patrons but she didn't think an intimate setting was right, unless they were dating, which they weren't, and she didn't want a chance meeting to get in the way of their professional interactions. "The bar." If Ryan was disappointed, she didn't show it.

"Here?" Ryan pointed to the end of the bar, away from patron traffic.

"Perfect." She settled onto a thickly padded stool with a contemporary back that was surprisingly comfortable.

Before Ryan sat, the bartender came from the back carrying a case of beer. He smiled when he saw her. "Ms. Lewis," he said before they shook hands. "It's been a while. Good to see you again."

"Likewise, Will. This is Daniella Brown."

"Nice to meet you, Ms. Brown. What can I get you?"

It wasn't quite dinner time, but she had tomorrow off. The week had been hectic with working every shift she could at the salon, and she was scheduled for both Saturday and Sunday at the restaurant to help support her indulgences. Ryan was one of them, no question. Inside, she smiled. "Pinot Grigio, please."

Ryan ordered a whiskey. "They have a quirky but fun menu if you'd like something to eat." As she turned to face her their knees brushed and the contact sent an electric shock up her leg to land directly in her center.

"I'm good for now." She took a sip of wine and then surreptitiously studied Ryan's profile. Her features were chiseled, but not harsh, reminding her of Greek statues. She wore dark gray slacks, a rust-colored shirt with a matching paisley tie, and a black suit jacket. When she glanced up, Ryan was staring at her, the corner of her mouth twitched.

"Do you like the view?"

"It's exceptional." She sipped again. "Do you always dress to impress?"

Ryan's gaze traveled over her in a slow, deliberate motion, and reminded her of their first time together when she'd looked at her the same way.

"When I'm working, yes."

"Do you ever not work?" She had the impression that Ryan was dedicated to running her business, leaving little time to enjoy life.

"On occasion." Ryan drank, then licked a drop from her top lip with the tip of her tongue. The move was sensual and erotic, and Dani became lost in the memory of the sensations Ryan's lips and tongue could provide. "Why do you want to know?" Ryan's voice jolted her back.

"I…" She took a breath. "I've never seen you in casual clothes." Ryan studied her and she wondered what she was seeing.

"If you're asking if I ever wear jeans, the answer is yes, I do. Is that important?"

"I don't know." She wasn't sure why she was asking, until her mind wandered to how Ryan would look in a tight pair of denim jeans, especially if she were packing. *Oh my God, where did that come from?* Her eyes got big as heat travelled up her neck and she hoped Ryan didn't notice, but of course, she had.

"What were you thinking about just now?"

Dani considered avoiding the question, but there wasn't any reason to with Ryan. "About you in jeans and packing."

Ryan's eyes flared with unmistakable desire. "Would that be something you'd be interested in? A lover who wears a cock?"

Glancing around and being relieved no one was in hearing range, she leaned closer and placed her hand on Ryan's thigh, the muscle beneath flexing. She was playing with fire, and she liked the way it burned. "I think I would."

"How do you know I'm not?"

Dani glanced at Ryan's crotch before she could stop herself. "I..." She fumbled for the words that refused to form.

Ryan's hand brushed hers. "I'm teasing, I'm not at the moment."

"Jesus. I should know better than to prod you." She raked her fingers through her hair in an attempt to tone down her runaway libido.

"I'll be sure to tell Drake. She loves giving women exactly what they want." Ryan finished her drink. "Can you stay longer?"

She was surprised by Ryan volunteering her next escort to indulge her. It also made her wet, thinking about them discussing what her sexual fantasies included, and a picture of the three of them in bed together flashed before her. Maybe she'd ask. She'd have to get a third job if she kept this up. The thought made her laugh.

"Something amuses you?" Ryan slowly smiled at her.

"I was thinking I'm going to have to work a lot more if I keep coming up with fantasies." She drained her glass. "And, yes, I can stay. I'm not in any hurry to go home." Dani wasn't sure of her motivation, or why she was willing to blur the established line by socializing with Ryan, but she also didn't want to examine what it meant. Ryan clearly cared about her, even if it was all professionally motivated. Besides, it was a pleasant change from the idle gossip she had to endure every day.

Ryan moved them to a table away from the growing number of patrons and they ordered appetizers to share. To an outsider, Ryan might appear aloof, but Dani had witnessed her genuine concern and kindness. Sophistication was her true, or maybe perfected, nature. She'd never seen her act rudely or as though she was better than those around her, even if the car she drove spoke of having more money than Dani would likely make in a lifetime no matter how many jobs she had.

"Tell me something about your life outside of the Agency." She wasn't sure where the sudden desire to know Ryan on a more personal level came from, but now that it was out, there wasn't much choice.

Sitting back a bit with her tumbler, Ryan stared into the contents before beginning. "I have good friends. People I can rely on to buoy my spirit and give me a reason to laugh. I appreciate their unconditional love. My family, the one I was permanently placed with and adopted by, gave me stability when I needed it. I'm grateful to them for that. But they've never *felt* like a family, not that I'd know what that felt like. Maybe because they aren't blood or maybe because I'm so physically different from them. Like the only brown egg in a carton of white ones. I've always stood out and apart from them."

Dani regretted causing Ryan discomfort when talking about what was obviously a very private topic. "You're very successful. Everyone who knows you should be glad they do."

Ryan caught her gaze and held on. "Are you glad you met me, Dani?"

There was the distinct feeling she was being asked more than the question implied. "Of course. You're charming. How could I not be?" She smiled and Ryan chuckled, the dour mood seeming to dissipate a bit.

The rest of their conversation centered around lighter topics after Ryan's revelation. Dani shared anecdotal stories of patrons at the shop and how a lot of the women were pretentious. Ryan spoke of her dislike for running and said she only did it because she got to spend time with her best friend, though it did help keep her in shape.

"I happen to like your shape," Dani blurted. Perhaps the second glass of wine hadn't been wise after all.

"Mine may not be the only shape you like, but you won't know until you've had an opportunity to find out."

Dani's curiosity rose to the top. Again. "Do you employ a variety of women? I mean, I've seen their faces, but not their bodies." She asked the waiter for coffee and Ryan ordered an espresso.

"There are a wide range of women within the Agency with a variety of body types. In terms you may be familiar with we employ femme, butch, androgynous, and nonbinary individuals. The only thing they have in common is that they enjoy being with and are attracted to women. Each has unique talents and is capable of satisfying a variety of needs. The business was built on the premise of women's desire to be with other women, and I would like to continue to promote that mentality, no matter the form of desire."

From what little Dani knew of the policies of the Agency, it was held to a foundation of principles that seemed to align with those of Ryan herself. Ryan's company provided a discreet, safe haven for women to live out both their desire for companionship and their sexual fantasies. She couldn't help but wonder if there were times Ryan was so committed that she denied herself simpler pleasures.

"Do you have a lover?" Dani asked.

"I have a few casual liaisons."

Dani pushed on. "I meant a partner."

"In my line of work there aren't many women willing to share their partner with other women."

Dani studied her, waiting for more.

"No. I don't have a partner."

The idea of Ryan having sacrificed personal relationships for her business bothered her, and she wondered if Ryan had something against long-term. Perhaps she'd had one that was a fiasco, though certainly that happened to a lot of people. There had to be more to it. She couldn't understand why someone like Ryan would choose a solitary life when she could have it all. And yet, the niggling feeling that all wasn't right in Ryan's world refused to go away. Dani leaned forward. "I'm sorry. I didn't mean to pry."

"There are many aspects of my life that I enjoy. Spending time with beautiful women is a hardship I gladly bear." The smile transformed Ryan's trouble expression into one of true beauty.

"I'm very happy you do." Even as she said the words, Dani continued to question if Ryan had swapped one type of life, one with a long-standing relationship, for a solitary, superficial existence. If so, had that happened by choice or circumstance? She had a feeling that was one thing about Ryan she might never know.

CHAPTER THIRTEEN

You wanted to see me?" Drake eyed her cautiously.

"Coffee?" she asked as she stirred a little cream into a china cup. The collection had been one her adoptive grandparents had bequeathed her, and she vowed to use them so she could remember something good from her early years.

"I'm good."

She faced her. "That's what I've heard, too."

Drake gave her a roguishly handsome smile. "So I'm here because you want to give me praise? That's nice."

She settled behind her desk, not in a role of authority though. Drake had never questioned who was in charge even when she thought Ryan *had* lost her mind a time or two. They were discussing business and her way of keeping the lines between employee and friend clear. "I didn't think you needed your ego stroked."

Drake laughed heartily. "You're right, I don't. I already know I'm good."

Ryan grinned. "I've had a conversation with Ms. Brown. She asked about women who pack, and since I know you enjoy showing off your stuff, I thought I'd pass it along."

Drake was all attention as she moved to the edge of her seat. "I like a woman who knows what she wants. Is there anything else I should know?"

"I'll admit she has a sexy way about her without being over-the-top, along with a killer body. A lot of our clients are attractive in many different ways. Dani is...*intriguing.*" She twitched her eyebrow as she recalled the word she'd initially used when she'd first called Dani. "She's uninhibited. She's not afraid to try or do new things, but she isn't altogether sure what it is she wants and keeps coming up with ideas."

"In other words," Drake's mouth quirked in a half grin, "she's a challenge."

Ryan laughed. "That she is."

"Noted." Drake stood. She could almost hear the anticipation in Drake's tone.

"Drake?" She turned to face her. "Wear leather."

Drake's eye color darkened. "Whatever the boss says."

She could always count on Drake to rise to the occasion, no matter what demand she put on her. After draining her coffee cup, she stood by the window, admiring the expanse of trees and architecture that dotted the landscape. The sky was darker now than it had been, and the impending storm wasn't just an atmospheric phenomenon. The storm brewing inside was just as ominous, and the change was both frightening and exhilarating.

As she rubbed her eyes, she thought about the evening she'd literally run into Dani, and visions of her sitting across the table, the candlelight reflected in her eyes. Not to mention her beautiful smile that had left Ryan aching in a nonsexual way. She hadn't thought about the consequences of her actions. Her initial reaction had been anger when she'd thought Dani was vulnerable to robbery, and her instinct to protect her had kicked in. When Dani emerged unscathed and she'd calmed down, she'd just wanted to spend time with her without the obligation of being paid to do so.

The offer of a drink had unequivocally turned into a date rather than a prearranged time to quell Dani's physical needs. The spontaneity of doing so was out of character for her, but then, ever since her first contact with Dani she'd not felt like herself. Sighing, Ryan took refuge in what had been her savior for more than a decade. All she needed to do was focus on work, and the rest would take care of itself, though she wondered if either of those sentiments were true.

❖

"What have you got planned this week?" Pam asked as she put the finishing touches on her client, a woman whose hair was tinged with blue highlights and cut in a severe fade on one side.

"Nothing tonight. Not after the day we've had." The shop had been full of nonstop demanding customers, all wanting next-to-impossible services that would make them beautiful. Unfortunately, many were rich and privileged, wanting a miracle worker, not just a stylist, to achieve the desired effects. Ryan was rich and liked the finer things money could buy, but she never put on airs. *Huh.* Random thoughts of Ryan were becoming a frequent occurrence and even more so since their impromptu dinner together.

"Want to grab a beer and a pizza?"

The shop was closing in fifteen minutes and Dani wanted to be anywhere but on her feet. "If it means I can sit down for the next hour without moving, count me in."

"I'll wait on you myself if I have to." Pam made a kissy face and she laughed.

Lucky for her, their favorite pub was only a short block from work. She changed into athletic shoes before they headed out, and her feet were already grateful. They slid into one of the empty booths, ordered, and Dani settled against the smooth wood. "What's on your agenda? Any hits?"

Pam had been cruising Cupid.com without much luck. "Seriously? The only hits I'm getting are for free haircuts or a quick fuck. Doesn't anyone ever date anymore?" Pam had married young and went through a divorce a few years ago. She was glad children hadn't been involved. The separation had been messy enough.

Dani swung her feet up onto the bench next to Pam. What she was doing wasn't dating either, was it? True, she'd been wined and dined well enough before tumbling into bed with a stranger, but being with Ryan hadn't felt awkward at all. In fact, she'd enjoyed the lack of entanglement that dating involved, with one or the other wondering if there'd be a follow-up call or text, or even worse, being ghosted.

"Hey," Pam said into the silence. "What are you thinking about?"

The waitress placed their beers down, along with plates and napkins. She sat up, debating if she should share any details with her co-worker. They weren't super close, like she was with Mark, but they were friends, and right now Mark was among the missing, shacked up with some "hot body" who promised to show him the best time of his life. She hoped the guy kept his promise. Mark deserved being treated like more than a blow-up doll to be used and then left deflated. Would it be terrible if Pam knew a bit of what had her excited about getting through tonight so she could enjoy tomorrow?

"I have a date tomorrow."

Pam's eyes lit up. "Really? Tell me more about tall, dark, and handsome."

Little did Pam know she had two out of three right. Drake was blond and green-eyed, and Ryan had shared a full-length photo when she'd asked. Drake looked about the same height as Ryan, with slightly narrower shoulders and hips. From what Dani could tell, her breasts might be fuller, but that was just a guess. Whatever she shared she had to remember to be discreet. The Agency was adamant about anonymity, and she wasn't about to screw up her connection for the sake of gossip.

"She's quite handsome for sure." She'd captured the headshot of both women on her phone screen so she could study them.

Pam was about to say something when the waitress brought the pizza over and set down a shaker of grated cheese.

"You gals good for now?"

"Yes, thanks." She slid a slice onto Pam's plate before serving herself. When she glanced up, Pam was staring with a shocked expression. "What?"

"I didn't know you were going to keep doing this. I mean, not that it matters." Pam shook her head as though she shouldn't have assumed.

"Well, I don't want to limit myself, you know. I mean..." Dani bit off a piece of pizza and chewed while she tried to put into words what she hadn't been able to talk about until recently. "There's never been that spark with anyone, and lately I've been thinking a lot about how different being with a woman is. It could be a one-time thing, you know, but if it isn't I may have my reason for never feeling emotionally or physically fulfilled."

Pam chewed and took a sip. "It's not like you would have gotten away with trying that when you lived at home, that's for sure."

Dani rolled her eyes at the understatement. Conservative Catholics didn't think there was any relationship other than that between a man and a woman, and it had been one of the driving factors behind her escaping her overbearing and controlling parents. But she wasn't under her parents' rule anymore and she was beyond idly waiting to discover who she was and who she was attracted to. "Right? I'm focusing on me, not finding a life partner. I don't even know if such a person exists for me. Marriage doesn't work for everyone." When she met Pam's eyes the sadness in them reminded her of the recent end of Pam's relationship. "Jesus. What an ass." She reached for her hand and squeezed. "I'm sorry."

Pam shook her head and gave a small smile. "It's okay. Listen, just because I chose the wrong person to love doesn't mean the same is true for others." She took a drink and leaned in. "So tell me what it was like."

She told her what she was comfortable with, not wanting to cheapen what she'd done with Ryan. The amazing first kiss. The heart-stopping first touch. The overall feeling of contentment. The unpretentious enjoyment of what they'd shared.

"Wow," Pam said. She finished her beer and pushed away her plate. "So are you going to see her again?"

"In a few weeks."

"Oh, I thought you said you had a date tomorrow night."

"I do. With a different woman."

Pam's smile was genuine. "Girl, you're living the dream."

She tossed money on the table and gathered her things. "That I am." Of course, those dreams were expensive, but so far they'd been well worth the sacrifice.

Chapter Fourteen

At exactly seven o'clock, a silver Audi roared to a stop in front of Dani's apartment. She watched through the peephole as the occupant, her escort for the evening, strode up the walk with a confident swagger and a cocky smile. Dani waited several long seconds before opening the door. Drake's gaze slowly traveled over her and the heat in her eyes felt like a tactile experience.

"Hi, I'm Drake, your escort."

"Hello, Drake." She extended her hand. "I'm Dani." Her hand was smooth and engulfed Dani's much smaller one.

"My pleasure. Shall we go?"

When she turned to get her jacket, she took a breath. Drake was stunning, in a male runway model kind of way. She slipped her crossbody over her shoulder then checked for her keys. When she turned back, she smiled, determined to have a good time, even though she couldn't quite ignore the tiny stab of disappointment that it wasn't Ryan at her door instead. "All set."

Drake wrapped her arm around her waist, then led her to the car. As Drake went around to the driver's side, Dani followed her movement and the electricity she emitted from where she sat made her skin tingle.

"I thought we'd go for a drink and get to know each other a bit if that's okay." Drake's hand gripped her thigh possessively and the contact made her clit jump.

"That's fine. I could use a stiff one." The words were out before she could sensor them.

Drake shot her a heated look and smiled knowingly. "I like a woman who knows what she wants."

Dani bit the inside of her cheek. The contrasting energy between Drake and Ryan was a bit disconcerting. Ryan's responses were unhurried, and her overall demeanor was one of sophistication. She sensed Drake was wilder, untamed. Demanding. The air in the car practically crackled from her energy, and Dani's body was on high alert.

A few minutes later, they pulled up to the valet service at Vapor Night Club, the "in" place to go in Saratoga Springs. Drake spoke to the attendant before meeting Dani on the sidewalk. Music drifted out to them as another patron entered. Drake grasped her hand and led the way. She flashed a VIP card at the door, bypassing the cover charge. The pulsing lights from the ceiling matched the beat of the song playing. It was fairly early to be at a club, and they found a couple of unoccupied seats at the bar.

"What would you like?" Drake asked.

"Grapefruit martini, please." The bartender nodded and Drake ordered a dirty martini. She almost snorted out loud. The drink choice fit Drake's personality.

"To enjoying tonight," Drake said as she lifted her glass in a toast.

Dani let the first sip of alcohol relax her enough that she no longer spun on the merry-go-round that was Drake. "How long have you been an escort?"

Drake sipped from her cocktail. "Let's see," she began as she looked at some distant point. "About twelve years."

Dani had only been doing hair for a few years, but she couldn't see herself doing anything else. "Do you like what you do?"

"I love sex and I love fucking women. So, yeah, I do."

"That's good." Maybe someday she'd consider a different profession, but she wasn't in any hurry to change her life. Well, except for being a lesbian. Was she a lesbian now? Did sleeping with a woman twice mean she'd never go back to sleeping with guys? Still so many questions to be answered. She couldn't see herself long term with any of the men she'd met, then she remembered seeing the shadow that had crossed Ryan's face when she asked about a partner. What memory had caused the momentary shield Ryan usually had in place to falter? She could have pushed and asked, but she'd realized some things were too private to share, especially since they weren't dating. She was startled from her thoughts when she heard her name.

"Dani?"

"Hmm?"

"Are you having second thoughts about being with me?" Drake's eyes had a questioning, almost wounded appearance.

After giving herself a mental kick, she refocused on the woman beside her. There was no reason to fixate on anyone else when there was a gorgeous woman right there. She shook her head and smiled. "No. Sorry. It's been a long week."

Drake studied her for a few minutes. "That's okay." Her gaze moved to Dani's lips before returning to her eyes. "I hope I can help you forget for a while." Drake's hand possessively held her hip. The bulge in her leather pants left little to the imagination and Dani's imagination needed no help in thinking about what Drake was going to do with the cock resting against her thigh. She'd been reading up on the subject, surprised at how much information was available on the internet, and glad she hadn't had to go searching in porn shops for answers to questions she didn't even have yet.

"Would you like to dance?"

At first glance, Drake's long blond hair and mesmerizing eyes gave the impression she leaned feminine, though that was in direct contrast to everything else about her. Dani sensed power in her shoulders that were nearly as wide as Ryan's. Her blood had begun to run hot the moment she'd stepped out of the Audi. She wouldn't regret a thing about tonight, and the freedom she felt of finally being in control of her life as well as what was happening in her bed, made her light-headed. She finished her drink. "Yes, but not here."

Drake's brow rose as her full lips formed a knowing grin. She pulled money from her pocket, leaving a generous tip, and took her hand. "Then let's not delay."

Her clothes felt too tight. The anticipation of what would happen when they arrived at whatever apartment they had for the evening made her break out in gooseflesh. She wasn't afraid. Drake didn't give off danger vibes, but the energy wafting from her was nonetheless intense. She glanced in her direction.

"I understand you're looking for a different experience tonight." Drake shifted smoothly as they cruised along the boulevard.

She laughed. "Am I the subject of many conversations?"

Drake looked over at her, then back at the road. "No. Just looking for clarity to make sure you're satisfied with this evening's events."

Of course. Ryan would have told her of Dani's request. "I couldn't help noticing you've come prepared." Their car entered the underground parking for another high-rise condominium and rolled to a stop in front of a wall displaying 8A in black lettering.

Drake turned off the car and smiled. "Please wait for me to open your door." She took a duffel from the trunk before reaching Dani. "Right this way." Hand in hand, they walked to the elevator where Drake swiped a key card and pushed eight. The elevator smoothly rose, soft music playing in the background.

The minute she stepped into the enclosed space, Dani again felt Drake's vibrant life force surround her. Drake leaned against the wall, looking her over from head to toe, the caress of her gaze so intense she could already imagine her touch, sending a shiver up her spine. The bell chimed and the elevator slowed. When the doors opened, she let out the breath she'd been holding, and her vision blurred.

Drake caught her. "Are you all right?"

The hallway in front of her stopped swimming. "Yes, just warm in that small space." Her smile felt awkward. Drake guided her to a door marked "A" and swiped the card again, then brought her inside. Once she was seated on the leather sofa, Drake went to the bar and produced a couple of waters, opening one.

"Drink some of this, please."

Grateful for something to do with her hands, she took several swallows and instantly felt better. "Thanks. I'm good now."

"Well, that's a relief. I'd hate to think we'd have to cancel our evening." Drake slid her hand over her ribs, her thumb against the side of her breast.

"That would have been a shame." She wanted Drake's touch. Longed to feel her against her and her cock at her soaked entrance.

Drake picked up a remote from the coffee table and the apartment filled with sultry jazz. "Shall we have that dance now?" Her eyes brightened.

"Oh, yeah. I'd like that." Once in her arms, Drake pressed the prominence in her pants against Dani's center. It was hard and soft at the same time.

"Can you feel me, Dani?" Drake's lips brushed the curve of her ear. "I'm going to enjoy fucking you so much."

If it weren't for the fact that she was paying a great deal for Drake's attention she would have told her to take her right there. That's what a guy would do, and while Drake may have an ambiguous gender name, she was every bit a woman. God. How could she have been so blind for so long? The sudden movement of being backed across the room as they danced jarred her to the present.

"What are you thinking about?" Drake spoke again when Dani hesitated. "Tell me."

"How much I want you to fuck me and how much I'm struggling with going slow."

Drake's hand wove into her hair and she pulled, exposing Dani's throat. After running her teeth down the column, Drake pinned her against the wall. "Why would you want to go slow?"

She groaned. Every fiber of every nerve in her body was alive, tingling with such anticipation she wasn't sure she could stop if she wanted to. "Because I've never been fucked by a woman. Not...not like that."

Fingers at the buttons of her shirt, Drake kept her there by pressing her thigh into her center. "Do you think it will be fast? Over before it's barely begun?" Drake flicked the blouse from her shoulders, then lifted her hands over her head and held them there with one hand while she kneaded her breasts with the unoccupied one.

Thinking became a chore. Nothing made sense. Drake teased her flesh incessantly and her nipples turned into hard pebbles. "No."

"Do you think my cock will go soft before you're satisfied?" Drake smoothed over her abdomen, cupped her crotch, and squeezed. She gasped. "No, no." She tried to push her away. Her mind warred with her body. She wanted what Drake was offering, but everything was happening so fast, she trembled in her grasp.

"Stop fighting me. Stop fighting yourself and what you want."

The kiss that followed made her weak-kneed. Drake was much more aggressive than Ryan. Not in a bad way. Different. Uncontrolled. Instinctual. Drake was as wild and dominating as a lion. A powerful animal intent on mating. Dani imagined that was also how she fucked. She'd had enough control in her life. It was time to enjoy what was happening. In the back of her mind, no matter how intimidated she might feel at the moment, she trusted Ryan wouldn't have sent Drake to her if there was any chance Dani wouldn't enjoy what she was offering.

"What's your safe word?"

"What?"

The weight of Drake's body against her disappeared and her whimper was real. With her hands still held above her head, Drake's vivid green eyes danced with desire. "You need a safe word because sometimes no doesn't really mean no, does it? Sometimes," Drake said as she used her free hand to undo the grommets encasing her hips in leather. "No means keep going. Don't stop." She grasped the bulge so close to the opening Dani could almost see it.

Her chest heaved. She was so turned on…so afraid of her own wanton needs, she almost forgot to breathe. Years of being under her parents' rule had done little to suppress her natural desires, and she'd found refuge in the books she read, her appetite voracious, devouring page after page. She could go anywhere, do anything, with no one to stop her. No one to make her behave or follow a righteous path. Those days were behind her. She would never again succumb to anyone's will unless she chose to, and here she was, wanting to succumb to whatever Drake wanted.

"Thunder," she blurted.

To Drake's credit, she hardly missed a beat as she withdrew her cock from the confines of her pants. The head of a dark purple dildo poked from the opening and Drake ran her fingers along the still covered shaft. "Is this what you want?"

"More than you know." Her bravery returned. Drake was a professional. She wouldn't hurt her, or use her, or abuse her unless that's what *she* wanted. And even then, there were rules.

Before she knew what was happening, Drake had her naked to the waist and facing the wall, arms splayed out and legs wide. Drake's hands smoothed over her heated skin while her lips played at her neck, kissing one minute, biting the next. A gush of excitement soaked her panties. Time stood still. In that moment, all there was in her world was Drake's mouth and hands, and the press of her body. Dani's legs shook. When she began to slide down the wall, Drake picked her up and carried her to the bed. She sank into the softness, content to let Drake lead.

Dani focused on slowing her breathing. She rarely thought about being in control of herself. Prior to Ryan, there wasn't much going on to get worked up about, and the few orgasms she'd had weren't all that pleasurable, they just…happened. Or not. Drake was not someone she could just go through the motions with. Especially not after she'd come prepared to please her, and Dani had no doubt she would do just that. There was something about Drake that drove her need higher in a way that was primal. She might never see Drake again, but she was certain tonight would be one she wouldn't easily forget. Ryan may have been her first, but Drake would likely show her there was more than one way to be with a woman.

Her remaining clothes were aggressively removed, as though Drake couldn't get her naked fast enough. When their eyes met, Drake's were heavy-lidded, and her body felt anything but soft. Drake's hand moved over her abdomen as she smiled.

"I love your curves. You're so fucking sexy."

She pictured Drake being buried deep inside of her as she captured her lips. Drake moved her mouth sensually before pressing her tongue inside.

"Tell me what you need to make your fantasy a reality." Drake took her nipple in her teeth, lightly tugged, then lavished attention on it with her mouth and tongue.

"I want to feel your naked body against me." She yanked at Drake's shirt as roughly as Drake, liking the surge of power by knowing she could ask for anything. Drake sat up, bringing her with her. "Take it off," she said. Once her breasts were freed, they hung heavy, as though they were larger than they actually were. She cupped them in her hands and brought one to her lips, making her wetter. Drake held her head and Dani had the impression she would have liked to take over what was happening before remembering this was her show. Her nipples grew incredibly hard and the surrounding flesh pebbled beneath Drake's fingertips, mirroring her motion before she pressed a tip to her mouth. If Drake kept sucking, she was going to come. "Stop, baby." Drake pulled away and her nipple popped from her mouth.

"Was I not doing it right?" Drake licked her lips. Her eyes were glassy, thoroughly lost in the moment.

She smiled. "You did it so right, I'm going to come."

With her head tipped and a puzzled expression, Drake asked, "You don't want to?"

Dani ran her fingers over her shoulders, then traced her collar bones. "I do," she said as she leaned closer. "But I want your cock inside me."

"Fuck yeah." Drake stood over her. "Help me get this leather off." Between the two of them, they peeled the clinging hide down until all she wore was a harness with a seven-inch dildo swaying from it. Dani stared at the appendage. "Do you want me like this?"

"Yes." Dani's voice cracked.

Drake reached into the nightstand and withdrew a condom. "Sheath me."

"Have you used this on other women?"

"The gear we all use and wear is new every time. I prefer you not having to worry about anything when I'm fucking you." Drake watched her as she tore the package open and rolled the cover down, the fit snug. "Lay back." She dropped to her knees and took her place between Dani's thighs. Drake kissed her taut stomach and continued upward. Once she was resting on her forearms, she lowered her center until her cock was pressed against Dani's opening. "Can you feel how ready I am to be inside you? Please let me fill you."

She spread wider and reached between them. "This is for me, right?"

"All yours." Drake trailed her tongue over her chin, down her neck.

"Show me." Dani gave the dildo a jerk.

Lifting to give her hand space, Drake grabbed the shaft and slid the head over her clit several times. Dani looked between them. Beads of arousal clung to her hair. When Drake pushed the tip inside she momentarily tensed before Drake eased in deeper and fully opened her. Drake pressed forward until her cock was buried all the way.

She groaned as her gaze lost focus. "Feels so good."

In and out, Drake slowly moved her hips as they kissed and tasted each other. "Do you want to come? Can you come with my cock?"

"I want to," she said between gasps of pure pleasure.

Drake began thrusting, each one deeper and harder until all that remained was the feel of Drake over her and the moans from both of them filling the air. "Harder. Fuck me harder." Drake's response assured her she was more than happy to oblige. Pressure began to build in her groin as Drake shortened her strokes. She was so close.

"Come for me, Dani," Drake said, her voice strained as she pounded against her. She kissed her hard, then moved to one tight nipple and began to suck as a counterpoint to her thrusts. Dani cried out and arched to meet Drake as Drake exploded in a gush that covered them both. Her hips continued to move in jerky strokes as Dani trembled through the last contractions. Able to finally lift her head, Drake focused on her and when a smile formed, she relaxed and withdrew. Dani sighed.

"Are you okay?" Drake wiped damp strands from her face.

"You're kidding, right?"

Drake's hand froze. "No."

"Hey." She stroked the furrow between Drake's brows. "I'm great. I just thought that after all the women you've fucked, you'd know when one was basking in the aftermath." She kissed her lightly.

"Well," Drake began, "I usually do, but not necessarily with someone I've been with for the first time."

Dani pushed on Drake's shoulder until she was on her back. "Now you do. And," she said as she peeled away the condom and tossed it on the nightstand. "You should also know I'm not done." She straddled her, rose up, then lowered herself onto the cock. "I feel so full."

"It's the position. I have smaller ones if you'd like me to change it."

Leaning down for a kiss that returned the fire to Dani's center, she smiled against Drake's mouth. "Let's give this one another workout, then I'll let you know."

Steam from the cup of lavender chamomile tea rose to greet Dani and she inhaled deeply. She blew across the surface then sipped, grateful not to have to hurry to get to the salon. Her days off were few and far between, and she wasn't about to squander this one by spending the whole day doing neglected chores. As she dropped onto a kitchen chair, she pulled a magazine from the growing unread stack. She flipped through not really looking at the pages while her mind wandered back to a few days ago and her time with Drake. *God, she was intense.*

Not that she hadn't enjoyed being with her. Experiencing Drake's masterful use of a strap-on had been amazing, and she'd enjoyed every sensation and position as well as the residual soreness she'd felt for the last few days, which was a constant and sensual reminder of the fantastic new experience. Though that's basically where it ended. Drake had been thoughtful and kind when they'd finished, but Dani hadn't been *moved* by her the way she was with Ryan. Ryan exuded not only confidence, but a genuine concern in providing not only the physical and sexual experiences Dani craved. She'd also taken time to explain things and answer her seemingly unending questions with patience. Most of all, Ryan had been able to read her thoughts even when Dani didn't have the words to express them.

Ryan didn't appear to rush through life like Drake seemed to, and she was coming to realize the calm energy and unhurried demeanor was more to her liking. All those factors combined to make her feel special and desired, like Dani deserved not only Ryan's undivided attention, but the singular focus bestowed on her too, like she was the only woman who mattered in Ryan's world.

Dani laughed out loud, chastising her runaway thoughts. Ryan could have any woman she wanted. There was no reason to think she was *that* special. But still...

Chapter Fifteen

It was foolish on Ryan's part, really. Her innate need for control had always kept her from letting emotions get in the way of business, and until now that ability had become second nature, but this instance felt different from her previous lack of involvement in what happened behind closed doors.

She'd been dying to ask Drake how her night with Dani had gone, but asking was against protocol, against the rules and guidelines she had put into place from the start. What happened between a client and an escort was private unless there was a problem, or the potential for one. Then she expected her employee to come to her to provide the information necessary to head off any impending disaster. The Agency took safeguards and precautions including having every client sign a nondisclosure waiver and the stated consequences of how breaking such agreement would be costly to both parties, but there was always the danger of scandal in their business. It would only take one disgruntled client to send the empire crumbling. Being able to take down even the most affluent customers, while possible, would be a lengthy and expensive process she'd just as soon avoid in most cases.

However, Dani wasn't affluent, nor did she consider her a potential threat to the integrity or discretion of the Agency. Those factors didn't give her the right to pry, and she wasn't sure if it was simple curiosity or something else that drove her need. The fact that she couldn't stop thinking about Dani and what she wanted to continue to do to and with her was a good indication she wasn't in control. All the things she never thought she wanted to feel. Terrifying, and exhilarating.

She stared at the screen. She should get away. From the business and the preoccupation with Dani. It was a rare occasion that she actually got to enjoy the money she made. Some R&R time would be a nice respite. Maybe she could go to a few plays she'd wanted to see, or travel a bit, even if only for a long weekend. The idea of going alone held little appeal and was likely the reason she didn't do any of those things. A sigh erupted from deep inside. The CEO of a lucrative escort service, and for the first time in years, she recognized her loneliness.

Something had to give soon. Maybe it was time to talk to Drake about taking on more responsibilities and less clients. The idea made her smile. Drake loved sex and would likely balk at the mention of less time with the ladies. It was worth a shot. She was next in line, a VP without the official title, if this was a typical business, which it certainly wasn't. Then there'd be no excuse for constantly hiding behind her desk.

Before tackling the next influx of emails, she went to the credenza. Lately, the espresso machine was doing overtime. Not only was the business booming, which was great for everyone's bank account, but being back in active status, albeit with only one client at the moment, threw a wrench in her previous day-to-day routine. Maybe that's why she felt off kilter and it had nothing at all to do with her overzealous curiosity. Besides, she'd be seeing Dani in a few days. Maybe she'd mention what happened with Drake, but Dani didn't come across as a kiss-and-tell person. Ryan shook her head. Obsessing wasn't something she did. It was time she dropped it and focus on what really mattered. The Agency, her pride and joy.

"Oh my God," Pam said.

Dani finished sanitizing her station between customers. She'd been going since eight that morning and the twelve-hour shift she'd signed up for threatened to kill her back. She'd tough it out like she always did. "What?"

"A female version of Adam Gregory just walked in."

She glanced over her shoulder and the air left her lungs. Ryan stood at the desk, chatting it up with the receptionist and smiling that killer smile of hers. "What is she doing here?"

"You know her?"

Shit. She hadn't meant to say it out loud. How was she going to explain her reaction to Pam? "Yeah. She's probably here for one of the other stylists." Though, she didn't think so. She'd never seen her at the shop, and she'd worked a lot the last few months. This wasn't a coincidence, and she knew it. Just then Melody called to her.

"Dani, you're up."

Fuck, fuck. She could do this. Ryan was in her territory, and she knew how to handle the elite. "Be right there."

Pam nudged her. "Which one is she?" Her eyes were saucers as she glanced at the waiting area. Luckily, Ryan had turned to look at the wall of hair products.

"My first, but don't you dare say anything."

Pam motioned locking her lips and moved away after winking.

Jesus. She took the paper from Melody and called out her next cut's name. "Ryan?" The killer smile returned as she took the few steps to get to her. "Right this way, please." Dani indicated her chair and pulled a fresh cape from the stack. "You're here for a cut, correct?" Her throat was dry.

Ryan's gaze met hers in the mirror. "I am. I have a date and I want to look my best."

Dani ignored the tremor inside. Was Ryan talking about her? She'd said she was the only client, but maybe that was no longer true. "Have you been here before?" She was fairly confident she hadn't seen her, certain she would have remembered her, but she needed to know the real reason she was there.

"No. I couldn't get an appointment with my usual salon and decided to give this place a try."

Dani studied her reflection, the intensity of her gaze touching her in places familiar to her. She refused to give Ryan the upper hand outside of the bedroom and raked her fingers through Ryan's hair. "Do you want to stay with this style?" The gaze that set her on fire was staring back at her. Not from across the table, or down at her as was so often the case in bed. The gaze she returned was meant to say, "I'm in control." But then, when it came to Ryan, she didn't really want to be in control, did she?

"I want something different. Something that will show my personality and who I am. Can you do that for me, Dani?"

Just then George, the ass who owned the salon, stopped at her station. "Ms. Lewis, so good to see you again. Dani is one of my best stylists. I'm sure you'll be pleased with the outcome." He brushed his hand over Ryan's shoulder and Ryan stiffened.

"I've got this, George." After he went on down the line as though inspecting livestock, she bent over so only Ryan could hear her. "Do you know him?"

The sideways glance and cold eyes betrayed Ryan's irritation. "He moves in elite circles but he's a piranha. And a womanizer." Ryan's gaze returned to her. "He boasted about owning a string of salons, but I didn't know this was one."

Ryan's reaction to his too familiar touch confirmed how much of a jerk her boss was. "I won't let him touch you again."

Ryan's hardened gaze cleared. "I'm fine." She turned and stared in the mirror, still looking irritated.

She lightly touched Ryan's arm. "You don't look okay."

After a breath, Ryan met her reflection. "I'm not good with men touching me." She brought her hand from under the cape and covered Dani's. "It's over now. How about that cut?" Ryan's grin returned.

She nodded, then put in an earbud, turned on her music, and did what she did best. She gave Ryan a low-fade quiff that suited her no-nonsense demeanor yet was soft enough to show her stylish side. She'd been tempted to do a skin design but thought better of it. Those were more suitable for artist types, not upper echelon positions. Dani might be capable of trusting Ryan's skills in the bedroom, but Ryan didn't know her as a stylist, and once a skin cut was done, there was no turning back. Perhaps they'd discuss it if she came back to the salon, but she hoped this was a one-time event. Ryan's presence, while nice in a blood racing kind of way, was distracting in the work setting. They'd already blurred the lines once, and as much as dating someone like Ryan might appeal to her, doing so would obliterate the boundaries of professional and personal. She didn't think that was a smart move on her part. What did she have to offer that was different from what any number of women could provide?

After brushing away any loose hairs and using a warm towel, she applied a molding paste and demonstrated the variety of looks Ryan could achieve. The thing she liked most about the product she used was the ability to change styles and "remold" throughout the day, and she explained that Ryan could change her look to meet with different clients on the same day. When Ryan gave her a little half smirk, she ducked her head shyly. When she finished, Ryan leaned closer to the wall-mounted mirror as she lifted a handheld so she could see the back.

"Is this how you see me?"

Dani flushed. "Yes." She wondered if she should go on and when Ryan nodded into the reflection she went with her gut. "Controlled, but not severe. Pliable when desired. All business when necessary."

Ryan's mouth opened, then closed. "It will take some time to see how much I can do with it." Then Ryan shared that slow smile that took her breath away. "I like it." She stood and Dani let out a breath.

She walked to the receptionist, filled out the charge slip, and handed it to Melody. "Thank you for giving us a try. I hope we'll see you again."

"I'm sure you will," Ryan said. "I'd also like to buy the product that you used."

She moved around the counter and picked up a container. "Just remember, a little goes a long way."

Ryan's brow lifted. "Professional advice?"

Her mouth twitched at the corners. "You could say that, Ms. Lewis. We all have our expertise. Have a great day." Somehow, she'd make it through the rest of her day and tomorrow until she saw

Ryan again. Only then Ryan would have the upper hand, and she was looking forward to finding out what Ryan had in store for her.

Ryan had been intrigued as she watched Dani in action. She obviously knew what she was doing and enjoyed it. Her scissor skills were evident by the lack of tentativeness when she cut. Her hands gently manipulated her head this way and that. The clipper buzz reminded her of a vibrator but too far north to do anything constructive, though the idea of using one on Dani made her adjust in her seat. The finished result, while not her typical style, was nonetheless attractive. A mix of business and leisure. She'd have to get used to that. Until recently, those lines had never blurred. Even when she wasn't at work Ryan was always in business mode. Strictly controlled and projecting the utmost decorum. It was how she'd survived when she was younger, and she'd never let go of what was ingrained.

Her eyes were gritty, and she glanced at the clock in disbelief at how late it was. Where had the time gone? She should have left at a decent hour for a change, but without plans and no one waiting for her, Ryan hadn't been in any hurry to escape the office to go to her beautiful though empty home. As she flicked off the lights the exit sign that buzzed over the stairwell door dared her to take the ten flights down and use some of the pent-up energy she'd been ignoring since seeing Dani.

"Not tonight," she said out loud before heading to the elevator.

"It's never a good sign when the boss starts talking to herself." Drake grinned and stood next to her, their shoulders almost touching. "What are you doing here so late?"

"I could ask you the same." She hadn't heard Drake's approach. The idea she was losing touch with her surroundings bothered her more than the comment.

"I had a backlog of summaries to complete and since I'm off a few days next week, I decided to clean my desk, otherwise the boss would have my head."

Drake was a professional like her, except she took time to enjoy life, a luxury Ryan rarely gave in to. "I would have understood, but thanks for your dedication." They stepped onto the elevator together, then she pushed the button for underground parking. She wanted a drink, food, and a fuck, not necessarily in that order.

Shrugging, Drake clasped her shoulder. "And even if you *didn't* say anything, it would have bugged you knowing I'd left them." Drake walked with her, their cars parked next to each other. "I'm going to stop for a bite and a nightcap. Want to join me?"

She was about to turn down the invitation before remembering she'd be alone. "Why not."

"Your enthusiasm is endearing. Meet me at Bixby's," Drake said as she opened the driver's door. "Last one there gets to buy." She jumped in and revved the engine before squealing the tires.

Son of a bitch. Ryan laughed as she caught up at the exit gate on the ground level. Drake turned left, but she went right. The shortcut she'd discovered about a year ago wasn't that much shorter, but it might give her enough of an edge to win the bet. Suddenly, she didn't feel all that tired anymore.

Once they got there and were seated with plenty of banter about who made it to the parking lot first, Ryan began to relax.

Drake put her hand on her shoulder reminding her of the tension that still existed beneath her fingers.

"What's got you so uptight?"

Maybe she was worried about the expansion project that was underway. She'd been interviewing potential escorts for weeks and supervising the acquisition of necessary resources, but she was kidding herself. "I'm not sure I want to talk about it." She took a sip of twenty-one-year-old scotch.

"Ryan, I'm your friend. You can't keep everything inside all the time and not expect consequences. How about sharing for a change?" Drake watched her intently, any trace of humor gone.

She smiled, but it was forced, feeling unnatural even to her. "I'm tired, hungry, and…" She paused and finished what was left in her glass.

"And?"

"I need a hard fuck."

From the way Drake stared, she was sure she saw a torrent of emotions, because the same ones coursed through her veins. Drake told her years ago she may be able to control her physical reactions, but her eyes revealed everything. She knew her too well to not see more than anyone else. As much as she would have…should have…asked for one of the escorts to be available and though she had before, she hadn't wanted her sour mood to rub off on an employee or make for any unnecessary awkwardness. She had great relationships with her staff. They trusted her judgment and her business savvy as well as her innate ability to get to the heart of an issue without making a big deal of it. She wouldn't subject them to her turmoil.

Drake pulled out her phone, typed a text message, and motioned to the bartender for another round and ordered a couple of appetizers. "You need to eat something and so do I." By the time their drinks arrived, her phone chimed, and she read the response. "Your fuck will be here in forty-five minutes, so tell me what's really going on."

For the first time since seeing Drake at the elevator, Ryan's smile felt real, and she laughed, shaking her head. "I can always count on you to brighten my mood."

"Glad to know I'm good for something," she said, winking and pointing to the plates that appeared. "Food, then words, and don't give me any more bullshit about it being nothing."

While they ate, Ryan admitted she was drained, and Drake seemed surprised when she asked if she'd be willing to take on more responsibility for the business while expressing her reluctance for asking because she knew how much Drake enjoyed being an escort.

"I think sometimes you forget I'm a partner in this adventure. Don't worry about cutting into my bookings," she said as the corners of her mouth rose. "I'll always make time for women."

"I have no doubt," Ryan said.

They were just finishing their discussion about what needed to change at the Agency when Jay walked through the door. She strode directly to her, whispered in her ear, nodded to Drake, then left. Ryan stood and reached for her wallet, but Drake stopped her. "I've got this. Go get what you need, even if it's only temporary."

Ryan stared at her for a long beat, then nodded before walking away. She felt her gaze follow her until she disappeared through the door. They'd been taking care of each other for decades, but Ryan rarely admitted to what she considered her own shortcomings, often forgetting that she was human and had frailties like everyone else. Drake had willingly taken on the role of reminding her.

Jay waited beside her car. "You want me to drive?"

"I can't leave my baby here." She pointed to the Audi Spyder that not only didn't belong in the area, but it also stuck out like a placard saying, "Here I am. Take me."

"Oh, wow. Nice car."

Ryan tossed the keys in the air. "Is your place far?"

Jay smiled and stuck out her hand. "Give me your phone so I can put in my info."

"I've got your number," Ryan said casually.

Leaning closer, Jay traced the edge of her jaw with her tongue. "And I've got yours," she said before giving the phone back and getting into her GT Mustang.

As Ryan followed Jay through the city, she almost called her to cancel. She couldn't deny she'd rather be with Dani, but Dani wasn't her girlfriend, and she had no right to have expectations neither of them should pursue. At least Jay would be a diversion and serve to remind her that there was a bevy of reasons to keep her personal feelings from interfering with her professional life. The situation with Dani would only become more complicated if she continued to cross the line. She'd never felt a need to complicate what should be simple. Fuck for the pure pleasure of it and be done. So why wasn't she able to do what had always been so simple?

Chapter Sixteen

How do you like your cut?" Dani asked.

Ryan took her jacket. The weather had cooled, and the forecast of rain added to the gloom hanging thick and heavy in the air. "It took a little getting used to, but I like it." She came close and pressed her thigh against her center. "I like it a lot." Ryan ran her fingers over her cheek and trailed down her throat. "Would you like a drink?"

She didn't want her senses dulled, but she was nervous and unsure what tonight would bring. "Wine, please. Grigio if you have it." Of course, Ryan made sure every apartment was fully stocked and she suspected this one would be no different.

"Dani," Ryan said as she handed her the half-full glass. "If you're unsure about giving yourself to me you can change your mind."

"I know." She took a sip, let it warm her. "I haven't changed my mind." She looked around at the décor. Each place she'd been in was different though all were tastefully done. "Why do you have apartments and not just rooms at hotels?" She sat on the leather sofa. The kind you could sink into, in a good way.

Ryan sat in the adjacent chair, her long legs stretched out and crossed at the ankles. "Because the women we service aren't casual tricks, and neither are the women we employ. I'd never want to cheapen the experience by having either feel as though they were being rented by the hour." Ryan met her gaze with an acuteness she hadn't witnessed before, even in bed. "Just because we make money doing what we enjoy, I never want our employees to feel like they're being pimped out. They deserve accolades for the services they provide. Not many women can handle the stress, and the cost of giving up a personal life isn't for everyone."

There was more than just the business aspect at play in Ryan's words. Dani needed to find the deeper meaning, but for now it was enough to know she wasn't viewed as someone willing to pay for a quick lay because she was in it for so much more. The wine had relaxed her enough that she was ready to experience another aspect of self-expression and testing her own limits in the physical world. Ryan had promised to take her there. She stood and set her empty glass down.

"Let's not talk about work anymore."

Heat flared in Ryan's eyes before she moved so quickly Dani gasped when she pulled her against her. "Tell me your safe word."

Dani trembled in Ryan's grasp, at the hard desire in Ryan's eyes and the firm grip on her waist. She swallowed and whispered, "Thunder." She was led to the massive bed covered in a red, gray, and black pattern quilt and black curtains on the windows. The trace lights in the ceiling glowed red. Her feet sank into the thick gray carpet with every step. At first glance, the vibe of this room was ominous, yet when she took a breath, then another and really looked, there was much more. A small vase of flowers on one nightstand. Nude prints of women in the throes of orgasm, pure pleasure in their eyes and written in their expressions. But the sense of power came from the dynamics forming between her and Ryan. Ryan turned her to face the massive mirror opposite the bed and began to slowly undress her.

"I know you're nervous," Ryan said, her voice low. "You're also excited and wet." Her nimble fingers unbuttoned her jeans and drew down the zipper. "Remember one thing, Dani." She met Ryan's gaze in the mirror. "A submissive has all the power in a scene. You can stop what's happening at any time by saying one word. Just be absolutely sure you want to stop before you do." Ryan turned her around, finger under her chin until their eyes met. "Understand?"

"Yes." Her head swam. Her knees shook, threatening to drop her to the ground. Ryan removed the rest of her clothes. As she stood naked and vulnerable something in Ryan's eyes assured her she'd be okay. She'd trusted Ryan to bring her into the world of women and all they had to offer. There was no reason to think Ryan would be any different now.

"Lie on the bed, facing up." Ryan's tone was stern, commanding, and just like that, she felt the power shift. "Don't talk unless you're asked a question. Do exactly as I say."

The room was warm, and she began to sweat. Funny, she hadn't noticed the heat a short time ago. Dani sank into the bedding, but the surface under her was firmer than the other beds she'd been in as though they'd been made for comfort and this one...this one was made to put her on display. Ryan moved around the room with practiced ease, opening a drawer here, checking for something in the dresser. Yet the armoire remained closed as it had in all the other apartments. Ryan stood at the foot of the bed.

"Do you trust me?" She stood stock still, but Dani could see her chest rising and falling.

"Yes."

Ryan reached beneath the bed and wrapped her ankle in a thickly padded cuff, moved her leg outward, and attached the cuff to a length of leather that hooked to the bedpost. She repeated the process until her arms and legs were immobilized and she lay spread-eagle, exposed and shaking. Ryan unbuttoned her shirt and bent, she assumed to remove her shoes, then she dropped her pants to reveal crotchless leather shorts that had a single piece of leather with a metal ring for where the dildo would go.

"Close your eyes and don't open them until I tell you to," Ryan said. She heard a latch snick followed a minute later by the sound of Ryan breathing close by. Her fingers traced the bones of her face, over her chin to her throat. "You're so ready to experience your body in ways you never thought possible, and I'm going to take you there." Ryan's breath caressed her face.

Soft material alternately trailed over her arms and stomach, and she fought an urge to look. Dani focused on the only thing she could. The sensations in her body, and Ryan's steady breathing. Not to mention how utterly perfect it was to be exactly where she was at that moment.

❖

It had been ages since she'd introduced a woman to the pleasures of a power exchange. Even longer since she'd *wanted* to be in that exchange. Dani's trust wasn't some frivolous fancy bestowed upon her because she was being paid. She almost believed it was due to how far they'd come together and the idea that Dani had picked her for any other reason was both disturbing and exciting. "Tell me what you feel."

"Soft material trailing over my body."

"That's what's happening externally. I want to know how you feel inside." She dragged the soft suede strips over each breast and Dani's nipples peaked.

"I'm...excited, and apprehensive."

Moisture pooled beneath Dani's center. "I can see you're excited. Tell me what makes you apprehensive." She brushed the leather covered handle over the juncture of hip and inner thigh. Dani gasped.

"I don't know what's going to happen next."

"Because you can't see? Because you have no control?"

Dani squirmed what little she could. "Yes."

She abandoned the instrument and pinched both nipples, then released them. Dani groaned. Moving her hand down the center of Dani's body made the muscles twitch and tighten in anticipation, but it was too soon for Dani to have the touch she craved, or the release Ryan would eventually allow. If she gave in too quickly, the heightening need growing inside Dani would be lost, and it would be no different than any other sexual encounter. Dani would have to ask for release and if she were ready, Ryan would give it...or not. "But you like not knowing."

"I'm not sure."

"Of course you are. That's why you asked me to bring you here." She pressed her lips to Dani's heaving abdomen. "You want to know what you're capable of enduring." Ryan picked up the flogger again, dragging the suede tails back and forth over Dani's mound. From the way Dani held her jaw, her head slightly raised, she was doing her best to figure out what was coming next. Ryan flipped the handle and pressed it against Dani's opening. It was too large to enter her, but Dani didn't know she wouldn't try. So much of the D/s relationship was about anticipation and in the giving and taking of power.

"Please."

Ryan flipped the flogger, catching the handle, and lightly struck her thigh, making her jump. "Did I say you could speak?"

"No," Dani answered defiantly.

"Punishment for disobeying will be swift." She smoothed her hand over the light pink area to soothe the flesh and reinforce that obedience would be rewarded. Ryan slipped her fingers around Dani's clit and lightly massaged. "Do you like that?"

"Yes, yes."

"Be a good girl and I might let you come soon." She withdrew her touch and straddled Dani's thigh, sliding up and back, her own soaked center hard against the tight muscle. Ryan placed her index and middle fingers on each side of Dani's swollen clit, careful to not stimulate the nerve endings. Dani moaned. Down farther, she spread the moisture around her puckered entrance and pushed ever so slightly. Dani clenched against the unaccustomed intrusion. "Relax. I'm not going to hurt you." To her credit Dani had yet to open her eyes, but she would soon. Very few people could resist seeing what was happening or about to. She gathered more slick heat on her thumb and pressed again, sliding two fingers into Dani's pussy at the same time.

"Oh, God." Dani's words were whispered, then she bit her lip and tensed, likely thinking she'd be punished for talking. But not this time.

"Do you want to come, Dani? Do you want me to fuck you?" Her excitement and desire were building, and Ryan fought the urge to rush to climax. She withdrew from Dani, then lay over her grinding her exposed center into Dani's. "Look at me." Dani blinked, her eyes were questioning and wary. "You are going to watch me tease you. You are not going to come until I tell you."

Dani nodded, her body covered in sweat. She was ripe and ready and wanting. Ryan inched her way down, placing light nips in her path. By the time she settled between Dani's trembling thighs she wasn't sure how long she could hold her off, but she was going to try. Ryan wanted Dani's need for release to obliterate all sense of reason, and for her to disobey. She licked the entire length of her gathering her flavor on her tongue. Dani moaned above her, hands clenching in the restraints. Another swipe, another moan. She kept up the maddeningly slow pace, pressing herself into the bed, her body surging and her climax approaching. She wouldn't allow it. Dani's pleasure came first. As her escort, and especially as her top, she would not disappoint.

"Please, please." Dani's entire body shook.

Ryan knew she was barely holding on and the rock-hard pebble between her lips began to pulse.

Still within her reach, she lifted the flogger and dragged the tails over Dani's abdomen. "You may come now." The added stimulation, and perhaps the hint of punishment, pushed her over the edge.

Dani strained up. "I'm coming."

"Yes, you are." Ryan took her fully into her mouth and Dani exploded with a guttural scream of ecstasy, bucking and shaking. Light oaths of the pleasure she'd drawn from her gave Ryan her own pleasure. As Dani quieted, she freed her feet, then her wrists and gathered her still shivering body to her with soothing touches and praise. "That's my good girl. You waited for permission so long." She gently rubbed Dani's wrists to return the circulation, amazed at her soft coos and the pink tinge still vibrant on her chest, in her cheeks. Ryan was lost in the reality of being Dani's first in so many ways, she was touched in the deep places no one had ever reached. Time passed before Dani opened her eyes again. She offered Dani a drink and smiled as she nearly emptied the bottle.

"Are you ready?"

Dani visibly stiffened. "For what?"

"You've asked to experience BDSM. To find out what you like and what you don't. I've only begun to do that. Have you thought about what things you want to explore since we talked? Do you want to find your limits of pain, or would you prefer to explore a different way to experience pleasure?"

Dani visibly shivered. "I don't think I'm ready for a..." Dani motioned with her hand, clearly frustrated by not being able to find the right words. "I don't want you to beat me, if that's what you're asking. Not to make it really hurt, I mean."

She caressed her face tenderly. "Even if that was something you wanted, I told you I'm not the person to wield a whip that way, and it's much too soon to go that far. But as a dominant, there are things I can do that may initially make you uncomfortable simply because you've never experienced them that will ultimately end in excitement and pleasure. That feel good." Ryan kissed her gently. "I hope you trust me enough to show you that side of BDSM."

Eyes wide, Dani appeared to be in deep thought before she asked, "How do I address you?"

Ryan's clit surged. "I prefer sir, but you should ask each domme before starting."

Dani moved to sit on her haunches, her head held high with her gaze cast down, waiting. Waiting for her to lead her on this journey of self-discovery. Ryan wasn't about to let her down.

"Kneel on the bed, face down." She opened the armoire and took out a riding crop, a short, slender dildo, a harness, and a packet of lube. Her harness in place, Ryan reattached the cuffs to Dani's wrists and adjusted them until she was satisfied Dani wasn't stretched out so far that it became uncomfortable. Finding what excited Dani was the only thing she wanted to do. "Remember the rules. No talking unless I ask you a direct question and then you must address me properly, is that understood?"

"Yes, sir."

Ryan smiled and knelt behind her, enjoying the view of Dani's shapely ass in the air and her swollen pussy begging for attention.

She smoothed her hand slowly over each cheek. "You have a beautiful ass," she said before lightly striking her cheek with the crop. She'd been taught by a very masterful dom who had Ryan use the implement on herself after demonstrating how to avoid cutting or causing deep welts. It had taken practice and patience on her part after baring a few misplaced hits of her own, but the reminder taught her to pay attention to what she was doing. Dani flinched and gasped at the contact. She knew she hadn't really hurt her and with no intention to do so, she repeated it several times until Dani's skin turned pink and she moaned when she stopped, an indication she had enjoyed it, at least to some degree. She ran her fingers along Dani's slit. Slick moisture covered them, and she pressed two against her puckered entrance. Dani immediately pulled away.

"Do not move or you will be punished." Her tone left no room for disobedience even though she wasn't angry. Resisting the unfamiliar stimulation was natural. She'd forgotten how intoxicating the surge of power could be, made all the more intense knowing Dani had chosen her to introduce her to this other form of intimacy, and she would not take that responsibility lightly.

Ryan smoothed her hand along the contours of Dani's body and lightly slapped her ass as she gently pushed her finger inside, blurring the two sensations into one of pleasure. When Dani no longer resisted her entering her and she knew she was ready for more, Ryan removed all physical contact. Dani wiggled her ass, seeking her out.

"Are you looking for more, sweet girl?"

Dani whimpered. "Yes."

Her crop strike was firm. Dani cried out. "You forget yourself."

"Please, sir." Dani's tone held an edge of sarcasm, but she was willing to let it slide. For now.

Ryan reached around and began to rub Dani's clit. She wanted her need to become so great, Dani would do anything to get off, and when Dani tried to move against her, Ryan knew she was ready. She tore open the lube with her teeth and drizzled some along the cleft of Dani's ass and smoothed the remainder along her sheathed shaft. Ryan guided the head while she continued to play with her clit, slowly entering her, pleased when Dani's groan was one of pure pleasure and she pushed back against her. Dani's clit hardened against her fingers.

"Do not come."

"Oh, God," Dani groaned. "Please, please."

Ryan closed her eyes, immersed in the surge of power that coursed through her and delighting in how turned on, and how wanting and needy Dani was at that moment. It gave her more satisfaction than she could ever remember in a scene. More than just her body was involved. Ryan cared about Dani and had connected with her on a level that no one had ever provided. She clenched her teeth and focused on the moment. She withdrew until only the tip remained inside.

Dani cried out. "No. Please. I want you inside me." Dani sobbed. "Please, sir. I'll be good," she begged.

She shuddered. Blood raced to her center, engorging her clit as she pressed herself in and filled her while she tugged Dani's clit.

"Ryan," Dani screamed as her body shook. "Oh, God. Don't stop. Ryan, don't stop."

Dani's strong cries turned ragged as Ryan continued to thrust into her. To give Dani what she wanted. Ryan's clit surged and she exploded with a deafening roar of satisfaction, her thighs steel against Dani's trembling ass. When she was sure Dani had no more to give, she slowly withdrew, unfastened the straps, and tossed her gear. She moved quickly to release the restraints and pulled Dani into her arms, cradling her against her body. Tenderly, she swept the sweat soaked strands from her face.

"I've got you. Such a good girl." She brought Dani closer still. "I've got you." Dani snuggled into her embrace as cathartic tears of submission fell from her closed eyes. Ryan knew without a doubt she'd found what had been missing from her life. Sorrow engulfed her. Falling for a client was forbidden and she had tasted the fruit one too many times. What was she going to do?

Dani let the tears fall, though she wasn't completely certain why they were there. She felt...emptied. Like she'd given over her whole self, like she'd allowed someone into her soul and been held in the most intimate way possible. Slowly, the overwhelming emotion subsided, and she relaxed into Ryan's embrace.

"No safe word," Dani said as she reached inside Ryan's shirt to massage her breast, but Ryan stilled her hand.

"You did well."

Dani struggled to sit up. After studying Ryan for a long beat. "You topped me, is that correct?" she asked, thirsty to understand.

"Yes and no. I took what I wanted and what you were willing to give, but it wasn't a true BDSM scene. I don't think you're quite ready to explore that dynamic."

"So there's a difference?"

"Yes. A top is someone who controls what happens in or out of a scene, but they aren't necessarily a dominant. It can get complicated, and people argue over the terminology and semantics all the time."

"Do you let women top you?"

Ryan glanced away and Dani thought she may have crossed an unspoken line. "Sometimes, when the need arises. I'm mostly a top, though I switch now and then."

Dani reached for water and took a long drink. "When do you know that's what you need?"

"When the responsibilities become overwhelming and..."

"And?"

Ryan sighed. "And I let someone else be responsible for a little while."

She sat quietly for several minutes, facing Ryan and sipping water. She put the near empty bottle down, knelt between her thighs, and rested her hands on her shoulders. "What you did to me," she said before taking a deep breath then continuing. "I felt myself let go and stopped worrying about what was going to happen next. I knew I could trust you." And she did. The one thing she knew above all else was the certainty that Ryan wanted to give her what she'd asked for. What she needed.

"Dani, I only ever want to please you." Ryan moved her thumb over her cheek and guided her forward until their mouths met.

The kiss that followed was tender and careful, as though Ryan was afraid if she let go, if she let her passion rise, there'd be no stopping. For her part, Dani needed to step back. A lot had happened to her in the last couple of months. More than she could have ever anticipated. That didn't mean she wanted the night to end. With Ryan so close, looking at her with so much emotion she might have thought hidden, she couldn't think of anything but wanting more. But God, was that explosion of emotion, that surrender, a regular occurrence? Could she take someone to that point herself? "Will you let me top you?"

Ryan hesitated.

"You don't have to answer." She broke eye contact, her hand trembling as it dropped to Ryan's thigh. "I have no idea what I'm doing. I'm not sure why I even asked."

Ryan lifted her chin with her fingertips and caressed her cheek with her thumb. "You asked because you want to experience everything, right?"

"As much as I can." Dani's heart raced.

"If you want to know what it feels like to top me you'll need to make another appointment. It's not easy to go from one role to another. I can't do that tonight."

"You'd be willing to let me try?"

"Yes."

She felt her eyes grow big. "It probably won't be particularly good for you, so I'll apologize now. I promise not to leave you hanging, though."

Ryan laughed. "I don't think you would, but that's not going to happen tonight."

"What is going to happen the rest of the night?"

"I could think of a few things."

Dani cocked an eyebrow. "Name one."

Heat filled Ryan's gaze. "I've brought a very special cock to fuck you with."

She shivered. "What are you waiting for?"

From a small black bag Dani hadn't noticed before, Ryan produced a double-headed cock already in a harness. From the armoire she produced a small spray bottle, then set everything on the bed. Ryan pulled off her shorts and stepped into the straps, stopping partway.

"This end of the cock," Ryan said and pointed to the end facing her. "Has a little bump that will rub my clit when I press the bigger end into you. It feels like you're fucking me, as I'm fucking you." Ryan focused on her. "Do you want to try it?"

Her sex clenched. "Absolutely I do."

Ryan smiled before she sprayed both ends. "This lube is my favorite because it's less messy and long-lasting." When she was done, she pulled the straps higher and guided the shorter end into her pussy. She shivered, releasing a low moan, then joined her on the bed.

"I'm here for you, Dani."

She spread her legs wider and smiled. "Take me."

Ryan entered her in a long smooth stroke and waited. The cock was big, and the lube helped her adjust quickly. Ryan settled over her, kissed her slowly and began moving her hips. "You feel so good." She groaned when they broke for air. Ryan was careful, going slow and deep, filling her and listening to her groans of pleasure.

Ryan's arms began to shake. "I'm going to come soon. Come with me, Dani. Please." Her half-lidded eyes were heavy with longing.

"Flip us." She wrapped her arms around her shoulders while Ryan held her hips and rolled.

"Easy. When you sit up my cock will be deeper."

She grinned. "I know." With her hands on Ryan's shoulders, she pushed until she was sitting, the cock buried deep inside, and she began to raise up and down, her ass against Ryan's thighs.

Ryan grabbed her hips and helped her. "Jesus, Dani. I'm going to come." She shook beneath her.

She may not have topped her, but she felt powerful just the same in a kind of all-powerful femme way that she adored. Dani rose up, then dropped again and the tingle of her impending orgasm rushed through her. She grasped Ryan's nipples and tugged. "Now." She panted. "I'm coming now."

Roaring, Ryan's hips thrusted upward. "Dani," she cried out, her eyes closed tightly.

Dani shivered and shook as she rode the cock. Stars burst behind her eyelids and all she was aware of was the fullness of Ryan beneath her and her oaths of pleasure. She never wanted their night to end.

Chapter Seventeen

Whistling a tune she'd been hooked on since she was a teen, Dani threw the last load of wash in the dryer. She'd been on a cleaning spree and the apartment's gleaming surfaces were evidence of her efforts. She couldn't remember the last time she'd felt this energized.

As she made up her bed, her thoughts returned to her recent night with Ryan. Their scene play was not only eye-opening, but the power exchange had been a new dynamic in her growing knowledge of the bedroom variety.

When they'd started, Dani hadn't been sure if she'd like being helpless and at the mercy of another person, but Ryan wasn't some random woman. They'd been intimate several times and they trusted each other. Well, she trusted Ryan. She wasn't sure if Ryan should trust her, but the end result had been amazing, and she'd done so without hurting her. That was important.

Dani wished she had someone to talk to. Everything was so new and exciting. She'd learned so much in the last few months, but she was still a novice. Pam would have listened, but she was also a bit of a gossiper, and Dani didn't want a description of what she did in the bedroom to spread through the shop. She didn't care if anyone knew she was sleeping with women, but the erotic scenes felt too intimate to share with just anyone. It had to be someone she could rely on to keep her confidence, no matter how shocking it might be at first blush. Dani reached for her cell.

"Hey, sweetness. What's shaking?" Mark asked in his typical, upbeat fashion.

"Want to come over for dinner tonight?" She hadn't seen him in several weeks and she missed him.

"I don't know. What are you going to serve me?"

"If you bring the wine, I'll make chicken parm." For some reason, Mark acted like her chicken parm was second to none. It wasn't anything special, but if it made him happy, that's all she cared about.

Is that what kinky sex was about, too? Doing what your partner liked? What they found exciting and meaningful on another level? Not to mention how hot she'd been afterward. Ryan had taken care of that lingering issue, too. Her lovemaking had been gentle and sweet, leading her into an orgasm that seemed to last forever with Ryan's fingers buried inside her. It had felt...special.

Dani scolded herself. The sex Ryan and any others provided was bought and paid for, nothing more. She wasn't interested in anything deeper. But she still wanted to explore more and really top Ryan. She had a hard time picturing what that would be like with Ryan not liking anyone to see her vulnerable side, but Dani knew it was there. And against all rational thought, she wanted to be the one to bring that out.

"Earth to Dani." Mark's voice jostled her back to the now.

"What? Sorry."

"Uh-huh. We'll talk about where you went at dinner, just give me a time and I'll be there." They made kissy sounds when they got ready to hang up. "I'll bring fresh Italian bread from Prinzo's."

She glanced at the clock. She had a few hours to kill before starting dinner and with nothing left to do in the apartment and the dryer still going, Dani grabbed her laptop and curled up in the corner of her couch with a cup of tea and opened her email. As she glanced down the list of new arrivals her breath froze. There was one from Ryan from an hour ago. Her heartbeat sped up while her body began to hum, and she held her breath as she read.

Dear Dani,

Thank you for an exciting and adventurous time. I enjoy how curious you are about your own sexuality and that of the world at large. Below are a few books and articles you may find interesting regarding sexual power, play, and scenes. I hope they help answer some questions and further pique your interest for more exploration to come.

Fondly, Ryan

After reading the message again, her hand hovered over the mouse. If she clicked, it would mean she was committed to more than idle curiosity. In all honesty, there was nothing innocent about her level of interest. Since entering adulthood she'd been fascinated by what little she knew of leather bars and kinky sex, wondering what it entailed and how far people went. Taking a deep breath, she prepared herself for whatever was on the pages Ryan had thoughtfully sent.

By the time Mark arrived her head was swirling with all kinds of new information, and she realized she'd barely skimmed the surface. It was a heavily nuanced world she'd be diving into, if she wanted to take it beyond the light experimentation she'd already begun with. Once the food was ready, she dove in and told Mark about her life lately.

"You did what?" Mark's shocked expression took her by surprise.

Maybe it had been a mistake to tell him about her kinky bedroom forays. "I don't know why you're getting upset. You were the one who told me to be safe and not jump into bed with just anyone." She sipped her wine and took a bite of chicken.

"These women you're sleeping with *are* strangers. A step above paid prostitutes if you ask me."

Mark's words stung. He had no idea the level of professionalism and decorum the Agency insisted on for their employees, not to mention Ryan was the fucking CEO. "It's wrong of you to be accusing these escorts of being prostitutes. I'm shocked you even brought it up considering you sleep with any guy who's upright with a pulse and a dick." Dani picked up her plate and went to the kitchen, her appetite gone. Tears blurred her vision as she pretended to look outside, wanting to be somewhere else.

"Dani," Mark said as he placed a hand on her shoulder. "I didn't mean to upset you. You're my best friend and I'm worried about you. I don't know these women. I should have realized you'd never keep seeing them if you thought you were in danger." He turned her to face him. "Forgive me?" He brushed away the tear that ran down her cheek.

"I thought you'd be supportive. This is all so new, and I wanted to talk with someone I could trust not to blab it." She sniffed and tried to get her emotions under control. "Was I wrong to expect you to understand?"

"I'm still human. That means sometimes I'm also a jerk." He hugged her hard before taking her hands. "Tell me all about it." Mark's nose wrinkled. "Maybe not all because, you know, I'm not into lady parts, but all the sexy stuff."

Laughing, she pushed him away. "You're right. You are a jerk. Pour some more wine and help me clean up and I'll tell you how amazing it's been."

The clock glared at Ryan, calling her bluff. She'd vowed to sleep in and recover from what had unerringly turned from a night of discovery for Dani to a night of self-discovery for herself. Dani had followed where she led, much as Ryan expected her to, but so much more had occurred. Ryan's emotions had risen to the surface, and for the top that she claimed to be, it should never have happened. And she was unable to stop it.

Somehow, Dani had managed to pull her from herself and exposed the core of her being. Had anyone ever asked her to explain why the need to relinquish control became so great that she had to find release at the hand of another? It wasn't often that Ryan gave in and willingly allowed anyone to take control of a scene, but even she occasionally craved not having to be responsible for the pleasure of another, or herself.

Naked, she stumbled to the shower and stepped under the cold spray, inhaling sharply. Ryan grabbed the sponge and lathered, her other hand following the same path. Except for a brief touch before she fucked her, Ryan hadn't let Dani touch her because she knew how much she *wanted* her to. She moved her hand lower and brushed over her hard clit. It wouldn't take long. A few well-timed strokes were all she needed, but it wasn't what she wanted. Her desire would be her downfall. If Dani called for her again, she wasn't sure she should say yes to her request, knowing it would only lead to her wanting more from Dani, but she'd promised to show her more and knew she couldn't say no.

She quickly rinsed, ran a towel haphazardly over her body, and picked up her phone. After two rings she heard a familiar voice. One she could trust to ground her. "Drake."

"Morning, boss. Something up?"

"I need a hard run. Are you up for it?"

"Are you okay?"

"No."

Drake's silence told her there'd be no holding back in telling her the reason. "Meet me outside in twenty."

For the last few weeks, Dani's attempts to ignore wanting to see Ryan again had been in vain. Their last time together hadn't been just sex. That had been clear from the moment she'd been tied down. The entire experience was from a different level of trust and intimacy. Ryan had done things to her she never would have let any of the people she'd dated do, each one followed by Ryan's typical show of how much she cared about her being okay with what was happening. Now she was going to show Dani the other side of a dynamic.

Ryan had promised Dani she'd bring another escort for their next session so Ryan could show her how to use implements to bring pleasure to someone who liked various types of stimulation. To say Dani was surprised was an understatement. The woman who'd greeted her and Ryan when they arrived wore black leather pants with a thick leather belt, a low-cut, long-sleeved black T-shirt with the sleeves pushed up, and black biker boots. She extended her right hand.

"It's a pleasure to meet you, Dani. I'm Jill."

She shook hands, her gaze drawn to the ties of a braided black leather bracelet on her right wrist that swayed with the motion. "Nice to meet you." Ryan's warm hand pressed to the hollow of her back, and while the touch was familiar, Ryan appeared rigid, out of her element, which never happened. They moved to the small bar that held an array of appetizers and bowls of snacks. Jill moved behind the display and smiled.

"What would you like to drink?"

For some reason, she'd expected someone…well…submissive looking. Whatever that was. However, Jill didn't look the role at all. She looked dangerous and dominant. "Red wine, please."

Ryan disappeared for a moment, likely to check the bedroom as she always did before she slid onto the stool next to her.

"Scotch. Neat," Ryan said, her voice low and sultry. The same voice that commanded her to such pleasure she could almost climax from hearing it. Ryan downed half the contents of her glass and turned to face her. "Jill is one of our most recent hires. She's characterized, for lack of a more suitable term, as a switch, and has offered herself for tonight's demonstration."

She must have appeared as confused as she felt.

"Looks can be deceiving in the BDSM world, but there are clues and cues to help you figure out the basics."

They'd discussed Ryan's role for the evening, but the display of her familiar power made her clit swell, and she adjusted her angle on the padded seat to relieve the pressure. Still confused, Dani drank some wine. "So dress has nothing to do with roles?"

Ryan shook her head. "It's not as simple as black and white. If we were at a club where members of the BDSM community gathered and scenes were played out, almost everyone would be wearing leather, or black, or a combination. The clothing has more to do with setting the atmosphere than conveying roles." Ryan must have sensed her ongoing confusion, and she looked at Jill. "Let's demonstrate."

Jill took her beer and stood at the end of the bar, her stance relaxed, and her gaze disinterested as she glanced around, not making eye contact with either of them. The bracelet was on full display as she raised the bottle to her lips to take a drink.

Ryan moved closer, drink in hand. "Jill is waiting to be approached. As a submissive, a display of aggression or blatant interest isn't welcome. That wouldn't work if she wants a top's attention." Ryan squared her shoulders, her black jeans hugging her ass. "This your first time at the club?" Clearly in her element, she moved into Jill's space, her legs spread, and her gaze locked on to Jill's face even though Jill didn't look directly at her.

"No, but it's been a while."

Jill's gaze was downcast, but Dani didn't miss the slow perusal of Ryan's firm body before stopping at the bulge in her crotch. A flare of territorial jealousy rose before she pushed it away. She'd paid for this scene, and she was going to get her money's worth even if it involved Ryan touching another woman as she watched.

Ryan traced the braid of leather with her fingertip. "Is this for real?"

"Yes." Jill looked up. An unspoken exchange happened between them before Ryan stepped back and returned to her.

"Did you get all that?" Ryan asked, then knocked back the rest of her drink and set the empty tumbler down.

Dani closed her eyes and replayed the scene, wanting to get it right, not knowing if she would. "Jill appeared indifferent but there was a sense of tension coming from her. She displayed her submissiveness with the bracelet." After a minute she went on. "She avoided eye contact until you made your interest known, then she looked up. I..." Dani took a breath. The excitement coursing through her gained momentum. "Then there was an understanding or acknowledgement." She shrugged, unsure if any of it was correct.

Ryan stroked her cheek with the backside of her fingers, and the intimacy of the touch brought another wave of desire. "Very good. When Jill said 'Yes,' she was consenting to a scene. One which..." she pointed to her wrist, "she knows I will lead." Ryan took her wine glass from her, coated her lips with the ruby liquid, and smiled that heart-stopping, seductive smile of hers. "Shall we?" She indicated the bedroom, then took Jill's hand.

They moved down the hallway as though they'd done this a hundred times. Maybe they had.

"Decide how you'd like to proceed," Ryan whispered, her lips close to her ear. Then she began to undress until all she wore was her boi shorts and the harnessed dildo concealed beneath them.

She chewed her lower lip, unsure what to do. Jill was standing near the bed, her gaze fixed on the floor. Ryan came behind her and pressed herself along her body, the cock against her ass.

"The most important thing to remember is that as a top, you agreed to please her when she agreed to let you." Her arm circled low on her waist and pulled her firmly to her. "What are you going to do, Dani?"

Her mind flashed on their previous encounter where Ryan was the top and she was in Jill's position. Maybe not in the way they were tonight, but the roles were the same and she understood she had an obligation. "Tell me your safe word." First and foremost, Ryan had made her promise if she were ever in a situation where the other person didn't ask, she would leave immediately. Jill revealed her word and Dani stepped away from Ryan's embrace, emboldened by the rush of confidence coursing through her. She stripped to her lace bra and briefs. Both black, both sheer. "Strip to your waist and get on your back in bed."

Once Jill was in position, she admired her face, her slim neck, and her full breasts with large nipples. Her chest heaved in shallow breaths, her excitement palpable. Dani recalled the words Ryan had used and repeated them now. "Is there anything you don't want me to do?" The tremor in her voice betrayed her own trepidation, but she was determined to prove she could do this.

"Don't make me bleed, and no ball gags."

Jesus. How could anyone actually want to be whipped to that point, or cut during sex? She still had so much to learn. Ryan came up behind her.

"Everyone has different personal limitations when it comes to this lifestyle. Knowing those limits, whether soft or hard, is an individual choice." Ryan ran her hands down her arms. "Do you remember how you felt when I led you there? To that sharply focused point when all you wanted to do was come?"

She shivered at the visceral memory of the tails of the flogger being dragged over her mound and the anticipation of what might happen next. Any pain was over quickly and followed by touches that drove her higher and higher until finally, she was given release. "Yes, I do."

"Give that to Jill. Watch her body, her face. Play with her tolerance. Be the top she craves."

Tingling sensations moved over her skin as her body quickened at the inciting words. She moved to the bed and attached padded cuffs to Jill's wrists until she was satisfied she was restrained but not in discomfort. Dani opened the armoire and selected several items. She looked to Ryan as she held out nipple clamps attached to a chain. "Show me." Ryan was extremely patient as she explained how a woman's nipples should be hard when the clamps were placed and even though Jill had told her what she didn't want, it was a good idea to be careful the first time she and a partner engaged in any untried or new way. She approached Jill, massaged her breasts, and gauged her willingness to participate. The look in Jill's eyes told her it was fine, so Dani attached one adjustable clamp and tightened it until Jill moaned and then repeated the process with the other. The surge of power from controlling what was happening was intoxicating and knowing Ryan was watching made it even more so. It was new and exciting even if she wasn't quite sure if this was a long-term role. For tonight it was great.

Over the next hour, Ryan guided her through a variety of play until Jill was begging her for release.

Ryan stood close, but not intrusively so. "You have to decide how far to push her while remembering she trusts you to take her there. She may already be to the point where one touch, one hot breath caressing her flesh will drive her over the edge and you have an obligation to accept she's reached her limit. Even if you told her not to come until you say, in her current state, she's vulnerable."

Dani ran her finger through Jill's swollen flesh, careful to stay away from the hard, distended clit. "And if I want her to come?"

Ryan shrugged and grinned. "Then take her. That power is yours."

Jill was ready and so was Dani. She entered Jill hard and fast, her thumb pounding into her clit. She bucked like a bronco as her orgasm claimed her, crushing Dani's fingers, and filling her hand with slick juices. She studied the transformation from tense, quivering muscles to the flush that rose over her chest and up her throat, to the arched neck and babbling tones of release and relief. Power, as Ryan so astutely stated, coursed through her and she bathed in it, all the while acknowledging she'd much rather be on the receiving end, though she was glad for the opportunity and experience. Ryan's voice broke through her revelry.

"Now she needs your assurance she did well and pleased you."

Much like Ryan had done with her, Dani released the cuffs and brought Jill's still shaking form into her arms, soothing her with softly spoken words and smoothing her hand over her naked body. She was content for the moment and that was enough, but her own body thrummed with a need much deeper than earlier, and she knew only one person who could bring the relief it demanded.

Ryan nodded to Jill as she dressed before joining Dani in the great room. The lights were low, and the city twinkled beyond the plate glass windows, filling the darkness with millions of pinpoints of light. Her clit throbbed painfully beneath the dildo pressed against her. She would need to relieve herself soon. Dani stood staring out at the vast open view, the robe she wore untied, and the reflection of her nude body enticed her. Refocusing her attention elsewhere, she tossed a few cubes in a tumbler and added bourbon. Jill approached Dani and she couldn't tear her gaze away from the intimate scene.

Jill placed her hand on Dani's shoulder. "Thank you." She leaned forward and kissed her cheek. Dani turned and smiled.

"I hope—" she began, but Jill silenced Dani by pressing her finger to Dani's lips.

"You were magnificent. If you ever want to do that again, just ask for me."

Dani nodded, her face flushing a deep pink. Jill glanced at Ryan, nodded once in acknowledgement, and quietly slipped out the door.

She closed her eyes and took a deep breath, her control teetering on the edge of jealousy and desire. When she opened them, Dani stood a foot away, her head tipped and her gorgeous body on full display.

"What are you thinking?"

Her mind worked to come up with a believable response. "You were amazing tonight." She brought the glass to her lips and sipped, her gaze never leaving Dani's.

"Maybe, but that's not what you were thinking." A step closer and Dani ran her hand down her naked chest before grasping her cock. She gasped from the sudden pressure.

"I was thinking..." she said.

"Go on." Dani stroked her again.

"How watching you with Jill made me want to fuck you." She wrapped her fingers around Dani's wrist, stilling her motion. It wouldn't take much to make her come and she didn't want to. Not like this.

Dani moved until the only thing separating them was the edge of her robe. "And now?"

She scooped Dani up in a powerful move and carried her to the bedroom. She flipped the covers down, not wanting her lust shared with what had happened prior, lifted the robe from Dani's shoulders and let it fall to the floor. "Get in." As soon as Dani moved, she stripped away her briefs and joined her. "Now I'm going to do what I've been wanting to do all night." Lying over Dani's body, she settled her weight on her forearms and kissed her slowly until both were gasping for air.

"Ryan," Dani whimpered. "Please touch me."

Shifting, she moved her hand between them, her fingers gliding through Dani's slippery folds. Ryan stroked in measured lengths, adding another finger until Dani was ready to take her without discomfort, her eyes closed as she moaned low in her throat. She held her cock at Dani's opening. "Look at me." She questioned her need for Dani to connect with her and why it mattered so desperately. When Dani's honey-brown eyes were fully open she pressed into her until she was buried all the way inside her. She was painfully close to coming and commanded her body to wait. She would not come until Dani did. Topping Dani, being the dom to her sub even if not fully in a scene and taking her to a place where nothing else mattered except the moment, made her heady with power. But power alone didn't drive her. On a deeply personal level, Ryan was compelled by her need to claim Dani as her own…a thought she'd been trying to deny until this moment.

Dani's slender fingers closed over her forearm. "What's wrong?"

Ryan pulled back, slid in. "Nothing except wanting you." A half dozen strokes later, Dani's fingers dug into her ribs, urging her to keep going until she cried out, and Ryan sank into her again as her own restraint broke free and the roar she released resembled the sound of victory, like a beast who had taken down her prey. The climax continued as she panted and groaned and pushed her body until she could do no more before she collapsed. Dani held her tight as they rolled onto their sides. After their breathing slowed, she brushed a wayward strand from Dani's face. "Thank you."

"For?" Dani ran her thumb over her swollen bottom lip.

She caught her hand, kissed her knuckles, and stilled her motion. "For the gift of you." Dani's trust *was* a precious gift, and Ryan's only wish was to never break it.

Chapter Eighteen

"Good morning," Ryan said as she settled in at the oval conference table with her steaming coffee. "I've called us together to review where we are in the expansion. Lane, you're up."

"Hey, everyone. The new condos are long-term rentals for a reasonable amount and suit our needs, so I've negotiated for two at LakeSide and two at Premier. Since we're known in the area, the owner assured us they can meet our requirements and is willing to finish and furnish to our specifications."

"Expenses?"

"Five thousand each for combined security deposit and to furnish requested amenities, then twenty-two thousand a year, not including electric for LakeSide. Premier is slightly higher, but so are the upgraded finishes, rounding out at twenty-eight thousand a year."

Ryan quickly did the numbers in her head. It was a great deal. "Anna, set up a meeting with the rental agents for next week so I can have a look at each one. I'd like them all on the same day."

"I'll get right on it, Ms. Lewis." Anna scribbled a note on her pad.

"Drake, any complaints regarding Beck Simon?"

Drake looked through her files and her mouth quirked up on one side. "From everything I've heard, she's a good addition. We do need at least one additional femme of center escort to fill the current demand, and maybe two more escorts who are into kink."

She glanced out the window for a brief instant. "And another masculine of center person wouldn't be unwelcome. Some of the staff are a little fatigued. It seems our clients are becoming a bit more challenging."

"Consumer demand." The last few applications she'd gotten were subpar of the standards the Agency required. "Anna, send out our usual feelers for more applicants."

"On it," Anna said.

"What about Jay?" Drake asked.

She had enjoyed her times with Jay, more so than even Trish though she wasn't sure why. She hadn't been aware Jay was interested in working for them. "Let's discuss it after we're done here."

Their numbers, which translated into income, had been soaring the last few months. Nothing had changed from the company's side and she was concerned about any publicity, good or bad, that might be circulating in the public sector. Anna was good at crunching client numbers and contacts, but she worried everyone was overloaded.

"One last item. How would everyone feel about an addition to our office staff? Someone who could take on the overload, do correspondence, maybe some of the day-to-day operations?"

Anna appeared stricken. "Are we falling behind?"

Ryan sat forward and made eye contact with each member of the team. "No. I'm assuming you all have lives outside of this office and I want to make sure you have the time to actually enjoy them. The busier we get, the less time we're all going to have." She took in the intense gazes and went on. "The last thing I want is for any of you to burn out. You signed on for the long haul, but I don't want anyone dragging their ass to get there. I couldn't ask for a better team and I want you all to know you're appreciated. We can afford to take on someone else to see to the time-consuming little details that we all make time for, even when we don't have it." She looked pointedly at Drake who nodded imperceptibly. "I believe in leading by example. Drake has agreed to help with hiring and other duties to take a little off my plate. I have also decided to officially name her vice president of the Agency." She glanced at the shocked expressions. "This adventure would have never gotten off the ground had it not been for Drake's untiring enthusiasm and support." It didn't take long for the others to voice congratulations, and although she hadn't told Drake of her decision, she looked amused. Time to get back on track. "If *I* can relinquish some tasks, so can all of you." Soft laughter followed. After several minutes, Anna spoke up.

"I've never minded the hours, but I wouldn't be opposed to having a day off every now and then."

"Everyone who works here deserves breaks, including our escorts." Her own life was slipping by without much notice. A change was in order for her, too. "What's the sense of making a ton of money if no one gets to enjoy it?" Consensus met, Ryan adjourned the meeting and stood before Drake lightly grasped her arm.

"Are you all right?"

Ryan smiled. "Yes. Why?"

"You seem…melancholy. Like the weight of the world is on your shoulders. It's rare for you to *ask* for a hard run, too. I know you didn't want to talk about it then, but I can't help worry, especially with all the changes you're instituting. What's going on?"

She gestured to Drake to sit back down. "I'm not melancholy, just reflective." Ryan hadn't voiced her loneliness because she'd willingly chosen the life she lived. She loved her few close friends, had a restrained but fun social life, and aside from a quirky adoptive family who had been financially generous when she needed it, had little to complain about. That was until she walked inside her gorgeous home and the hollow sound of her own footsteps gripped her heart in a painful way. Chester only made his presence known when his dish was empty, though the rare times he curled beside her were comforting. At thirty-seven she couldn't imagine she'd tire of living the dream of sex as often as she wanted and in ways she learned could give hours of pleasure while being paid an outrageous amount of money for doing it.

Over the last few years though, the newness and excitement had dulled, and she'd been left feeling adrift and alone. That's when she stopped seeing clients of her own, using the business as an excuse that had worked…until Dani.

"But?" Drake asked.

Ryan blew out a breath. "I can't stop thinking about the bigger picture." She was quiet for a minute, choosing her words carefully. Drake was the only woman Ryan had ever trusted enough to let inside, but she had to tread lightly because Drake *wanted* to be inside in all the ways that should matter. "Do you ever think about the connections we haven't made? The girlfriends who weren't girlfriends in the true sense, but women we weren't paid to be with?"

Drake stared at her notes, tapped her pen. "You mean have I thought about having a partner, a wife?"

Was that what she meant? "Maybe."

Drake leaned forward. "I love the connections I have with several women. We have fun and I love my life." She glanced down and hid her hands under the table before looking up again. "If that ever changes, I'll do something about it. Until then, I plan on enjoying every minute." Her mouth quirked. "Like the times I get your lazy ass to go running."

"Ha. You mean with my out of shape ass."

"Oh no, you're not going to get me to make a disparaging remark about my boss. No way, no how."

Ryan smiled. "Not that much of a boss anymore."

"About that. You just spring the news on me like that?"

She threw her arm around Drake's shoulders. "I thought you liked surprises." Actually, she was the one surprised by how easily the decision to give part of the helm to Drake had been. Now maybe she could spend some time on her personal life since she was starting from scratch. She couldn't help but wonder if it might include Dani.

"The Agency," Anna said. "How can I help you?"

"Hi. It's Daniella Brown. I'd like to speak with Ms. Lewis."

"I'm sorry, Ms. Brown. She's in a meeting at the moment. Can I help you?"

She didn't want Anna's help. She wanted to hear Ryan's voice and feel the rush it always gave her, but maybe it was better if she didn't. Her feelings for Ryan were growing in a direction she wasn't sure she wanted them to go. Maybe if she was with another woman she wouldn't continue to have them. "Will you let her know I'd like to schedule an escort?"

"Of course," Anna said kindly. "Will you be available in the next hour?"

Dani confirmed and hung up. Maybe Ryan would suggest Drake, but her energy was more than she could handle. She didn't need her intensity with track season in full swing and the shop brimming with of out-of-towners. She pulled up the file of photos Ryan had provided. It was time she went in a direction other than Ryan, though even the idea wasn't as appealing as it should have been. Ryan would be there for more kink, or whatever. Until she called back, she had to decide who her next escort would be. Her gut twisted uncomfortably whenever she felt like she was being careless with Ryan's feelings. She had to keep telling herself they weren't dating. It was only work for Ryan. But when they were together it didn't feel that way at all. And if she were honest with herself, it was Ryan she wanted.

Chapter Nineteen

Ryan loved seeing Drake's surprised expression at the announcement. She hadn't expected nor asked for a promotion, but she deserved it. Even though she'd finally given in and asked for her help with some of the day-to-day operations, which in and of itself had left Drake speechless, she was the cofounder of the Agency, and it was beyond time she received her due. Though she'd practically run the entire operation single-handedly from the beginning and only relinquished minor parts to both Drake and Lane, Ryan saw it for what it was. She learned years ago that having control in every aspect of her life was a necessity if she wanted to survive.

Behind the safety of her desk, she pulled up the file she hadn't opened in years. Ready for the pain that would surely come, Ryan clicked on the icon and an image filled her screen. Flowing auburn hair surrounded the alabaster skin and the fine features that had initially drawn her to Sarah. They'd met outside of the Agency while attending a track event for a local charity. At one point during the evening they'd ended up dancing together, and Ryan had been charmed by her sweet nature and sincerity. When they began dating, Ryan had refrained from sharing the true nature of her business and the wealth she was beginning to accumulate, afraid Sarah would stop seeing her if she knew what she did for a living or, maybe worse, continue to see her for her rising social status. She closed the file. The whole thing had been a tragic mistake on her part.

Once the pain of rejection from Sarah had subsided, she'd been resigned to the circumstances of her profession and the difficulties it entailed. Since then, she'd had safe, unattached sex. She smiled. Jay had not only let her enjoy some control in bed, but she'd also gotten her to let Jay wield her own the last time they were together. And like with Trish, letting go *had* taken a lot of pressure off, at least for a few hours.

Dani had been the last person she'd been with, and it had been spectacular as always, at least for her, and she wondered if Dani felt any of the emotional elements that Ryan continued to fight against. Clients were supposed to remain clients. Telling herself that little nugget of reality did nothing to quell the connection she'd felt. If she ignored it, that flame might turn into a fire that would engulf her. But every time they were together, the lines blurred a little more. Like when you lean against a chalkboard and the words became fuzzy, and if you kept doing it, sooner or later they disappeared, leaving nothing but an undiscernible smudge. She couldn't help considering that Dani was responsible for helping her move past the pain Sarah's leaving had caused. When she thought about it she was taken off guard by what little pain remained. Maybe she was finally letting go. Finally realizing maybe she didn't have to be alone forever.

She had to get moving and get away from the montage of thoughts and feelings assaulting her since they just kept going round and round in her head. Ryan headed to the lobby. "Anna, please send all the documents on recent hires and any accounts with pending actions to Drake and copy me on them."

"You could have just called you know." Anna smiled at her.

Since the day she'd walked in the office when there were no clients and only the barest hope for success, Anna had never wavered in her sense of duty or confidence the business would be a great success, and her attitude had been a welcome boost to their egos. Not to mention she was the most efficient administrator Ryan ever had the pleasure of knowing. "And miss a chance to see your beautiful smile? No way."

Anna blushed at the compliment. "I'll pull the files and send them shortly."

"Thanks." Ryan turned to walk away but stopped. "Do you think I've changed?" She hadn't been able to shake the unease of recent conversations. If anyone might have noticed a difference, it would be Anna, though she never said anything.

Anna folded her hands on her desk before looking up, her expression serious. "You've got a lot on your mind. The expansion, juggling all the new escorts, and interviews, not to mention the dozens of little details that often go unnoticed. Lord knows you've likely already spent countless hours considering every angle." Anna still looked thoughtful. "I imagine any changes you've felt will be temporary. Giving Drake some responsibilities can only help. You know she's been wanting to do more for the business."

She rarely reflected on how others at the Agency might see her, but maybe it was time for that too to come to the forefront. "Thanks, Anna."

"Ms. Lewis?"

Ryan met her gaze.

"I know you and Drake are close, but if you ever want another ear, I hope you know you can always talk to me."

She reached over the desk to take Anna's hand and gave a gentle squeeze. "I know. I don't tell you nearly often enough how much I appreciate everything you do, including looking after me."

Perhaps Dani seeking her out had been cathartic in many ways. For the first time in a long time she found herself thinking long-term, and it was something she should have done years ago.

A little while later, Anna called her on the office phone. "Ms. Lewis, your eleven o'clock is here. Shall I send Ms. Carson in?"

She glanced at the picture on the wall. The nude woman posed in such a way as to suggest sensuality and sex, but without actually showing anything. It reminded her of all the reasons she needed to remain removed from close bonds with anyone. She had an appointment with Dani to engage in more kink and she'd agreed to let Dani practice topping a little more, but this time it would be just the two of them. Maybe she'd let someone else step in. Of course, that would be the wiser thing to do. But the thought of Dani submitting that way to anyone else made her feel slightly ill. Regular sex was one thing. Power exchange was another, something deeper and more intense, and damn it if she didn't want Dani experiencing that with anyone else.

"Yes, Anna. I'm ready." Just how ready remained to be seen.

❖

A shiver of excitement coursed through her. She hadn't thought about Dani tying her down, taking her pleasure, but the images flashing in her mind's eye made her long for being touched in ways she had only dreamt of over the years. Yet, a part of her, the part always in control, had a hard time letting go. Dani must have sensed her unease and she pulled away.

She hadn't allowed herself to come with Dani, and she wasn't sure if she wanted to. "Where do you want me?"

Dani pointed. "Take off your shirt and lie down." Dani took it from her and carefully hung it over the back of the chair. Then she cuffed both her wrists and stood chewing on her bottom lip while she looked her over.

"If you want to leave the shorts on, I may let you use the cat later."

Dani gasped. "I might hurt you."

She lifted an eyebrow. "That would be the point of a lashing."

"You like that?"

"It can be very exciting with the right person providing the experience." Apprehension clouded Dani's expression. "Remember, you don't have to do anything you don't want to."

Dani moved to the ankle cuffs and worked them until she was in the same position Dani had been in earlier. She'd requested that they go over a topping scene because Dani wanted to get it right. The idea of Dani giving her pleasure in a different way excited her. Standing in front of the armoire, Dani opened the doors, then took a step back. Every shape and size of dildo, harnesses, vibrators, whips, canes, and a plethora of other instruments she likely had no clue about using were displayed inside. Dani reached forward then stopped and looked over her shoulder.

"Can I touch them?"

"Just remember whatever you touch will be removed when we leave, so only remove things you're sure you want to try."

Dani picked out several items. As she climbed onto the bed, she dumped the items beside her outstretched leg. A small pair of clamps, a mid-sized dildo, a finger vibrator, a small packet of lube, and a condom. Inwardly, Ryan chuckled. Dani was amassing quite a collection since she'd told her to take home whatever she wanted. She didn't appear nervous, but as she looked over the items, she could see Dani's determination. Ryan's stomach muscles rippled.

"Okay, I think I'm ready."

Her mouth twitched. "Aren't you forgetting something?"

Dani's lips pursed as she reviewed the items. "I don't think so, unless you want something different." Dani glanced at the open armoire.

"You need to know my safe word."

"Oh." She lowered her head and studied her hands, then glanced at the instruments again. "I don't think I can…"

"Dani." Ryan held Dani's gaze for a brief moment, and the connection between them was unlike any she'd ever experienced. Dani's hesitation came from wanting to please *her*, and she would grant herself permission to enjoy her explorations. They would travel this road together. "Yes, you can. I trust you. I'll teach you."

"Tell me your safe word."

She smiled. "Romeo."

"As in the suave lover?"

"As in fated love." She inhaled sharply. She'd never told a soul why she'd chosen that word and what it meant to her. But then, no one had ever asked. Dani asked about a lot of things she was unable to ignore.

Dani looked at the nipple clamps.

Christ. With Dani sitting naked on her haunches and the toys scattered around her, she was more than a little turned on. Dani picked up the cat.

"How is this different from a flogger?"

"The leather is meant to caress or sting, although a braided cat can cut if wielded without control. In scene play, a lot of what is exciting is the anticipation of what will happen next, and whether it be pain or pleasure, because that power is in the top's hand, and the unknown is what brings heightened awareness to the bottom. You may want to get a suede flogger instead. It's a different sensation and easier to control." When Dani returned with it, she talked Dani through using it on her own thighs and after a few minutes she seemed more confident about the instrument. A trickle of wet heat seeped from Ryan's cunt. She was going to explode without Dani even touching her if she didn't rein in her body. Not an easy thing to do when tied and in need.

Dani slipped the finger vibrator on. "You mind being penetrated?" she asked as she moved closer.

"Not at all."

When Dani straddled her abdomen, her wet heat covered her as she leaned closer. Her mouth was warm, her tongue slowly tracing the tips of her nipples. Dani turned on the vibrator and she moved it lightly over her bicep, across her shoulder, then downward to circle first one nipple, then the other.

"Is this okay?" Dani asked before closing her lips over her pebbled flesh and gently sucking as she continued to trail the vibrator lower.

The thought of Dani touching her after the intensity of their first scene together drove her toward the edge. She gritted her teeth. "A top doesn't ask for permission." Ryan pressed into her as much as she could.

"How do I know when to stop or keep going?"

Ryan took a breath. She needed to hold on. "Tops *know* how close their sub is by their body's reactions. They pay close attention." She jerked at the next touch. "I'm going to come soon."

"Mmm. And you're telling me because I'm still a..." Dani seemed to be searching for the word. "Novice?" Dani asked as her finger slid against her throbbing clit, then yanked it away. "Do not come," she said firmly.

Her body stiffened. She knew how to stop the involuntary reaction, and she was baffled by not wanting to. She *wanted* Dani to drive her over the edge of control, to give her the freedom giving in would provide. "I'm trying, mistress."

Dani stilled at her words. "Should I reward you for trying to obey, or punish you for being so needy?"

She opened her mouth to answer when Dani silenced her by softly licking her clit. Not enough to make her come, but definitely enough to have her hanging on by a thread. Her body began to shake as she wielded the barest of control, her body screaming for release. From her lips tumbled a word she rarely used during sex. "Please."

Dani kissed her inner thigh as her gaze traveled upward to find hers. "I want to see and hear when you do." She nipped at the tender flesh. "Got it?"

All she could do was nod. It took every ounce of concentration she possessed to wait for Dani's permission. When Dani's mouth opened and covered her sex, and her tongue moved over her clit in firm strokes, she climaxed. Her entire body hardened before she heard herself crying out in exquisite pleasure. The same kind she'd felt the first time a woman much older and wiser had taken her. As her body still convulsed, Dani removed the cuffs and held her against her, stroking her. Ryan briefly fought the wave of exhaustion that washed over her. She was safe and satiated. For once, she wasn't interested in fighting against what felt so good.

Chapter Twenty

The shift dragged on even though the restaurant was busy as usual. Dani was flagged down at every turn, not giving her more than a few stolen moments in the rest room to gather her thoughts. But no matter what chaos she found herself in, all thoughts returned to Ryan. She hadn't heard from her since the night she'd topped her, not that she was expecting to. In this case, Ryan was the employee, and it was rare as such to initiate contact. Right? But seeing her so open, so expressive when she climaxed, made her feel things she hadn't expected to. Not because Ryan was being paid, though that should have been reason enough. But because Ryan had been willing to do so. With her. A client, and as an employee Ryan was governed by rules of behavior. Maybe Ryan had a pass on rules as CEO. The question remained, had Ryan broken them? Or was she simply performing her duty? Dani's chest froze at the idea.

"Dani," another waitress said. "Table eight needs another round of drinks."

She nodded and pulled up their tab. One more round and she'd either get a really generous tip or they'd forget altogether. As she smiled and replaced the empty glasses for full drinks, one of the men caught her eye with a predatory glance. Dani continued to serve and smile, ignoring the creep. If Ryan were there…Dani turned away and shook her head. Ryan wasn't there, and even if she was they weren't dating. They had prearranged sex and kink lessons. *Then why did it feel like so much more?*

❖

Ryan's dislike for hiking was second only to running. She'd much rather spend two hours sweating at the gym than tax her body in ways it was never meant to endure. The only reason she'd agreed to go with her screener, Kim, was to hear her thoughts on the type of escorts the Agency needed more of. Her current predicament had come into play when she'd relinquished letting Kim pick where they would go for the meeting. Just one more reason why she didn't give up control unless she had no choice

"Come on, Ryan. You're doing great. Almost there."

Kim appeared to be sprinting up the steep incline while she huffed and puffed and mumbled under her breath for the dozenth time. Finally, they stopped climbing and Kim stood with her hands at her waist and gazed around, smiling.

"Isn't it gorgeous?"

Ryan bent over, hands on thighs, gasping for air. They'd started off at a reasonable clip on a gentle incline, but the treacherous terrain turned taxing without any warning, and she hadn't been able to ease up for the last forty-five minutes. "For Christ's sake, are you trying to kill me?" She was in good shape. She ran five miles once a week with Drake and worked out at the gym four or five days, rounding out her routine. Ryan focused on strength training and had obviously underestimated her need for endurance too. Tomorrow, if she could walk after this, she'd talk with one of the trainers at her gym on how to fix that.

"Oh, come on now. This was your idea after all." Casting a glare in her direction, Kim continued. "Okay, so not exactly *your* idea, but you did let me pick." She took off her backpack and started digging around inside. "You should drink something with minerals."

Ryan sat on a smooth, sun-warmed boulder and pulled a water from her pack. "I know when I need to drink. Just because you're a sprinter doesn't mean I don't know how to take care of myself." It was a grumpy response, and Kim laughed. She cracked a bottle open, dumped a packet of Ultima in, and gave it a vigorous shake. It didn't take long for the electrolytes to kick in and she finally stopped panting. Sweat ran down her neck and between her shoulder blades.

"I've brought us lunch and we'll dig in soon. In the meantime, I'm going to take in the view. Maybe you could do the same instead of thinking about the business like you are right now."

Caught without a plausible retort, Ryan moved gingerly. Her thigh muscles quivered the same way they did when she engaged in marathon sex like she had with Dani. She pushed the thought away and shook her head as she went to stand near the edge of the cliff. Soon she'd be engaged in shop talk, and she couldn't be distracted by random images of Dani with someone else. Of anyone else but her.

Kim was right. The open vista before her was breathtaking. Beneath her lay a lush forest of thick pine trees divided by a slow, meandering river. One small patch of flat land could be seen where dark green grass grew and several deer nibbled away. A mountain range rose up in the distance, its peak shrouded in a thin veil of fog. The sun she'd been sheltered from while climbing along the forest ridge peeked out from behind fast-moving clouds. It had been years since she'd taken a real vacation and even longer since she'd allowed herself the simple pleasure a view like this could bring. Ryan took in a deep breath and cleared her mind. For a few blissful minutes, she could let go of everything and everyone, and she sank into the peace that surrounded her. The hand gently placed on her shoulder brought her back to the present.

"I didn't want to disturb you, but you began to weave a bit and I was afraid…" Kim glanced at the edge not more than a foot from where she stood.

"Sorry. I took a little break from reality. I'm back now." She turned and squeezed Kim's hand. "Thank you."

"Let's get down to business while we eat." Kim began unpacking a variety of small containers and an icepack containing a thick sandwich. "Nothing fancy, but there's lots to choose from. I know you're used to fine dining."

Did everyone view her as a pompous, stuck-up CEO? "Simple is sometimes the best of all." She had to ask. "Is there a rumor mill where people think I have a stick up my ass?"

Kim laughed out loud, her eyes wrinkling at the corners. "Of course not. If there's something up your..." Color bloomed in her cheeks. "What did you want to meet about?"

Ryan cocked a brow. She rarely spoke with Kim aside from the evaluations she conducted, and they'd never engaged in a sexual encounter. Ryan didn't want to skew her opinion of a potential employee because she'd slept with the boss. "We're going to be bringing on more escorts and I want to know if we fall short in any way with the services we provide. You know what each woman excels at in the bedroom. Are there any areas we need to expand in? Do we need more dominants or subs? That kind of thing." She shoved her empty water bottle into her pack and took out another.

"How many are you going to bring on?"

"As many as necessary, but I'd think a maximum of six right now."

"Wow."

Ryan nodded. "The staff needs time off. Just because I live, eat, and breathe the Agency doesn't mean everyone else should." She took a hunk of cheese and a cracker, wishing she had a crisp white wine to wash it down. Maybe she should cut back on her alcohol consumption.

"Are employees complaining?"

She couldn't remember Kim ever telling her she was unavailable for an evaluation. Not that she was called in every day, but even those that had been employed for several years were reevaluated every so often to be sure they hadn't gotten sloppy or lazy or forgot they were being paid to provide a service. "It's not that. People have a right to enjoy life when they're not working and that means not working all the damn time." Frustrated, she stood quickly, and her legs screamed in protest, making her groan. "Jesus, I'm getting old."

Kim was instantly at her side. "You're far from old, Ryan. You aren't used to mountain climbing is all." She ducked to catch her gaze. "What's wrong?"

What *was* wrong with her? She took a hard look inside. "I've rarely worried about anything...the Agency or anything else. Lately, that's all I seem to do." She attempted a smile, but the result felt forced. "You've heard about Drake taking on more?" When Kim nodded, she continued. "I love what I do, and I hope that never changes, but...there's something missing." She should be having this conversation with Drake, but sometimes Drake was too close, and she already thought seeing Dani was a huge mistake. Ryan ran her hand over her face, determined to go on. "I had an ulterior motive for asking you to meet me. You spend time with all the escorts in a limited, but unique capacity." She took a step away, not wanting Kim to see the inner turmoil that was getting harder to hide. "Would you ever consider a relationship with one? I mean if, you know, things clicked. Even knowing what they did for a living?"

"That's a tough question with no easy answer. I think it would depend on how special I thought the person was, no matter their profession." Kim tipped her head. "What else is bothering you?"

"My ego is bruised. I've been seeing a client and she's definitely special, but she's asked..." She couldn't finish.

"Are you worried you've lost your edge?"

Wincing, she held Kim's gaze. "You're awfully brave asking me that."

After a long beat, Kim picked up the conversation. "Are you?"

"Fuck. Maybe. I don't know." She pulled her hand through her hair. "If I knew I probably wouldn't be talking about it."

"I could let you know." Kim winked, smiled.

Of all the scenarios about their meeting she'd played out in her head, this certainly wasn't one of them.

Ryan laughed. "I appreciate the offer, but if I can be honest with you, my performance isn't in question."

"Ryan, whatever it is, your secret is safe with me."

She blew out a breath. "I don't want one of our clients, Dani, sleeping with anyone but me." There. She was finally able to admit what was bugging her.

"Ah, the age-old reason for self-doubt." Kim handed her half of the sandwich, and when she hesitated she held it closer, nodding. "A woman."

"Thanks." She took a bite, not really tasting it.

"You have feelings for Dani?"

"I'm…I don't know. It's complicated. Do you remember Sarah?"

Kim's gaze softened. "Yes."

"So, I'm guessing from your expression you have an idea of what happened."

"Ryan, it's none of my business what happened between you two and I didn't ask. All I know is that you were gone for a while after you two broke up. I can only imagine something tragic happened between you."

"You're close. Anyway, not since then have I had feelings for a woman. I mean, I'm fond of the women I sleep with, but there's nothing emotional." She took a second, hesitant to open up any more than she had. "It's bad enough I'm very close to breaking a rule I put into place when expecting everyone else to follow it."

Kim took a bite of sandwich and chewed before responding. "You've never been anything but professional, Ryan. Maybe you should try looking at the idea differently."

"How so?" She grabbed a couple of grapes.

"If, let's say, Drake were to become involved with a client and she was truly happy, would you be angry with her for breaking the rules?"

"Of course not. Drake's happiness would be more important than any rule." The light bulb went on. "Touché." She swallowed hard. "It's more than that, though. Unlike with Sarah, I wouldn't want to fuck up with Dani, in any way."

"What makes you think *you* were the one who caused the breakup with Sarah?" Kim squeezed her hand. "Everything I know about you leads me to believe you'd put your entire being into making a relationship work."

"I thought I had. In the end, it just wasn't enough." That was a long time ago though, when she was younger and headstrong.

"There's a gulf of experiences that separates us." She met Kim's kind expression. "The sex is phenomenal, but everything else…" Ryan swallowed around the knot that had formed. "Dani has awakened those long-forgotten feelings, and I have no clue if she feels the same about me."

Kim was quiet for the time it took to pack away the leftovers before she looked up. "Don't you think it's time you found out?"

Ryan agreed with the sound advice. The part she wasn't sure about was finding out if Dani had no interest in her other than professionally, and how she would deal with it.

Chapter Twenty-one

"I wish I could tell George to kiss my ass," Dani said as she stormed around the salon cleaning stations and filling empty bottles of product.

"Why don't you?" Pam asked as she set up her own station with her implements before her first customer waltzed through the door.

She dropped into a chair and sighed. "You know as well as I do why. I need this job and the tips. Otherwise I'll have to wait a year to indulge my habit. And I'm having to forgo every single extra in life to scrape the money together as it is."

Pam's eyes widened when it clicked what Dani meant. "That's a habit I wouldn't mind indulging in myself."

Dani giggled. "It *is* addictive for sure." She chewed her bottom lip. Since her little introduction to scene play, she'd been craving more. She'd made two more appointments over the next few weeks. One to be accompanied to a retirement party, and one with Beck just because seeing Ryan so often wasn't good for her. But she was having second thoughts about both when she could have... *should* have...asked for Ryan. Wouldn't the rest of the attendees be surprised to see her on the arm of a very handsome woman? Though she'd made it clear to Ryan she only wanted an event companion, not sex, it still didn't quite sit right with her.

As she stomped around still fuming, Dani thought about her options. Sure, she'd asked for more hours knowing it was extra busy during track season, when all the socialites were busy posing for photos with horses they didn't even ride, but in a rage at her being late by ten minutes due to traffic, George had given her the delightful duty of opening the salon every day for the next week. That meant getting there at the ungodly hour of six a.m. There had to be another way to earn money. George didn't have the only salon, but this one was in a high-traffic location, and they got a big share of walk-ins. Maybe she could go work for the Agency. That idea made her laugh out loud. She was doing okay in the bedroom, but she was far from living up to the skill standards the rest of the escorts possessed if they were anything like Ryan or Drake. She unlocked the door, checked in Pam's customer, and growled when the phone rang. "And so it begins."

"A Cut Above, Dani speaking. How can I help you?" She cringed at the edge in her voice. She'd pay for that if it was George.

"Good morning, Dani."

She took in a quick breath. There was no mistaking Ryan's rich, deep voice. "Good morning, Ms. Lewis. What can I do for you?"

"I could think of a few ways you could do me," Ryan said, sending tingling sensations down her spine. "But I imagine you're not allowed to give me that kind of service in the salon. Are you?" Ryan's tone was deeper, similar to the one she heard in bed.

"Not that I'm aware of."

"Pity. In that case I'd like to schedule a cut with you for today. What's your latest appointment?"

Dani couldn't help smiling at the idea of seeing Ryan again as she checked the book. "I'm only here until six. I have a five thirty opening, though by then I might be running a bit late." The client scheduled at four thirty was a royal bitch, but she tipped well, and Dani endured her never ending complaints for the thirty dollars she always slid her at the end.

"I don't mind waiting if you don't mind staying a bit late."

"I don't mind."

"I'll see you then. Have a good day, Dani."

She scribbled Ryan's name in her column, then ran her finger over the print. Her day wasn't going to be as shitty as she thought after all.

❖

Ryan opened the salon door and walked into mayhem. Voices and shouts greeted her as she stood trying to take it all in. The atmosphere was nothing like the first time she'd been there. Dani was working on a customer whose hair stood out in folded foil sheets as her hands flew in animated conversation. After several minutes, a petite redhead hurried forward.

"I'm so sorry." She glanced over her shoulder. "It's a bit crazy here today. How can I help you?"

"No worries. Ryan Lewis. I have an appointment with Dani for five thirty." She glanced at the wall clock that displayed five twenty-five.

"There you are." She checked the book and then looked over her shoulder. "Oh goodness. I'll be right back."

The woman hurried to Dani and whispered in her ear before Dani looked over. Her features were pinched, her cheeks red, and she looked like she wanted to cry. She bent to her customer before heading over.

"I'm running behind." She rolled her eyes. "By a lot. A simple cut has turned into a frost." She ran her trembling hand over her face. "I don't know when I'm going to be done."

Ryan couldn't stand to see her in distress. "Do you have anyone scheduled after me?"

"You're my last."

Against her better judgment, which was happening a lot these days, she smiled and went on. "Finish your human antenna and call it a day. Then I'm going to take you to dinner since you probably haven't had a chance to eat much today."

Dani's eyes welled with tears. "But what about your cut?"

"I can wait a few more days." Ryan pressed on. "Unless you have a date tonight, I still want to take you to dinner." A beat passed. Then two. "Say yes. Please?" Her clit twitched when Dani bit her lip.

"Yes, but I don't know when I'll finish. It could be another hour." Dani glanced back to where the client was looking at her pointedly. Dani raised her finger, but it didn't look like the one she really wanted to raise.

"Go. It doesn't matter how long. I've got my laptop. Text me when you're almost done, and I'll come back for you." She handed her private card to her.

Relief washed over Dani's face. "Thank you."

As Ryan walked to her car, she allowed herself a minute of pleasure at having the chance to see Dani outside of a prearranged situation. Stress was something she'd learned to deal with before becoming a teenager. If she could, she'd help Dani see how harmful it was to her well-being. She stopped short. She cared about Dani. Her preoccupation had changed to something much deeper, and the fact that Dani's mental health mattered so much held implications she didn't want to dissect.

She settled in the passenger seat, reached back for her laptop, and pulled out her phone. There was never a shortage of things to do when you ran your own business. The demands of her job were her own doing and she loved it. Most of the time anyway. After entering her password to the Agency's email, Ryan began weeding out the curious vs. the serious, something she'd gotten good at spotting.

Forty-five minutes later, her phone pinged. *Ryan, just go without me.* She stowed her stuff and walked to the shop quickly. Something was wrong. The redhead met her at the locked door and let her in.

"She's in the restroom," she said and pointed down the hallway.

Ryan found Dani standing in front of a sink dabbing at some dark liquid splashed on her clothes, tears running down her face.

"Hey." Ryan met her gaze in the mirror. "Are you okay?"

"You should have gone on to dinner by yourself. I don't want you to see me like this." Dani stared at her hands.

She lightly grasped her shoulders and turned her. "What I see is a beautiful woman who's had a bitch of a day." She trailed her finger over Dani's cheek, caught a tear, and pressed it to her lips. "Do you have a change of clothes?"

Dani stared into her eyes as though looking for some deeper meaning. "I think I have jeans and a T-shirt." Her shoulders were slumped, her eyes still watery.

"Good." Ryan wet a clean towel and gently washed away the evidence she'd been crying, took her hand, and led her to the front where the lights were low. "What do you need from here?" Dani grabbed her purse from a drawer and her jacket from a hook, then waited. Ryan pulled her along and turned to the redhead who was counting money. "Dani's leaving now. Thanks for your help." The redhead stared at her.

"Uh...you're welcome. See you Thursday, Dani."

"Which one is yours?" she asked. Dani pointed to an older model green Subaru that had seen better days. "Let's get your clothes."

Dani unlocked the hatch and dug around until she produced a reusable bag with a few items of clothing in it, then locked the car.

"Will it be safe for the night?"

Confusion creased Dani's brow. "Yes, why?"

Ryan hit the remote and the lights flashed on her car. She opened the door and guided Dani in. After tucking herself into the driver's seat, she met Dani's questioning gaze. "You're coming home with me. You can take a shower while I cook dinner." Dani nodded silently, still looking dejected, and Ryan drove. Comfort wasn't something she often gave to anyone, including herself, but it felt right with Dani. Maybe because Dani had looked so lost it reminded her of her much younger self when she had no idea how she'd survive another day. And damn if it didn't feel good to come to Dani's rescue. She wanted to be the one Dani turned to, and that was one more thing that resided in dangerous territory.

Chapter Twenty-two

On the outside, Ryan's home, while not sprawling, couldn't compare to the grandeur inside. Dani stood in the tiled foyer surrounded by modern, yet classic accoutrements. Tasteful paintings, unobtrusive lighting, warm, inviting colors all made for a welcoming feel. The tray ceiling offered soft bluish white lighting, unexpected and pleasing to the eye.

"Your home is beautiful, Ryan." Stunned and feeling incredibly out of place, she was unsure if she should go any farther since she was covered in hair product, so she stayed planted where she was. A gray tabby peered around the corner and eyed her suspiciously before disappearing.

"That's Chester. You likely won't see him again unless it's to complain his dish is empty." Ryan turned to move farther into the house, but when she didn't follow, Ryan stopped. "What are you doing?"

"I'm a mess." She gestured to her clothes. "And your home is so nice"

Ryan took her hand. "Don't be ridiculous." She tugged her gently until they entered a large, open living room. "Do you want something to drink?"

Dani gathered her bags closer. "I want to get out of these."

"Give me a minute." Ryan went to the spacious kitchen, pulled several items out of the refrigerator, and then the freezer before turning on the oven. "Let's go take care of you."

Hand in hand, they entered what had to be the master suite. A huge bed with plush coverings took up a large portion of the room and the wall of windows were surrounded by flowing tapestry curtains. The colors were hard to distinguish in the quickly fading light. There might have been hints of mauve or gray with white trim and more softly glowing cove lighting. The wooden floors were dark, broken only by a thick white carpet on either side of the bed. Three matching pieces of furniture, two dressers and a desk, helped balance the grandeur. Dani was speechless.

"Right through here," Ryan said.

Wanting to see everything, Dani quickly followed. The bathroom was just as opulent with a large, tiled shower, a low-profile garden tub, and double sinks. Ryan produced several luxurious towels and set them on a small stand near the shower. When their gazes met, her sex clenched at the feral look in Ryan's eyes, but she didn't say anything as she approached, shedding her clothes with each step.

"Will you let me take care of you, Dani?" Her voice was deep and soothing. She took the bag from Dani's fingers and set it on the floor.

"I don't belong here," she said. It was true. She'd thought she was out of her element when they'd dined at a five-star restaurant, and then again whenever she went to one of the posh apartments. There wasn't any doubt she didn't belong there with Ryan, someone so out of her league.

"You belong wherever you are." Ryan's lips brushed over hers and traveled down her neck. Her hands moved slowly downward before inching the edge of her shirt up.

"What do you want?" She was trembling. A mix of excitement and wonder coursed through her, making her breath catch in anticipation.

"I want..." Ryan said as her warm hands smoothed over her stomach then back. "For you to give yourself over to me."

Dani moved her hands to the snap on her pants in answer. She wanted this. Wanted someone to erase the anger of her youth and the discontent of her adulthood. She wanted someone to care for her like a lover, like a partner. Dani didn't want to think anymore, she just wanted to feel. Ryan seemed to understand her...know her... in ways no one had ever taken the time to do. Naked, she gazed at the familiar contours of Ryan's body with new eyes. Her generous mouth, her wide shoulders, her ridged abdomen. She lifted her hand and placed it in Ryan's waiting one.

Their shower together was intimate without being sexual. Ryan gently washed her while she leaned against Ryan's firm body. She spoke softly in Dani's ear, telling her all manner of things to make a woman feel worshiped. Ryan washed her hair, massaging her scalp. It all felt so good, she could have stayed there for hours, but when the water started to cool, Ryan turned it off and wrapped her in a towel, ruffled her hair, and kissed her lightly, encouraging her to take her time before she left her alone.

As she sat on a padded stool drying her hair, she couldn't help wondering whether Ryan was as wet as she was. But she didn't crave sex, which was rather strange. Or rather, not *just* sex. Instead her body was reacting to the memory of Ryan's touch and the pleasure she could give, as well as the comfort and understanding she'd found in Ryan's embrace at the end of a terrible day. It was a little disconcerting, but she didn't care right now. For the moment, she'd just enjoy being taken care of.

She went to find her clothes and smiled as she looked at the two piles on the bed. One of her own clothes neatly laid out and another of loose silky pants and a short sleeve matching shirt. No underwear in either pile, but she didn't mind. Dressed and more relaxed than she'd been in weeks, Dani went to find Ryan.

Chapter Twenty-three

Ryan added ingredients to the dinner she'd ordered the other night but hadn't eaten. Fixing a nice meal for Dani gave her pleasure, and she gently hummed as she worked. A soft sound nearby made her glance up from the counter.

Dani stood at the island. "What are you making?" she asked.

"Two dishes. I wasn't sure what you'd like. Shrimp scampi with angel hair pasta and petite filet mignon with red beet puree. Arugula dressed in a vinaigrette and a delightful, unobtrusive white wine." She held out a glass and Dani took it as she settled on a barstool opposite her. "Feeling better?" Dani appeared relaxed, her skin still lightly pink from the hot shower and her ministrations. She was beautiful.

"Wonderful." Dani sipped and sighed. "Like I've been to the spa all day."

She smiled again as she refocused on dinner preparations. She couldn't remember the last time she'd cooked for another woman other than Drake, who didn't really fit into the category since she was her friend. *Huh.* In fact, she hadn't had another person in her house in so long she couldn't remember who it had been or why. She pushed through that thought and got back on track. The kitchen was equipped with state-of-the-art appliances and the finest cookware money could buy, yet she rarely enjoyed either to its full potential. Maybe now that she was relinquishing some of the day-to-day activities she'd allow herself the pleasure of entertaining once in a while. "I'm glad. You looked a bit overwhelmed earlier." She'd been pleased Dani had appeared in the loungewear she'd set out. Though the pants were too long, Dani didn't seem to mind.

"Frustrated was more like it. At least until I dumped that bottle of dye and had a full-blown meltdown." Dani rolled her eyes and sighed deeply. "I was looking forward to dinner out with you."

"I'll gladly give you a rain check or I can dump this in the trash, and we can still go." When she'd left Dani to have some alone time, she'd chosen soft cotton pants and a long-sleeve T-shirt. Dani had once asked her about what she wore when she wasn't working, and she liked the idea of Dani seeing her in non-work clothing. Thinking about redressing wasn't horrible, but she'd much rather stay home for a change. Especially now. Dani glanced down as she poured more wine.

"If you don't mind, right where we are is fine." She smiled sweetly and stretched, the bottom of the shirt revealing an expanse of creamy flesh.

She glanced away, willing the unbidden desire that flared deep inside to retreat. "The steak needs to rest a bit before serving. Why don't we drink our wine by the fire?" Ryan pointed to the love seat that faced a gently crackling fire. Even in summer she enjoyed the ambience a fire added, and often lit a small one, if she wasn't too tired to bother. She sat down close to Dani, enjoying the intimacy of the moment. It almost felt like something real.

"Every room is massive, yet you still managed to make it feel warm and inviting." Dani moved her back against the corner and tucked a leg under her. "How did you do that?"

She debated answering honestly, but this wasn't the time for avoidance. Not if she wanted more between them in the long run. "My childhood was trying. I didn't receive much in the way of nurturing and I've always wondered what people meant by saying a place felt comfortable or welcoming. So, when I had this house built, that's how I wanted it to feel." All too well she remembered the hard, broken-down furniture and filthy bedding she often endured, not that she knew any better until her last foster home. And even then, the slightly worn furniture and fabric, while clean and sturdy, gave her a sense of lacking. Of being ashamed of where she came from and how she got there. No, she never wanted to feel like she didn't deserve better again. Dani touched her arm, startling her from the past.

"Is there something you want to share, Ryan?" Dani's eyes spoke of empathy and understanding, and she almost gave in until she remembered her desire to be the caregiver.

"No. Tonight I'm taking care of you." She set down her glass. "Put your feet up here." She patted her thighs.

"Ryan..." Dani hesitated.

"Please?"

Dani slowly unfolded and stretched out.

She began massaging her feet with strong, measured strokes. The resultant sighs and moans were enough to test how hard a handle she had on her reaction. After five minutes she glanced at Dani. Her eyes were closed, lips slightly parted, and a bit of a smile rounded off the view. She could have been sleeping except for the rapid rise and fall of her chest.

Ryan gently lifted her feet and Dani's eyes opened. "Stay here and relax. I'll call you when dinner is ready."

"Mmm. Only if you're sure." She reached for her wine.

"I've got it." Ryan extricated herself and took a breath. She could get used to taking care of Dani like this. She silently laughed. She didn't even know she *wanted* to do the simple things she was enjoying doing for Dani. She fixed plates and brought them to the bistro table, poured wine into fresh glasses, and went to rouse Dani, who was in a semi sitting position, her head resting in her hand.

She approached with a bow, then held out her hand. "Dinner is served in the solarium, madam."

Dani's laughter rang softly. "Oh, fancy."

Ryan took the empty glass, setting it on the counter as they walked to the small room off the kitchen. She hadn't known what to do with the space until Drake suggested a breakfast nook, which then morphed into an all the time place for solitary meals and morning coffee. The stone tile floor was heated and warm beneath her bare feet.

"I've never seen anything like this," Dani said in awe as she slid onto one of the thickly padded chairs and looked around at the plants.

Ryan removed the cloches and took her seat. She'd hung strands of tiny lights throughout the compact room, liking how warm and romantic it made the space feel. As she looked at Dani, and saw the candle's flame reflected in her eyes, all she could think about was how badly she wanted to take her in her arms and make love to her. To share passion without a contract stating what was expected of her. Her stomach tightened. Dani was a client, not a lover. She'd do well to remember that. Ryan lifted her glass in a toast. "To destressing."

"I'll drink to that." Dani's gaze was unreadable. "Thank you for everything. I've never felt so pampered."

"That's a shame. A beautiful woman should always be treated special." She sliced through her steak as though it were butter, and the results of her culinary skills gave her some comfort despite the mixed emotions coursing through her.

Dani spread the compound butter over the still warm steak and cut a delicate piece. Ryan watched her mouth open, her tongue appeared to be waiting in anticipation as the fork moved toward her lips. When she closed over the morsel, Ryan's center clenched in response, her clit swelling. She covered her moan with a sip of wine, but her body would not be reined in again.

"Oh my God, this is fantastic," Dani said after she'd swallowed. Their eyes met and Dani's cheeks colored. "Why do you look like you want to eat me alive?"

Not prone to avoiding the truth, she responded the only way she could. "Because I do. But I'm not going to."

Dani drank before asking, "Why not?"

"Because I asked you to let me take care of you and I keep my promises." Her body was on fire. Dani's seductive gaze shot jolts of electricity through her, her heart racing to a tempo only she could hear.

"Even if I want you to?"

She sighed. "You're not going to make this easy for me, are you?" She grinned, not really minding the challenge.

Dani gazed down at the table as she set her silverware aside before their eyes met. "I'm sorry. I didn't pay for tonight."

"Is that why you think I'm not taking you to bed? That the only reason I would is if you paid me to service you?" When she'd offered to care for her, the reason had been altruistic, but the more she was around Dani the less professional her feelings. And now Dani thought the worst of her. To be fair, it was the reason she'd decided not to go any further with Dani, so she could keep things professional. But hearing Dani say it out loud hurt. Ryan didn't want to be thought of as someone unavailable except when paid.

Dani's confusion was clear. "I'm not sure I was thinking at all. You offered to take me away and I accepted, but I'm not clear what's going on, or what's next."

Ryan wiped her mouth on the cloth napkin, pulled Dani's chair back, and then lifted her. She headed down the hall to her bedroom, intent on showing Dani how very wrong she was in her assumptions.

Chapter Twenty-four

Dani wrapped her arms around Ryan's solid shoulders. There'd been a much different look in Ryan's eyes, and she wasn't sure what it meant. Maybe it was all in her imagination and there'd be nothing different about tonight than had been in their previous times together. Ryan set her on her feet, and began to unbutton her top, then abruptly stopped.

"Unless you tell me no right now, I'm going to make love to you until you tell me to stop. Not with your safe word, but in your own way. Do you understand?"

She swallowed around the lump in her throat. "Yes."

Ryan pressed her lips to her skin as it was revealed. Stepping behind her, she kissed the nape of her neck, below her ear. As the material slid off her shoulders to the floor, Ryan pulled her against her and cupped her breasts, kneading as she worked her nipples into hard points of cutting pleasure.

"I'm going to take my time, Dani. I'm going to worship every inch of your body." Ryan lifted her hair, exposing her neck and covered her with the softest kisses she'd ever felt. "Tonight there are no rules. I'm going to touch you because I want to, not because you've paid me to."

Her legs began to shake as she fought the overwhelming sensations. Then she was lifted and placed on the bed. Ryan peeled her T-shirt off her well-developed body, exposing the small ovals of her breasts, her nipples pointed.

"Close your eyes." Ryan's voice was gentle.

In the darkness, she heard a drawer open, and soft sensual music, perfect for this moment, began to play. Rustling noises she couldn't decipher above the insistent beating of her heart bated her curiosity and she almost looked. Then the bed moved, and she knew Ryan was beside her. Something soft traced her cheeks and continued to follow the contours of her body.

"Keep them closed for me, baby. You can open them soon."

The earlier tone of Ryan's voice, while still soft and gentle, had deepened, and Dani hoped it was from desire. The softness trailing her limbs and chest became both soothing and erotic, like a hesitant lover's touch. But she knew Ryan, and Ryan didn't hesitate when she wanted something. That much she had witnessed on more than one occasion. Never overbearing or demanding, yet there was no question who was in control in any situation. Control was the one thing she'd wanted to escape most while living with her parents, and now here she was again giving in...but damnit, this was one time when she wanted to give it up to see a different side of Ryan, the mystery woman.

Ryan's weight shifted. "Slowly open your eyes for me."

She blinked several times to clear the haze from her vision. Ryan knelt next to her, the lounge pants she'd worn replaced by thigh length boxers. The bulge along one side was unmistakable as she rolled over her and the unencumbered thigh pressed to her center. She kissed her breast, dragging her lips as she moved to the other. Dani snaked her hand through Ryan's thick hair and tried to guide her. Ryan smiled against her skin.

"There's no hurry. Neither of us are going anywhere." Ryan's mouth came close to hers as she flicked her gaze between her eyes and her mouth. "You don't have anywhere to be, do you?"

Her breath caught with a sharp inhale. They'd been intimately close since they'd arrived, and Ryan had yet to touch her. Really touch her. Did she want to leave? End the control she cherished and most certainly would lead to regret? Or perhaps she'd celebrate a different type of freedom when Ryan was done. "No."

"Then we need not talk about it anymore."

Ryan kissed her carefully, slowly, and the passion of that kiss coursed through her in gentle waves of desire. While her heart pounded in her chest and her center grew heavy, she relished the attention, the pure heat of yearning for more...wanting more. Long minutes passed with Ryan's mouth on hers, on her neck, her chest but avoiding her painfully tight nipples. Her clit throbbed, shielded by silk alone. As Ryan moved lower, she tried to anticipate what sensation she would feel next. Unable to, she grew frustrated. "Ryan, please. Please touch me."

Ryan stopped moving and looked up. "I promise I will soon. I know you're hard and wet and ready. Enjoy what you're feeling." Ryan untied Dani's pants, edged them lower on her hips, and groaned. "I'm not sure I could have resisted so long had I known there was so little in my way." Her lips pressed to the arc of her hip, first one side then the other. A little lower, and her mons was revealed. Ryan inhaled and sent a shiver through her as she sighed.

"The scent of an aroused woman is such a turn-on." Their eyes met. "I want you, Dani. I want all of you." Ryan's tongue flicked over the soaked material barely covering her. Her hips rose of their own accord, so great was her need. "I'm going to taste you, worship that sweet pussy of yours." Ryan drew the material down and off, then settled between her thighs.

Ryan's soft warm tongue outlined her folds, then slipped inside.

"Oh." She gasped at the exquisite pleasure even the small amount of contact brought her. "More, please, Ryan. I need more."

Ryan closed her lips around her clit and gently sucked. Her head was going to explode.

"I know what you need, love. I'm going to give you what you ask for."

Ryan's masterful tongue slid over her throbbing knot and brought moan after moan from her lips. Her hips chased the sensations until she could barely breathe. As she opened her mouth to beg for more, fingers filled her and Ryan's lips closed around her clit again, gently sucking. Tremors began low in her belly and spread outward. Her heart was pounding. Ryan's fingers stilled.

"So beautiful." She kissed the inside of her thigh, making her whimper. "Will you come for me, Dani?"

Ryan had always shown desire for her, but this time there was a deeper emotional connection. Not with the professional Ryan, and certainly not with Drake. This version of Ryan, the lover, was unsheathed, open, and so much more.

"Please, Ryan. Please." Dani gasped. The music playing was drowned out by the roaring in her ears. Ryan's mouth claimed hers, and her fingers thrust deeper. Her body twisted and turned to find the promised pleasure. Her orgasm broke free and her hips rose as Ryan hung on. Thrashing, she cried out oaths at the mind-numbing release. Ryan kissed her still heaving abdomen and slipped out before moving over her. The ridge of her cock pressed against her, and her lips glistened as she smiled.

"I love watching you come."

The kiss that followed was slow, tender, and deep. Ryan's tongue caressed hers and she tasted herself everywhere. Desire rose in her and Ryan began to move against her. She hungered to be filled. Dani snaked her hand between them and grasped the hard bulge. "I want you inside of me." She pulled on her length and Ryan shivered.

"Whatever you desire, Dani." Ryan stripped away the only layer between them.

Her sex clenched. Ryan's cock hung between her muscular thighs, her eyes hot. Lust-filled lasers that drew her to the magnetism of them. Ryan raised over her and Dani's gaze traveled to Ryan's hand wrapped around her shaft. She spread her legs wider and accepted Ryan into her.

Ryan groaned. "This is what I want too, Dani," she said as she pushed inside. "To give you all of me."

Ryan's mouth covered hers, her tongue outlined her swollen lips. Long, drawn out moments of tongues that teased and taunted, and the heat inside her was nearly unbearable. She couldn't help feeling this side of Ryan…this unrestrained side…was what she'd been longing for. The part of her that was driven by yearning and controlled only by the desire to go slow. To name the need that drove Ryan into her arms. Breathless, she gasped for air and Ryan extended her arms. "You feel so good," she groaned.

"I'm going to fill you over and over until all you can do is feel me." Ryan pumped her hips slowly, driving deep, giving her every inch. When she circled her cock and her shaft ground against Dani's clit, she cried out.

"Oh, God. I'm going to come."

"Can you wait for me?" Ryan asked as she lowered again. "I want to come with you."

Dani's mind reeled. The tables had turned, and all she wanted was to give Ryan some of what she'd given her, even though her body screamed for release.

"I know you can feel me." Ryan pumped harder. "I'm going to come with you, baby." Her hips moved like pistons.

She grabbed Ryan's shoulders, dug in, knowing she wasn't going to last.

"I'm coming." Ryan groaned as her arms begin to shake while she rocked her hips, roaring in release.

Dani's muscles tightened, locking Ryan inside, and she followed her over the edge into ecstasy. Ryan kissed her, slowly and methodically until everything else faded away and all that was left was her body swaying to the rhythm of Ryan's touch and the music that played.

Chapter Twenty-five

Ryan shot Drake a look. The last twelve hours had done nothing to diminish her feelings for Dani. She'd wanted to make love to her. To erase any traces that might have lingered regarding any other lover, and she had no idea where that left them.

"Well, I'm not typically one to say, 'I told you so' but..." Drake shrugged, an *I told you so* expression clear on her face.

"Yes, you are." She reached for her drink and stopped.

"Truth. All I'm asking is do you know what you're doing?"

She'd never done anything remotely unprofessional with a client. Hell, she barely relaxed enough to enjoy a real date. "It's... Christ." Ryan swept her hand through her too long hair. Another thing she never neglected. Her personal appearance was everything even though clients rarely saw her, and the staff didn't care how she looked. "I remembered a time when I felt that lost and downtrodden. All I wanted was for Dani to stop hurting."

Drake placed her hand on her shoulder and squeezed. "Noble as your intentions might have been, just admit you fucked up and move on. There are plenty of escorts she can choose from and I'm sure she won't mind."

"Dani trusts me in scenes." Ryan finished off the scotch she'd been nursing. That wasn't the reason she didn't want Dani with any other escorts, but it was believable. Sort of.

Drake finished her cocktail and the waiter placed appetizers in front of them. "A bottle of Albariño, please." Drake studied her for a few beats. "What has you so worked up about her? I haven't seen you this way in ages."

"If I knew we wouldn't be having this conversation." She was pissed off at the world. The more she fought against feelings she shouldn't be having, the more overpowering they became.

"I'm not saying you shouldn't take care of her kinky side if that's what she wants and she trusts you. After all, she's still a client. Just get your head out of it."

More like my heart, actually. But Drake didn't need to know that, and if she guessed, she'd vehemently deny it. Drake wouldn't want to hear that she was more than physically attracted to Dani, even if she asked.

The waiter poured and Drake took a sample taste, then nodded. When he left, she went on. "We've got a lot of interviews coming up and I need to know you're up for it."

As she set her glass down, her body stiffened, and her entire demeanor changed. "Of course, I'm up for it. I'm still the CEO. Just because I had a moment of weakness with one woman doesn't mean I'm not capable of running the company." Her anger rose to the surface. Drake had pushed too far, but that's what Ryan expected from her, to be the voice of reason when she needed it.

"Jesus Christ. What the fuck is wrong with you?" Drake hissed the words so only she could hear them.

Embarrassment heated her face. Maybe Drake was right. Maybe she *was* losing it. "I'm sorry." She glanced down at her untouched plate. "Can we get out of here?"

"No," Drake said matter-of-factly. "This," Drake pointed to the bottle of white chilling in a bucket, "costs a small fortune. Besides, I'm starving." She dove into her lobster risotto. "You'll just have to sit there and pout until I'm done." After a few slow bites, Drake glanced at her, the corner of her mouth twitching.

Ryan slowly smiled in turn and began eating again. "I'm so glad you're in my life, for a lot of reasons. One being you keep me grounded and don't put up with my shit."

"So you've come to your senses, have you?" Drake pushed away her plate and finished her wine. The waiter appeared, poured for both, then whisked away their plates.

Ryan laughed. "I don't know if I'd go that far, but at least I can admit I stepped over a line."

Drake leaned forward. "What is it about her that made you want to? I mean, she's beautiful, but so are dozens of women you've slept with, and you've never been this twisted over anyone."

Ryan stared into her goblet, searching for answers, but when she looked up, she wasn't sure she wanted Drake to read the truth that was likely revealed in her eyes. "Dani is the first woman in a long time that I want to know on a deeper level, but I don't think I'll get the chance."

"Why not?"

"Would you want to be with someone who slept with other women for a living?" She said it with more anger than she'd intended. The old wound felt fresh, as if she were still bleeding. Perhaps she was, and for an instant she imagined Dani could be the balm for her soul.

"I don't think I'm the best source to ask. I *do* sleep with women for a living. But if I were to ever find someone who could accept me as I am, I don't know if I'd be able to let her go. Not for work." Drake visibly swallowed hard. "So the question isn't mine to answer. The real question is do you want to pursue what might be between the two of you?"

She was quiet for a long time before she finished her wine, stood, and shared a wistful smile. "I have no idea."

"I'd like to book a session with the gray-haired woman, Beck," Dani said as she nibbled at the inside of her cheek. It had been almost a week since her night at Ryan's which ended with Ryan taking care of her in many nuanced ways, and now that she had time to analyze what had happened with a clear head, she was convinced a date with someone other than Ryan would help cool her compulsion to be only with Ryan. But as she said the words she knew that wasn't what she wanted at all.

"Of course, Ms. Brown. How soon would you like to be scheduled?" Ryan asked.

Dani heard the tension in Ryan's voice even if she was doing an admirable job at concealing her annoyance. They'd been together enough that she could detect the tightness in Ryan's tone. "This week or next." She would have preferred to tell her the next bit of news face-to-face, but she wasn't sure she could keep her face neutral, and Ryan deserved to know. "My confidence is growing, in a large part thanks to you, so I'm not sure if I'll require the Agency's services much longer." She held her breath. Sometime over the last twelve hours, she'd argued that Ryan's reactions were simply rote, the thing she was good at...hot women, hot sex. Dani was one out of many. Right? It was just a one-time thing. Better to break ties now than to have her heart broken later.

"I'm glad we've been able to help you on your journey of self-discovery."

"You certainly have, and I appreciate your patience."

"I'll be sorry to see you go, Dani." Ryan's voice was soft, like a caress, and her body responded like it always did to the smooth, velvety tone.

It was Dani's turn to be silent. She hadn't meant for the current conversation to be good-bye, but it certainly sounded that way. Thinking about their last time together and Ryan's unmistakable passion, she regretted making the call and, ultimately, ending whatever was between them. *It's for the best.* She'd much rather be on the receiving end of Ryan's attention, but to whose benefit? Reasoning the why nots didn't change how her stomach tightened at the thought of not seeing Ryan anymore. Later she could say she changed her mind and schedule to see Ryan. She didn't want to end their conversation on such a solemn note. "You can always see me for your next haircut." She tried to keep her tone light, but the decision weighed heavily between them.

"Perhaps. Would next Wednesday at eight fit your schedule?" Ryan's professional demeanor was back in place.

"Yes, that's fine." Again, she searched for a reason to keep Ryan on the phone. "Is there anything I should know in advance about Beck?"

"I think she'll suit your needs, but you can discuss the details with her."

Obviously, Ryan wasn't giving her any wiggle room. "Okay. Thanks again, Ryan."

"Good-bye, Ms. Brown."

Her screen darkened and she instantly wanted to hear Ryan's voice again. The call had been more difficult than she'd imagined, and now that it was done, she'd feel foolish calling for another date with Ryan. "It's for the best," she said out loud to her empty apartment. She'd never been good at intimacy, and if anyone deserved it, it was Ryan. She inhaled sharply, her hand on her mouth. Was that what she was doing? Avoiding the one person who had treated her the way she'd dreamt of? Was she afraid if she acknowledged it, then she'd have to treat Ryan as more than an escort, and maybe it wouldn't be enough, especially with someone of Ryan's caliber?

"God, what a fucking loser I am." It was just as well they were done. Ryan deserved much more than she could apparently give.

"I heard you were rescued by a knight in shining armor," Pam said.

"What?" Dani had been nonstop since the minute she stepped through the door at noon, and for the first time since then, she didn't have a customer. She dropped into her chair, slid off her shoes, and rubbed her aching feet. The memory of Ryan's massage made her smile.

Pam sat next to her, eyes sparkling. "Cindy couldn't wait to tell someone that a very handsome woman swept you away after a shit day. I could only come up with one person to fit that description." Pam's brow rose.

"She had an appointment for a cut, but Ms. Tierney demanded a frost when she got here and George eyeballed me, so I couldn't say no. It meant having to ask Ryan to reschedule, but she wasn't put off by waiting."

"So you were having a busy day?"

Dani slipped her feet into her shoes. "You could say that. But then I reached up to get a bottle of toner and ended up taking a bath in it."

"Oh no. What did dreamboat say?"

After a starry-eyed look at Pam, she smiled. "She took me to her place, and I got to have a long, hot shower while she made dinner." She wasn't going to tell her about how she'd been bathed, or the foot massage, or the rest of the night. The entire evening was intimate and something she wanted to keep to herself.

"Sounds like Ryan has more in mind than what you two usually do." Pam said it casually enough, but there was an undercurrent of meaning.

"What do you mean?"

Pam shrugged. "I don't think casual fuck buddies take who they're bedding home and make them dinner." She leaned in. "Maybe she wants to know you in an exclusive way."

Busying her hands by straightening her station, she let the statement hang. She had similar thoughts, and that didn't change how wonderful Ryan's attention had felt. Ryan had given her pleasure in so many ways she could still feel her warm, wet mouth on her, and those long, strong fingers that played her with so much care. Ryan had drawn her to the edge again and again until finally... *finally*...letting her come. Her orgasm had gone on and on while Ryan pulled her close and held her with her fingers still buried inside her, stroking, teasing, until she had nothing left but a whimper and a choked plea to stop. And then...and then she'd held her. She'd snuggled in against her and been held safely throughout the night, and when she'd woken, Ryan had left a sweet note on the pillow to say how wonderful the night had been, that the keys to an Audi were on the counter, and that she'd see her soon. She'd let herself out, though the desire to stay there and be waiting for Ryan when she came home had been strong. It felt like something honest and real was happening.

Her body heated at the memory. Dani's hand shook as she reached for her spray bottle. Like it or not, her body craved what Ryan offered. But more than that, her heart was getting involved, too. Whether she would give in and let her lead again remained to be seen. The reason she'd liked the idea of a hired escort was because *she* was in control of everything that happened. Dinner, no dinner, sex, toy play, being dominated. *Dominating.* She'd found freedom in the bedroom that was spilling over into her everyday life, and she liked it. Dani trusted Ryan. She didn't worry Ryan would push her too far, or hurt her physically, any more than she wanted, if she wanted it. Those instances that Ryan had gently pushed her pain/pleasure threshold, Ryan had backed off before she'd used her safe word and the orgasms that followed were so intense, she worried if she'd ever come again.

"'Night, Pam," she said on her way out. Once in her car, she thought about what lay ahead. She had a date scheduled with another escort. This time she'd chosen someone who looked decidedly different from Ryan. Though not nearly as sexually attracted to her as she was to either Ryan or Drake, Dani had decided it was foolish to think Ryan wanted her for more than paid attention. On the short drive home, Pam's words replayed in her head, and she fought against what they inferred, though she was beginning to wonder why. Ryan had been sympathetic to her distress and had helped her in ways she thought Dani would appreciate. She'd gone into this adventure without any desire for a relationship, with Ryan or anyone else. But it was getting harder to keep what happened in the bedroom and outside of it separate. What would happen if she didn't push the possibility of more away?

Chapter Twenty-six

So how much is the conversion therapy costing you?"

Dani shot Mark a glare full of daggers. "Not funny."

"That much, huh?" He sipped his cocktail through the thin straw, then smiled before leaning closer because the music had changed to a dance number, the booming bass traveling up through the floor. "Is it worth it?"

Mark had been poking her to spill for weeks. She'd resisted giving anything up since their last conversation when Mark had made what she'd done feel dirty, but she was dying to talk to someone about the night Ryan had let her top her after being topped. Dani finished her drink and smiled. "Every fucking cent." Memories flooded in. Ryan's deep, commanding voice. The darkness that surrounded her with her eyes closed while she waited for Ryan's touch, and the anticipation of the next stroke or sensation or lightning strike of pain gone so quickly, she wasn't sure it had happened and made her breath catch. Then when she'd been in command and Ryan had revealed herself so openly. Even now, there were times when she replayed that night and questioned how much was real and how much had been her imagination.

"Come on." Standing, Mark took her hand. "I came to dance, not watch you come in your jeans just thinking about it."

She laughed as he led her to the dance floor. The people there were in full swing. Bodies hot and sweaty pressed together. Others showing off their moves by following a rhythm so primal there were likely a lot of them who were wet and wanting, just like her. But as she glanced around, none of the women could compare to the one who'd awakened her to the pleasures she'd been denying. While she moved her feet and hips, slipping her fingers through her hair, she wanted those moments again. Dani could hardly wait.

"Earth to Dani," Mark said.

Her unfocused gaze returned to normal as she realized the music had turned to a slow, sultry serenade. *Christ.* She needed to get her act together. "Sorry," she said as they moved back to the bar.

Mark placed his hand on her shoulder. "Don't be sorry." He smiled. "Are you sure they don't have any men at that place? From the look on your face I'd be willing to spend a small fortune for a night."

She laughed and shook her head. "Women only."

"Pity." He caught the bartender's eye and ordered another round. "So what's next for you?"

Biting her lip, Dani hesitated before remembering who she was talking to. "A threesome." Mark choked on his drink and coughed hard. "Not what you were thinking, huh?" She glanced around to see if anyone was close enough to hear her. She had no idea if anyone there had used the Agency's service and she didn't want to be the one to out them. "Just kidding. That's already happened in a way."

To his credit, Mark recovered then narrowed his gaze. "You've been holding out on me."

Talking to Mark about the kind of sex she was engaged in should have made her uncomfortable, but it didn't. "You know I wanted to explore in different ways, and Ryan suggested a third person so she could demonstrate how to use certain toys. She said it was the best way to learn."

"Fuck. Can I volunteer?" He fanned himself with his napkin.

"No. Jerk." She loved Mark for so many reasons, but the idea that he'd be in the same room with her and Ryan naked wasn't something she wanted a visual of.

Mark nodded. "Makes sense though." He sipped, then licked foam from his lip. "How much did *that* cost you?"

"Same as usual. Ryan said since the logistics of the lesson wasn't something I'd requested, she'd take care of the other escort's fee."

"Hmm." Mark tapped at his drink, looking thoughtful.

She knew that look and it meant whatever he was thinking would likely piss her off. "What?"

"It's just that Ryan seems to be quite invested in your lessons."

"What are you getting at?"

"I mean, introducing you to the wonders of same-sex sex, not to mention fulfilling your kinky fantasies. Then rescuing you from a horrendous day at work on a strictly personal basis." He drank again, then looked at her in a different way. "What do *you* think it means?"

Dani hadn't really thought about the implications, though it had crossed her mind that the fee she paid had always been the same and always at the lowest rate. Was Ryan supplementing the real cost with her own money? And what did it mean when they'd made love? Fuck. She hadn't thought about the difference, sexually, between dates and the night at Ryan's, but there was no mistake now that she took a hard look at it. Ryan *had* made love to her. It was tender and slow and sweet. "Shit."

"Uh-huh. Look at the bright side, she's charming, wealthy, and one hell of a looker. You could do a lot worse."

What Mark was saying was true. "I just came out of the closet. I'm not looking for a permanent hookup." Even as she said it, she felt the tang of the lie in it. Ryan was special.

"Why not? That's what lesbians do. Haven't you ever heard of U-Haul lesbians? It's all the rage. You meet, have sex, and within a few weeks, one of you is moving in."

"That's bullshit."

Mark's hand flew to his chest. "I swear it's true." He glanced around and tapped the shoulder of a woman near them. "Excuse me. My best friend is new to queer life and doesn't believe that U-Haul lesbians is a thing. Care to enlighten her?"

The roguishly handsome woman settled in and gave a five-minute recital on the better known sayings, beliefs, and truths of lesbian life. Dani was both mortified and mystified that she was so naive and uninformed. Maybe she'd quiz one of the escorts about what life was like for them, though they were pretty close-mouthed when it came to their company and other employees. Considering she'd only met three so far, she should expand her pool. After all, she couldn't go on paying for the service forever. She'd end up bankrupt. Dani chuckled to herself at the idea of conjugal visits while serving time for tax evasion or some other outlandish charge.

After Mark finished his last drink, he threw his arm around her shoulder. "I need to eat."

She looked around the immediate area. "I don't see any guys sidling up to you, so I guess you're out of luck."

"Oh, so you're an expert now?" He chuckled. "Food, love. I need sustenance. I plan on prowling the gay bar in Lake George tonight, and those dudes wear me out."

His knowing smile was infectious, and Dani couldn't help wishing she had the guts to strut her stuff the way he did, but she wasn't quite there yet. With the realization of what happened between her and Ryan sitting uneasily in the pit of her stomach, she doubted she could eat, but she wasn't ready to be alone with her thoughts. "Let's go." Mark was good at distracting her from the tough stuff, things she'd rather not face because she couldn't figure out what to do. Her feelings for Ryan were falling into that category. She'd started this adventure to validate her attraction to women, and then to discover the nuances of being with women in a variety of ways. And while that still held true, the only one she truly wanted to be with for all of it was Ryan.

Ryan hid her disappointment. She'd dropped in at the salon on a whim, hoping to see Dani, but when she'd discovered she wasn't due in until that evening, her insides knotted in dismay. Lately, all her fantasies had a common denominator. Dani.

This thing with Dani that she couldn't name and wasn't sure she wanted to, had somehow gotten out of hand. The connection was more than just Dani's inquisitiveness or her open attitude to all the ways power and sex intermingled. Ryan's emotions ran much deeper than with anyone prior, and the implications scared the shit out of her. Maybe she could pull Beck from her appointment with Dani and entice Dani with more lessons on dominance or topping. Beck was more than capable as a top and Dani was exploring her fantasies in every way possible, but the thought of anyone with a whip in their hand when it came to Dani brought out a fierce reaction. One she found harder and harder to resist, for good or bad.

After making a haircut appointment with Dani for the following week, Ryan slid her sunglasses over her eyes and shoved her hands in her pants. She was fidgety and unsettled, characteristics she wasn't used to. Sunday was the one day she made herself stay away from the office. It wasn't healthy for her mental well-being to be so singularly focused that she had to be there every day. Besides, if she was really bored, she could always work from home. Perhaps it was time to host a dinner party. She'd held them monthly when the house had been finished and she enjoyed showing off the architectural masterpiece to her friends.

Ryan shrugged off the melancholy. She'd moved on after Sarah and embraced her satisfying life, one in which she wanted for nothing. She pulled up short and someone behind her yelled, "Watch what you're doing." She mumbled an apology and moved close to the building she'd stopped in front of. The realization that she did *want* something weighed heavily in her chest, and it was time she did something about it.

Chapter Twenty-seven

Dani folded her legs under her and sipped prosecco from a fluted glass. She found the finer things in life, even the littlest like the champagne glass, were a nod to her hard work and that she deserved pampering. A sentiment Ryan reinforced every time they were together. All she'd been doing was working every waking hour, some weeks as many as eighty, not to mention the occasional dinner service where the tips were outrageous and the clientele elitist. The few evenings a month she wasn't working, she was seeing escorts. "Not a horrible life," she said to the empty living room. Sooner or later, she would have to stop the insanity and start living her real life again, not stay in her fantasy world like she was now.

Ryan had become more like a lover than a paid escort. She catered to Dani's every need like her teenage dream boat. She giggled at how different her life was from the days when her parents monitored her every move. *If they could see me now, they'd have a stroke.* Dani thumbed through the latest issue of *InStyle*, looking but not really seeing what was there. When her glass was empty, she tossed the magazine on the coffee table then went to rinse it. She had a busy schedule ahead and needed a good night's sleep. Tomorrow was her double shift and the next followed by a ten-hour day at the salon. She'd finally scheduled herself off for a weekend at the end of the month. That Saturday night she was attending a fundraiser with Mark. She could do with her own fundraiser.

She pulled out clothes for the morning and her restaurant attire of black pants, a white three-quarter sleeve shirt, and a black vest. Satisfied she had everything in order and more than a little exhausted, she stood staring at her reflection while she brushed her teeth. Her hair could use some highlights and a trim. A facial wouldn't hurt either, and her nails had been neglected for far too long. Since she had to be mindful of hurting the women she had sex with, she'd been trimming them on a regular basis, but they definitely needed some work. Tiffany would fit her in the Friday before the gala. At least they'd look good for one weekend.

She slid into cool sheets and pulled the summer comforter over her. As she closed her eyes, images of the women she'd been with began to slowly flash across her mind's eye, like the old-fashioned View-Master her grandmother had let her play with when she was young. Click, Ryan. Click, Drake. Click, Ryan. Click, Ryan. The common denominator was enlightening. She and Ryan were getting very close. And, God, sex with her was off the charts. Even with exhaustion pulling her toward sleep, she remembered her touch, her mouth, her scent. She'd examine the intensity of her attraction when she could think. All she wanted to do right now was sink farther into her bed and let visions of Ryan lull her to sleep.

"Why so glum, chum?"

Drake's levity increased Ryan's already annoyed mood. "Funny. Maybe you should change professions to comedian. I'm sure you'll make a fortune." She focused on the stack of intake applications. Women were contacting them in staggering numbers. For every new client there was a second from their allowed one-time referral, and from there the numbers snowballed into their current base of over two hundred. With only twenty-two escorts, they were still stretched thin, and unfortunately Drake and Lane were right. They were going to have to start turning clients away, or expand exponentially, and that would mean a lot more work for everyone involved.

The good thing was the constant flux of active clients. People found partners, or the itch no longer needed to be scratched, or a fantasy had been fulfilled. Ryan couldn't help thinking about Dani. She'd hadn't talked with Dani since she'd made an appointment for her with Beck, and a few days ago Anna told her Dani had canceled. Unsure what that meant and not hearing from Dani again made her edgy. Not that she expected to get a call. Dani had made it clear she didn't need their services any longer and the thought of never seeing her again twisted like a knife in her gut.

Drake rapped her knuckles on the desk. "What the fuck is wrong with you now?"

"Nothing." She shuffled papers refusing to look at Drake, knowing she'd be able to see the inner turmoil that hadn't left since she spoke to Dani.

"Bullshit. I've known you too long. Even when life fucked you over on a regular basis you never turned into a bitch like you have been lately, so what gives?" Drake dropped into the chair facing her.

If she looked up Drake would be singularly focused and waiting for an explanation. Trouble was, she wasn't sure she had one. "Fuck." She leaned back and ran her hand over her face. "I'm sorry. I'll get my shit together."

Drake leaned closer. "Just tell me what's wrong." Her expressive eyes revealed empathy and kindness, and she regretted not being the kind of friend Drake deserved, especially the last few months while her focus had been on Dani.

"I can't." She looked away, unwilling to see the hurt that would be there.

Memories flooded in. Sarah had turned away from what she'd thought was a good thing between them. Now Dani had pulled away, leaving her in much the same way though Dani obviously wasn't as invested as Ryan was. Crazy as it might be, she didn't want to live her life in a cloud of indifference. It wasn't Drake's responsibility to save her from despair. Again.

Drake's face remained tight.

She stood and went to the large window where she often told herself the world lay at her feet. She shoved her hands into her pockets and closed her eyes. Her current world was void of the kind of emotional connection she'd been looking for since Sarah, even if she hadn't admitted it, because the one person she cared about no longer cared to spend time with *her*. The weight of Drake's hand on her shoulder and soft voice were a welcome distraction.

"Ryan, talk to me. Please."

Sighing as she turned, Ryan couldn't miss the deeply etched concern on Drake's face. "I've fucked up. Royally."

Drake's gaze softened. "You've fallen for Dani and you have no idea how to handle it."

"Christ. Is it that obvious?"

Drake turned to pour two fingers of scotch into tumblers and handed her one. "Only to me." She clinked her glass then tipped it in her direction before taking a swallow. "You, my friend, have fallen down the veritable rabbit hole."

Ryan acknowledged how right she was by downing the contents. She dropped onto the couch and looked at the ceiling for help. Not finding any, she responded. "What do you suggest?"

Sitting across from her and smiling, Drake shook her head and poured more into Ryan's glass. "Damned if I know. I've managed to stay out of it."

She laughed. Leave it to Drake to not only point out the obvious but to also give her reason to laugh at her predicament. "Lot of good you are."

"You know I'm your only source of reason when you've managed to box yourself in a corner." Drake sat back and her face became serious. "So, what *are* you going to do?"

"It's not like I've ever been in this situation before. At least, not with a client." Ryan shook her head. She'd been naive back then and their business was thriving. Sarah had waltzed into her life and just as quickly waltzed out when she couldn't handle the freedom Ryan's position demanded, even if she initially said she could. "I don't fall for women. I enjoy their company and the sex we share, but that's where it's always ended." She finished the drink before setting the glass down.

"Until now."

Ryan blew out a breath. "Yeah. Until now." She'd denied the inevitable truth as it slowly made her cranky and on edge, but her veneer had begun to crack. She missed Dani. Missed her indominable spirit and her smile. Her laughter and her stubborn attitude. And yes, she'd missed her enticing body, the sex they shared, and the connection to another person she'd felt. And missing her only made Ryan want her more.

Drake leaned forward and swirled the remainder of her drink. "There's only one thing to do." She finished it and set her glass on the coffee table. "Go see her. Not a text or a call." She rose and Ryan mirrored her movement. "The only way to know if you need to get over her is to face her and ask her if there's any chance for more."

This time her laugh was a harsh, hard sound. "We both know what fucking women for a living means. Do you honestly think she's going to want me in her life for anything more?" Her stomach churned until the pain was blinding. Drake gripped her forearm.

"I don't know and neither do you, but you'll never find peace if you don't try." She pulled her in for a hard hug and spoke in her ear. "Not knowing will eat you alive."

Drake seemed to speak from experience, though she'd never shared whatever pain she bore like Ryan did. She held on for a long time. Drake's solid form grounded her and reminded her for the millionth time why she cherished their friendship more than any other. Resolve set in before she was able to slowly withdraw. "I love you. I don't know where I'd be without your friendship."

Drake straightened her tie before meeting her gaze. "Probably doing hard time, but still surrounded by women." She grinned.

"A picture I could do without," she said, grimacing.

Still smiling, Drake moved toward the door. "Let me know what Dani's response is. Don't forget to be charming."

"Aren't I always?"

Drake's brow rose, but she said nothing as she left.

Nervous energy coursed through her at possibly seeing Dani again. It had been several weeks since the heart-wrenching phone call, and while one part of her always knew it was a possibility, she'd hoped it was months away. Perhaps even more, she'd hoped to establish a meaningful relationship between them before it ever came to that. Fate hadn't been on her side. Then again, that's how her life had started, so why wouldn't it come back to bite her in the ass every now and then?

Chapter Twenty-eight

The next evening Ryan and her date, Michelle, a svelte blue-eyed blonde, were greeted at the door by a young woman in a shirtless tuxedo. "Ms. Lewis, it's a pleasure to see you again. Cocktails are being served on the veranda." The annual fundraiser for LGBTQIA youth was a notorious event that all the wealthy and affluent attended.

"Thank you, Kyle. May I introduce my companion, Michelle Finch." After a nod of acknowledgement from Kyle, she guided Michelle toward the group milling outside. "Would you like a drink?"

"Surprise me," Michelle said, then moved to the side to make room. She wore a stunning burgundy floor-length gown that shimmered as she walked. In three-inch heels, she was still several inches shorter than Ryan.

"Thank you for agreeing to this." Ryan handed her a martini then motioned to the crowd of strangers. As much as she enjoyed getting out for a night, she despised all the small talk and shallowness of events like this. Intimate settings were more her thing, but she hadn't had one of those in weeks. Not since—

"It's not that bad. I get to spend time with the most handsome woman I know, and if I'm lucky she'll be pressed against me at some point." Michelle sipped from the rim of her glass.

Ryan studied her for moment. She was gorgeous, and as with all her dates, there was an unspoken understanding that sex would likely be part of their evening together. Unfortunately, there was no excitement coursing through her in anticipation of being naked with Michelle. Her jaw tightened. She had yet to act on Drake's suggestion, using the business as an excuse for the delay, but that wasn't the real reason. The likelihood that Dani felt the same as she did was slim. Dani knew what living her life and running the business entailed. No wonder she'd pulled away. If she were in Dani's shoes, Ryan might feel the same way. Perhaps she should enjoy the evening for what it was, a feeble attempt at ignoring the nagging need for Dani in her life.

"Let's start with a dance." She motioned to the wooden flooring inside. The band was setting up and would probably begin playing soon.

"That *would* be a nice way to begin." Desire flared in Michelle's eyes as she looked over the rim of her glass.

She smiled. Michelle was charming. As she swallowed the fireball of alcohol, she moved her gaze over the length of her. What Michelle offered was definitely something she would have enjoyed a few months ago, before meeting Dani. Before the night she'd taken care of Dani and they'd made love. But now, the only person she wanted in her bed was Dani. There was a problem though. Dani didn't know her withdrawal had hurt Ryan more than anyone who'd ever left her.

They moved around the crowd, greeting familiar faces and engaging in discussions about why they were all there. LGBTQIA youth were suffering from many forms of rejection and displacement. A cause close to her heart. She gave large, anonymous donations throughout the year, but the gala was the one place she didn't mind showing her support. Initially, it hadn't hurt that it had also provided some wealthy clients, but now she had more than she could handle, so it really was all about the charity.

The familiar gong sounded, and guests moved toward the doorway of the ballroom. From there, they were escorted to their tables. It was a grand affair. Anyone looking from the outside would think the opulence was a waste, but every part of the event was secured through special donations set aside for this night. Ryan held Michelle's chair, then took her own. They had a great view of the lectern where the organizers would thank them for their support and donations before the band played and dancing began. Waiters appeared with bottles of wine and began pouring. She briefly wondered who was supposed to occupy the seats directly across the table before the distinguished gentleman next to her leaned closer and began talking with her. Movement out of the corner of her eye distracted her, but she ignored it. Probably the late-comers. It wasn't until there was a lull in the conversation that she looked across the table and stopped at the woman sitting there. Her heart skipped a beat and she forgot to breathe.

Dani was engaged in a hushed conversation with a man about Dani's age. He had a head full of tight curls and wore a stylish, if not quite appropriate navy-blue pin-striped suit with a white silk collarless shirt. Dani's lips pursed briefly before she put on a smile and looked at the other occupants at the table. When their eyes met, she visibly sucked in a breath.

Her abdomen cramped. Perhaps Dani had decided to return to her former life of dating men. She'd been so sure Dani had found her true self when they'd been together. But then she'd been sure of a lot of things, and had been wrong about most of them, so why would Dani's sexuality be any different? The pain in her chest refused to leave and she turned away, unable to look at her without wanting her. She'd made a horrible mistake by falling for Dani and she had no one to blame but herself. Dani had been honest from the start by telling her she was looking for multiple partners and into exploring her feelings to see what she wanted out of life. Obviously, she wasn't looking for a relationship, even though they'd crossed a few emotional lines and Ryan had really thought they might have shared a mutual attraction.

Michelle touched her leg. "Are you all right?"

She forced a smile she didn't feel. "Yes, I'll be fine. Something didn't sit well is all." She had to get out of there. "Would you excuse me for a minute?"

"Of course. Do you want me to go with you?"

Ryan bent down and kissed her cheek. "No need. I'll be right back." She turned away, refusing to look in Dani's direction as she strode purposefully toward the restroom. Once safely in a stall she leaned her head back against the wall and willed her churning gut to quiet. She would never have imagined seeing Dani again before going to talk with her. She was a mess. After relieving herself, Ryan stood at the sink and let the cold water soothe her. Nothing about tonight felt right. She used the towel she'd dried her hands with to wipe her face and the cool water helped. She straightened her Gucci tux and bowtie. When the door swung open, she almost groaned. Dani stood near her, looking up at her with her big, doe eyes, her brows creased.

"Ryan. It's good to see you." Dani stared at her, then her gaze fell to her lips before returning to her eyes

"You as well," she said and took a step forward. She couldn't let the opportunity go. "Dani, I was going to call you. We should talk. I..." The door swung inward and two guests in animated conversation rushed in. The women smiled and gave her the once-over, but she didn't want their attention. Dani was so close, yet it felt as if miles separated them. She wouldn't be able to breathe if she stayed. "Have a nice evening, Dani." She brushed by Dani, and a jolt of electricity shot through her from the brief contact. Once she was away from Dani, she was able to gain her footing again, though her body continued to thrum.

She sat before leaning toward Michelle. "I apologize for my abrupt departure. I'm better now." To her credit, Michelle studied her for only a moment before smiling.

"I'm glad. This is the first course, so you haven't missed anything." She pointed to the shrimp cocktail. "I ordered you a club soda with lime to help settle your stomach."

"Thank you." She began to eat, more because it was expected rather than from hunger. There were moments when she could feel Dani's gaze on her, but she ignored the impulse to make eye contact. The gentleman on her right re-engaged with her, and between him and Michelle, she could survive the meal. She had to.

In Mark's arms, Dani moved across the dance floor like they were a professional couple thanks to his insistence they take formal

dance lessons so they could show off at weddings and events like this one. She would have been having a really good time were it not for catching glimpses of Ryan and the gorgeous woman she was with as the music played on and the crowd began to thin.

"I know that wasn't meant for me," Mark said as they slowly circled the floor.

She tipped her head back. "What?"

"You sighed, heavily."

"Oh." She'd finally told him the name of the mystery woman she couldn't stop looking at. "I didn't realize she was working. That's all."

Mark spun them. "Maybe she isn't, but either way, the woman she's with is hot."

She accidentally stepped on his toe.

"Ow."

"Sorry."

"No you aren't. You're jealous."

Dani was grateful when the music ended a few seconds later. "I need a drink." She stalked off toward the bar, leaving Mark on his own. When he caught up to her, she felt the heat in her face. She'd never acted like that with him, or anyone else. She flashed a glance in his direction.

"Apology?"

She closed her eyes and gripped the edge of the bar. *What the hell am I doing?* "I'm sorry for acting like a total jerk. I don't know what's gotten into me." She knew precisely what the issue was. *She* wanted to be the one in Ryan's arms, not the glamorous woman currently there. Dani ordered him a seltzer with a splash of cranberry and a lime twist, then threw a twenty on the gleaming surface. They moved away with their drinks and stood at one of the high tops. She fought the urge to search for Ryan while Mark sipped through his straw.

"They left," he said.

"When?"

"Right after you stomped on my foot." Mark must have read the disappointment she was irrationally feeling. He put his hand over hers. "I'm sorry, hon, but aren't you the one who said it was getting too heavy with Ryan and you wanted things to cool off between you two?"

She might have said it, but she didn't mean it. After the last call she'd made to the Agency, she'd begun to miss Ryan, especially knowing there wasn't an upcoming date with her to look forward to. "I was wrong." Tears welled in her eyes, blurring her vision.

"You said you had a real connection with the kink stuff. You trusted her. Do you think she'd agree to see you for that? At least use it as an excuse to talk to her?"

It wasn't a horrible idea, but she wanted more than kink.

Mark looked thoughtful. "You're making assumptions about how Ryan feels. Didn't you say she wanted to talk to you when you went to the restroom? Maybe she wants to see *you*."

She jerked her gaze from the drink she'd been stirring. "I doubt that's it. Ryan looked ill when I saw her, but I didn't get to ask and Ryan left before I could say anything else." She downed her drink. Since the minute she'd seen Ryan across the table from her, her mind and body had given mixed messages, fluctuating between surprise and arousal, and then something else, something she couldn't deny. Mark stared at her, and she wondered what he saw.

"Are you ready to go, or do you want to keep dancing like Ginger and Fred?"

Dani laughed. She couldn't help thinking they were nowhere close to that level of perfection, but they'd been pretty damn good. Her heart just wasn't into it anymore. "I'm ready to go. It's been a long week and I can't wait to sleep until noon."

They gathered their things and made their way through the lingering guests to the valet stand. She thanked Mark for bringing her while they waited for the car. All the while, all she thought about was how good Ryan looked and how much she should have said, if only she'd been willing to take the chance.

Ryan dropped her suit into the dry-cleaning bag. The shower seared her skin, though the temperature wasn't hot. Dani's gaze had burned through the outer protective layer. The chance encounter shouldn't have thrown her so hard that her insides had turned to slush. Then in the restroom when Dani had spoken to her and she recognized the longing in her gaze, she'd had all she could to do to not take her in her arms and kiss her.

Michelle had been gracious when she had asked if they could call it a night. She gave no excuse and hoped Michelle didn't ask. Relief coursed through her when Michelle told her she understood. She knew if she brought Michelle to her bed, the only woman she would see when she closed her eyes would be Dani. Even the thought of another had no appeal. It wouldn't have been fair to Michelle, and she didn't want to lie to her either. Ryan promised to call to make it up to her, but she thought they both knew she wasn't going to.

Dani had been so close, and her perfume still surrounded her with its heady scent. God, how she'd wanted her. Her date didn't seem like he cared that she was staring at Ryan for most of the meal. She got the feeling they were friends, or work associates rather than lovers. The idea that Dani would seek her out at some point for kink might make sense to an outsider, but she wasn't going to settle for being Dani's escort. She wanted Dani in her life, not just in her bed. She'd had a plan for what she needed to tell Dani. Nothing had changed her mind, whether or not Dani had taken to dating guys again, that wasn't what Dani wanted and she knew it. Dani had embraced being with her and even with the idea that Dani might be bi, their connection had been real.

Tomorrow she would remove her picture from the list of escorts. After that, she'd make some changes in her life. She wouldn't give up running the Agency, nor would she drag her feet about contacting Dani.

She rolled onto her side and pulled extra pillows against her, imagining a woman in their place. She called up images of Jay, then Trish, and when each quickly faded only to be replaced by Dani, she sighed deeply and let the image of her carry her to sleep.

Chapter Twenty-nine

Monday morning Ryan sat in her office with Drake screening escort applications and deciding which would be interviewed. Her phone buzzed and she pressed the intercom.

"Yes, Anna?"

"Ms. Daniella Brown is on the line for you, Ms. Lewis."

Her body stiffened and that unpleasant feeling in her stomach returned. She still hadn't called Dani, using one excuse after another. First, Dani needed more time, then *she* needed more time. But no reason she came up with made sense except her fear of rejection. Drake watched her intently. She hadn't told her about the fundraiser, or how she'd begged off a night of sex with her date.

"I need to take this call."

Drake nodded in silent understanding as she stood, her smile encouraging.

"Please put her through, Anna." She took a deep breath, and her hand shook as she picked up the receiver. "Hi, Dani." The silence was foreboding until she heard her voice.

"Is this a bad time?"

Talking to Dani was never bad. Hearing her voice sent shivers coursing through her. "No, it's a good time. Dani, about the other night—" she began.

"It's more than just the other night, Ryan, at least for me. I don't want to have this conversation over the phone."

"You're right on both accounts." It was the first of what Ryan hoped would be more admissions of her true feelings for Dani, and the relief from finally admitting it left her dizzy. "When would be good for you?"

"Wednesday night. Can you come to see me?"

"Anywhere, anytime. How about seven. Is that okay?"

Dani's breath whooshed out. "Yes, perfect. Thank you, Ryan. I have to go."

Hearing Dani's strained voice was exhilarating and left her wondering at the same time. Forty-eight hours to get her head on straight. One thing she used to be good at, but nothing she did seemed easy any more.

Dani stormed through the door like her ass was on fire because being fired was the last thing she needed. "The whole God-damned world is crazy," she hissed.

"What's wrong?" Melody asked from behind the counter as she worked the computer.

"You mean aside from leaving forty minutes before I needed to be here only to get stuck in a traffic jam with everyone refusing to move? I'm officially late!" She swiped in as she talked and when she whipped around to see her bookings for the next four hours, she gasped. Ryan sat not far away, smiling with an unmistakable twinkle in her eye. She covered her face with her hands, mumbling her embarrassment as her heart pounded in her chest. A few deep breaths later, she looked up to find Ryan standing near the counter. Melody chuckled in amusement and Dani shot a scathing look in her direction.

"I've got a rinse to do." Melody slipped away, but the grin remained on her face.

"So," she said, not knowing how she was going to redeem herself. "I guess you find this amusing, too."

"I assure you, if you're concerned about your job, the situation isn't amusing at all." Ryan reached across the counter and stopped before she touched her. "Though I must admit the look on your face when you saw me was rather priceless."

"What are you doing here?" Her voice cracked and her insides turned to liquid. For a minute she thought she might be sick. Ryan was beyond handsome. Sophisticated and debonair. Under her clothing lay strong, muscular arms that she remembered well from when they wrapped around her. Staring into the fathomless Mediterranean blue of her eyes took her places she'd only ever dreamt of until Ryan made them real.

"You said I could come see you for a haircut." Ryan's gaze pleaded for understanding, patience.

"Is that all you came for?"

Emotions played in Ryan's eyes and shadows danced across her face before she spoke. "No. I know we agreed on tomorrow, but I couldn't wait."

Innumerable questions flew threw her mind, some she didn't want answers to. "Why?"

"Because I'm not as patient as I once was."

She didn't want to go round and round with Ryan. "You mean aside from getting a haircut?" She glanced around. "Let's stick to that for now."

Ryan's name was first on her list, and knowing she'd gotten there when the salon opened pleased her. "Give me a minute to check my station."

Ryan's mouth opened, then shut before she nodded. "Of course," Ryan said, as if the unanswered question hanging between them had little effect on her.

Dani focused on laying out her implements and a fresh towel. The purple spray water bottle was full, and an array of gels, mousse, and other products stood at the ready. After donning her smock, she pulled a clean cape from the stack, took a breath, and called Ryan's name. In her heart she hoped she knew why Ryan was there, but her head yelled for her to get a grip. She wasn't sure which one she wanted to listen to more.

The silence between them was loud and clear. As the scissors snipped and pieces of her hair fell, Dani continued to avoid looking at her and Ryan fought for clarity. Had she been wrong in thinking this living, breathing thing between them was one-sided? But her heart wasn't something she could control and the idea of feeling that crushing blow of being turned away again came roaring back. She wanted to cover her ears against its incessant noise. Dani's voice startled her.

"Ryan?"

"Yes?" The pounding of her heart drowned out the inner voice screaming in panic, telling her to flee.

"What do you think?" Dani asked, her hands gently resting on her shoulders.

After regaining some equilibrium, she met Dani's reflected gaze and the blood rushing through her veins slowed enough that she could smile. Then she glanced at her own reflection in the mirror. Dani had given her a different style from the last time. This one started close cut, almost shaved, on the right side and longer on the top, before blending on the left.

"I hope it's okay. I think it suits you better than the last cut. The severe fade is in style, and the textured layers highlight your facial features so much more, especially your eyes." Dani looked in the mirror but was clearly speaking directly to her, and she needed to keep hearing her voice.

"What about my eyes?"

Dani took a breath before she moved her hands to frame her face. "They're so vivid and mesmerizing. Definitely a feature you want to draw attention to." Her hands shook and she lowered them out of view. "I purposely brought the heavier focus to the left. Your dominant side."

Her sex clenched. She was right-handed, so Dani could only mean one thing. She swiveled her chair to face her. "Have dinner with me."

"What?"

"Say yes, Dani. Please?" The drumbeat in her chest was back, and the roar of blood in her ears made her lightheaded. She hadn't wanted anything this much since she'd opened the Agency, but this wanting was quite different. *Dani* was different from any woman she'd ever met. The connection she felt with Dani in a scene couldn't compare to any other either and she longed for her in every possible way.

Dani took a step back. "I don't think it's a good idea to—"

"I know. Say yes anyway." Her nerves twitched; her fingers ached to touch her. A sea of emotions played on Dani's face, and for the briefest moment her chest froze as she waited.

"I don't get off until eight."

The air escaped her lungs in a whoosh. "Eight is good." She went to stand, and Dani stopped her.

"Hold on there," Dani said, a small smile playing on her lips. After a few quick passes with the blow dryer, she sprayed something on her hands and worked it through Ryan's hair, pulling and playing with the strands until she was satisfied. Dani brushed away loose hairs, then removed the cape. "Now you're done."

Was she ever. The rough manipulation and tugging of her hair was intimately erotic in a way, and the result left her wet and throbbing. She prayed her legs would hold her as she stood. They walked to the counter together and she handed over her credit card, adding a generous tip before completing the transaction. "I'll see you here then?" She didn't want to give her an out, but Dani might want to go home first.

"How about I meet you at your place instead?"

The idea that Dani might not show was brief. If Dani changed her mind, at the very least she'd text her and that would be that. "You have the address?"

Dani pulled her phone from her back pocket, swiped the screen and tapped a few times, then handed it to her. "Just in case I get lost."

She entered her address. "Thanks for the cut and for saying yes."

"Technically, I didn't say yes." Dani chuckled. Her anxiety must have shown. "I'll be there by eight thirty."

Being tongue-tied wasn't a normal affliction, but she couldn't find her voice in her sudden elation. She smiled, nodded, and left before she made a total fool of herself.

"You know this is a bad idea, right?" Dani said while glancing in the rearview mirror. Yet here she was almost at Ryan's house and chastising herself for giving in so easily. The clincher had been the moment when Ryan had looked so…lost. Like she would melt into a puddle if Dani declined. In the end, she hadn't had the heart to disappoint her, nor did she want to, she had ached to reach out, but Ryan had practically run away, and she pretended it didn't hurt, but it had. What happened from here would determine if she'd been foolhardy or there was more between them than kink.

As she entered the driveway and approached the house a feeling of coming home settled over her, calming her frayed nerves. Warm, ambient lighting shone from several windows, and as she got closer, the flicker of the fireplace added to the welcoming atmosphere. At the last minute, she grabbed her jacket, remembering it was cooler up here than in the city. The porch by the entryway was backlit by more ambient lights, and she stood admiring it for a minute before ringing the bell. Inside, the sound of soft chimes made her smile. When the door opened, she forgot to breathe.

"Hi," Ryan said, her eyes as welcoming as her home. "I'm glad you found me."

Gone were the formal clothes Ryan always wore, replaced by stone-washed jeans, torn in a few tantalizing places. The long-sleeve flannel shirt looked soft and comfortable with just a hint of having faded from many washings. She'd showered and the clean scent of soap along with Ryan's cologne wafted on the gentle breeze. Ryan took a step back.

"Come in."

For a second, she wasn't sure her legs would move, and she had to make a concerted effort to get them going. *Breathe. Just breathe.*

"Would you like something to drink?"

A shot or two would be good. She giggled and Ryan tipped her head in question. She cleared her throat. "Please."

"I've got wine, beer, bourbon, scotch, and water."

When Dani glanced at her hands, she also caught sight of Ryan's bare feet and silently groaned. Not that she didn't look good in suits, but this casual, at-ease look was sexy in a different way. "Wine?"

"White or red?" Ryan asked as she headed for the fully stocked sidebar. She couldn't help but follow.

"You must entertain a lot," she said as she took stock of the offerings. "Red."

Ryan shrugged. "Not really. Not in a long time. Drake comes for dinner on occasion, but she's pretty busy."

She watched as Ryan's long fingers grasped the open bottle and poured into two glasses, and then she looked up. "Are you and Drake..." She accepted the glass, knowing it wasn't any of her business but wanting to know anyway.

One side of Ryan's mouth lifted. "Lovers?" Ryan sipped. "No. She's my best friend and my voice of reason."

"But you *do* have lovers." She didn't really want to know but couldn't stop from asking either.

"I have casual sex with women, but none that I'm emotionally connected to." Ryan gestured to the couch facing the fireplace, and Dani sat a discreet distance away. "I didn't invite you here to discuss my sex life."

She turned to fully face her, needing to see her eyes as they talked because Ryan revealed her soul through her eyes. "Why am I here?"

"For dinner," Ryan said. "And because I very much enjoy your company."

"Is there more?"

Ryan shifted her gaze and looked uncomfortable, then she looked at her without wavering. "Your absence from me hurt. I..." Ryan shook her head. "I've missed you."

It was time for honesty. "I'm not sure what to say. We come from different worlds." She glanced around at the home that screamed wealth. "You're used to the finer things in life, and I've learned to make do with what I have. I work two jobs and scrape every penny I have to do anything beyond pay my bills."

"This," Ryan waved her hand, "is a direct result of the success of the Agency."

Dani knew there was more, and she quietly waited for her to go on, sensing what she was about to share was either painful or extremely private. Maybe both.

"I was orphaned as a toddler and turned into a rebellious child who didn't understand why I didn't have parents until another foster told me my mother had given me up. That she didn't want me." Ryan was quiet for a long time, perhaps deciding how much more she could share. "As a teenager, I found out the only way to survive was by being in control. Keeping my feelings hidden. After some really hellish homes, I finally landed with a wealthy couple whose only agenda was to give another child what their own children had." Ryan's head dropped back on the couch, and she stared at the ceiling.

Dani held her hand, needing the physical connection. "I can't imagine what you went through." She rubbed the firm flesh with her thumb.

Ryan turned toward her and her tentative smile was a mixture of sadness and relief. "I was one of the lucky ones. But when I go spend time with them, I still feel like an outsider. We don't share any physical characteristics, and I'm sure my stepsiblings dislike the fact that their parents treat me as their own, although my foster parents don't approve of what I do for a living."

"Were they upset when you came out to them?"

Ryan laughed without humor. "That was the easy part. It was the escort service part they didn't understand."

Dani's childhood had been so sheltered, she hadn't ever met a gay person until Mark. What would she have done if she'd never had her parents' love? "How did you explain it to them?"

Shrugging, Ryan pulled her hand away. "I told them sometimes casual is all anyone is looking for and it was all I was interested in providing."

Her mind was a whirlwind of conflicting thoughts. "I have one more question."

"Go ahead." Ryan draped her arm along the back, her fingertips nearly touching her shoulder and she swore she could feel their heat on her skin.

"Is all the sex you have with clients casual, too?"

Ryan studied her. "You have been the only one I've seen in more than a year, Dani, and you're the last.

"I'm sorry?"

Ryan set her near empty glass down and slid a bit closer. "I said client as in singular. I've only taken on one client in the last year or more."

Her hand went to her throat as the implication set in. If what Ryan said was true, she'd been the only one for the entire time she'd been involved with the Agency. As much as Ryan enjoyed sex, and especially the kink they'd played with, she couldn't imagine why she'd deny herself opportunities. "How can that be?"

"Don't misunderstand me. I've had years of enjoyable client interactions and honed my skills and abilities as a top with each one, but that's where it ended. I went into retirement as a service provider because I wasn't really enjoying it anymore. Besides, most women don't want to date someone who has sex with others for a living."

She scoffed. "Men do it all the time. I see nothing wrong with it, as long as there are clear boundaries." She drank more as she weighed her next words. "Why am I the last?"

Ryan's gaze held hers. "I don't want another."

"But why?"

Ryan shook her head. "Come with me to the kitchen while I finish making dinner. If you want to continue this conversation while we eat that's fine, but I reserve the option of asking you as much as I want in return."

Dani had never been with anyone who wanted to know her or hear the details of her life. "Okay." Once in the spacious and well-appointed kitchen, Ryan refilled their glasses. "Can I help?"

Ryan removed a glass pitcher from the refrigerator. "Can you fill our water glasses?" She pointed to a small wooden table nestled in front of a bank of windows that looked out onto the yard and the trees beyond, a glimmer of water visible in the distance. A tall vessel held homemade bread sticks, the scent of garlic making her mouth water.

"I hope you like fish," Ryan called to her from where she stood at the counter scooping food.

"Depends on the fish." Her mouth twitched at the inference, her thoughts these days often running in sexual innuendo directions.

Ryan's eyes twinkled mischievously. "It has to be fresh." She winked. "This is Chilean sea bass. It's one of my favorite meals."

The plates were expertly arranged, and Ryan indicated the open bottle of Pinot Grigio and two clean glasses. "If you grab those, I'll come back for the salads." Ryan poured the wine before raising her glass. "To the women who aren't afraid to go after what they want." She tapped her glass to Dani's hoping she understood how much she believed in those words. Not just for Dani, but for herself as well.

"This is very nice," Dani said after tasting the wine. "And the food looks like it came from a five-star restaurant." She forked a piece of the delicate fish and slowly chewed, then swallowed. "Oh, that's good. Flavorful and light."

Ryan was pleased by the compliments, but they paled in comparison to Dani's company and her beauty. "Thank you. I believe eating well should be everyone's right, among other things." She broke off a piece of fish and scooped up some risotto with it. The flavors melded together on her tongue with just the right amount of buttery goodness. They ate in silence for a few minutes before Dani's voice broke the quiet.

"Getting back to why you took me as a client."

It was Dani's nature to satisfy her curiosity and one of the reasons Ryan had been drawn to her. "You intrigued me. You came to the Agency ready to explore another side of your sexuality and you knew what you wanted. You were excited for the adventure, and I wanted to be part of that excitement."

"God, I was terrified."

As Dani took a bite of food Ryan witnessed the emotional journey she was reliving. "You certainly didn't sound terrified. You sounded confident, self-assured. Your words and your voice made me hard, and *that* hadn't happened to me in a very long time."

Dani stared at her wide-eyed. "Seriously? You got a hard-on when we spoke."

"It's a compliment, I assure you." She noted Dani's cheeks turning a lovely shade of pink as she drained her glass. She picked up the bottle. "More?"

"The whole bottle would be good."

Ryan chuckled at her embarrassment and poured for both of them. *We could have an amazing life together.* "Your cheeks are the same color when you come."

Dani choked on her food, coughing hard. She took a sip of water, then another. "You're timing is really bad."

"I could have sworn you thought my timing quite good, but I've been mistaken before."

"Are you horny?" Dani asked as she looked over the top of her glass, her long lashes framing her expressive eyes.

Her dinner invitation had everything to do with wanting to see Dani and spend time with her, not purely for sex. But now that she was sitting across from her with the lights low and the sexual tension high, she couldn't deny wanting to make love to Dani. "I want you, but only if you want it too, Dani."

Dani's gaze held hers steadily until it briefly fell to her lips then back again. Her stomach tightened in need, a live raging beast intent on stealing her control and she forced herself to remain seated, watching and waiting for Dani to respond. Either way, she would enjoy the opportunity of having time together and the closeness they shared.

"You make it awfully difficult to say no." Dani set her glass down and pushed her plate away.

"Then don't." When Dani hesitated, she went on. "I'm trying very hard to not sweep you into my arms and carry you to my bed." She took a breath, then another. "But I invited you here for dinner and conversation, so I'm doing my best to honor my original intention."

Dani slowly pushed her chair back, then stood, and stepped forward until she was within inches of her. "And that's not your intention now?"

Ryan drank in all of Dani's curves until their eyes met. "I'm trying to do the right thing." She rose and brushed her knuckle along Dani's jaw before bending to do the same with her lips. Dani leaned into her and trembled against her, making her groan. "Not helping," she said through gritted teeth as she wrapped her arms around her.

"Take me to bed."

She scooped her up and carried her down the hall. All the while, her heart pounded and her blood rushed through her veins like a swollen creek quickened by a springtime thaw. Ryan set Dani on her feet and began to undress, wanting the barriers between them gone. Dani stilled her hands.

"This look is hot, and you wear it well." Dani's nimble fingers finished with the buttons and she pushed the fabric from her shoulders. Her nipples tightened when exposed to the cool air. "Kiss me."

She cupped Dani's ass and lifted her until their mouths met. The searing heat between them bonded their joining, like forged steel. Dani pressed her tongue against hers, the caress so intimate and gentle compared to the urgency she couldn't control brought a moan from her depths. Yes, she wanted Dani tonight, and the next, and the one after. Ryan pushed away *that* need…for now. One day soon, her needs would come first, with a woman who would take her as she was and for who she was. A woman who would love her no matter where her life had started, or what she did for a living. A woman who understood her strength as well as her weaknesses. Ryan knew in her heart that woman was in her arms. All she had to do was prove how special their life together could be.

CHAPTER THIRTY

Dani had made a clear decision that even if Ryan wanted to control what happened in bed, she could run with that. It was time to give herself over to her on another level because Ryan was the one who had awakened her body and soul and embraced her naivety. The revelation that she had rekindled something in Ryan was not only shocking but pleased her in a way that was hard to explain.

Ryan's full lips and soft mouth stoked the fire in her belly that had begun the moment Ryan had opened the door. She struggled for air and filled her hand with Ryan's thick hair, tugging her head back. The heated gaze wasn't unwelcome and the more she looked into the blue depths, the more she wanted to lose herself in them.

"Dani." Ryan's voice was rough and deep. "Let me touch you," she said as she lowered her.

She yanked her shirt over her head and reached for Ryan's belt. Her nipples were pointed, the flesh around them puckered, and she placed her mouth over one and began to suck, her tongue brushing against the tip. Ryan grasped her shoulders, head back, clearly enjoying the attention.

"You're driving me crazy, you know that, right?"

She undid Ryan's belt, drew the zipper down, then slipped her hand inside her jeans. Ryan was warm and wet. She pushed into her, finding the hard nub that quivered under her touch. Just as quickly, she went from seductress to wanting to take Ryan to a place Dani believed Ryan rarely let anyone. "Do you have cuffs?"

"Yes." Ryan's pupils contracted to pinpoints of naked desire.

"I want to use them on you." She withdrew her hand and began playing with Ryan's neglected nipple.

"I thought you preferred being on the receiving end?"

"I do." She began to work the jeans over Ryan's hips. "But you make me feel powerful, and I want to use that power to please us both." She pursed her lips. "Is that okay?"

"It's very okay." Ryan caressed her throat, framed her face in her hands, then kissed her with slow-building intensity. When she broke away with her lips next to her ear, she whispered her safe word.

Dani swallowed her sudden nervousness. She'd been taught by the best and she would do all she could to bring pleasure to Ryan in a way that showed their growing trust and connection. She hadn't thought she wanted it. Had denied it. But not seeing Ryan had been much more painful than she'd thought it would be. Dani had feared the loss of directing her own future and of not being able to make her own decisions, but Ryan had never tried to control her, and had always encouraged Dani to wield her power, sexual or otherwise.

In fact, there were moments like now, when Ryan appeared content to *not* be in charge. Was that how their life might be? Could she accept who Ryan was and all that came with her as the CEO of an escort service? If Ryan decided to return to taking clients, could she view it as being her job rather than cheating on her? Did she want to be the type of person who would stifle another's lifestyle for her own sake? Ryan's fingers snaked into her hair. She had time to consider her future, their future.

"What are you thinking?" Ryan was so patient with her.

"Show me the cuffs before you take off your pants." Ryan reached beneath each of the four bed posts and placed the restraints on the bed, then stripped. "Lie down and close your eyes." Without hesitation, she complied.

During the past few months, Dani had played out dozens of scenes. This had been a frequent player for a number of weeks.

She trailed her blunt nails up the inside of Ryan's calves and along her thigh until just shy of the juncture of her groin. Ryan's muscles twitched. She grasped her ankle and attached one cuff, then repeated with the other.

"Reach up and hold on to the headboard. Do not let go."

Satisfied, she crawled between Ryan's open legs. Beads of moisture clung to the close cropped, downy hair, the same shade as the hair she'd meticulously cut earlier, dark as a starless midnight sky. Dani slipped her thumbs inside, careful to avoid her crimson, glistening clit before sliding along the silk-like folds.

Ryan's chest heaved, her breathing fast. "I'm not going to last." Ryan moaned.

She withdrew her touch. "Not until I say." She watched as her abdomen rippled, coated with sweat. Dani moved higher until she straddled her, slowly lowering her denim-clad center just above Ryan's. She tweaked the hard knots of her nipples and Ryan softly swore. She smiled thinking about how different Ryan had been during their first encounter, and the more she asked the more Ryan showed herself by letting go. Dani closed her mouth over a stiff peak and bit down with enough pressure that she thought it possible Ryan was going to snap the wooden dowels in the headboard.

"I can't hold on," Ryan said.

She spoke in her ear. "You can and you will, because you want to please me as much as I want to please you." Dani kissed the tender flesh beneath her lips and the exposed places of Ryan's throat. "Open your eyes and focus on me." She moved to the foot of the bed, took off her clothes, then slowly crawled on hands and knees until her center was over Ryan's again. She spread herself over Ryan, lowering until their clits touched.

"Christ," Ryan said. Every muscle in her body twitched at once.

"Soon." Moving back and forth, Dani created just the right amount of friction and the first tingles of her impending orgasm spread from her center outward. "Almost there," she gasped, her body covered in moisture, a mix of sweat and arousal. Ryan jerked beneath her.

"I'm sorry," Ryan said breathlessly, her eyes squeezed shut. Her body stiffened and color rose up her chest before she cried out.

A gush of hot liquid coated Dani's opening and she thrust against Ryan once more before her orgasm struck. Her entire body trembled as she moaned and called out Ryan's name. The world blinked out of existence as she watched Ryan's climax rage on, all of her focus on the ecstasy written on her face. So perfectly open and so vulnerable, and she was responsible. A perfect power exchange. She lay on top of her and mumbled, "Let go," hoping Ryan understood, then she closed her eyes. At some point, Ryan embraced her and kissed the top of her head without speaking. She didn't have to. A shift had taken place. Dani wasn't sure what it meant, but she wanted to.

Seeing Dani had been exhilarating and heartbreaking. Ryan would be kidding herself if she said she hadn't hoped they would end up in bed, although she'd also hoped for some more intimate, deeper conversation about the possibilities between them. But conversation had taken a back seat to desire when she'd seen the lust in Dani's eyes. Sex with Dani was mind-blowing, but so was being with her, talking, laughing. Anything at all. She wanted to have more personal conversations. To find out all she could.

More than that though, her heart ached for Dani having to work so hard to get what she wanted. Sure, everyone who ran a business put in an inordinate amount of time, but that was okay because success came at a price. Working that hard for someone else, someone who didn't appreciate her dedication, like Dani's boss, left a person hollowed out. She knew George. He was a first-class prick, not to mention the fact he thought he was a lady killer and had the gall to touch women when he'd neither been invited or been shown interest. Ryan had disliked him the first time she met him, and after discovering he was Dani's employer, she despised him even more.

When they'd parted the following morning, Dani had promised to call her before the week was out, and there'd been a gentleness and openness in her eyes that had Ryan hoping there really could be a future for them. Until then, she needed to refocus her energies on the work piling up on her desk. The expansion had been necessary, but overwhelming. She pressed the speaker button on the phone, then the first speed number.

"Good morning, boss."

"Morning. Do you have time to meet? I want to find out where everyone is on the expansion."

"Sure thing. When?"

Ryan pressed her fingertips to her temple. The dull throb that had been there since she woke was back. "I'll have Anna set it up and message the staff, but I'd like it before noon." She hung up after a few more words and called Anna. Five minutes later, she received the invitation for the meeting set for ten thirty.

Once she had her papers organized and saved her slides to a USB drive, she went to the credenza. She'd cut down on her caffeine consumption the last month, but there were times when she still craved the jolt, a modified version of sex, to take off the edge. While it brewed, she pictured Dani standing at the foot of her bed, commanding her before she pressed their centers together. She groaned as her clit surged. Telling Dani how she felt about her had been a relief, in a way, and revealing her feelings had been long overdue. Though she still wasn't sure it was the smartest thing to do. Dani hadn't been put off by it, that's for sure. She'd taken her, commanded her body, and Ryan hadn't been able to stop her climax. Now she realized it was because she hadn't wanted to. Dani was the only woman she'd let her guard down for since the last time. The major difference this time was she didn't believe she'd pay the price for her carelessness with the shredding of her heart. The loud beeping brought her back to the present.

She fixed her coffee, gathered her things, then headed to the conference room. No matter what else was going on in her life, she had a business to run, and failure was not an option.

❖

Ryan rotated her shoulders, rubbed her neck. She and Drake had been immersed in expansion details for the last two hours. Her eyes were fatigued, her muscles sore from being hunched over. She needed food, a hot shower, and she wished she could head home to someone waiting for her. Not just anyone, though. *Dani.*

Drake came back in with two tumblers of amber liquid, set one in front of her, then took her former seat. "To all the details of expansion. May everything fall into fucking place."

Ryan laughed, tapped her glass, and downed a meager amount. Drake knew what she needed without her saying a word. "Spoken like a true VP."

"Honestly, I don't know how you did everything. I thought I had a pretty good handle on what was needed every time we took on a client or hired an escort, but there's so many other details involved it will take me years to remember them all." Drake tipped her glass and took another swallow. There was something going on with her that she hadn't shared, but Ryan wasn't able to read her.

"It's just business. We'll get through it. We always do." When the silence became uncomfortable, she leaned closer. "What's going on? Are you unhappy in your expanded role?"

Finally, Drake eyes met hers. "No, no. I like the extra responsibility and learning the intricacies of the business." She grinned sheepishly. "I've always been a bit too preoccupied with the ladies to be concerned about the behind the scenes operations."

"Yes, and that's one of the reasons I hesitated giving you more. But honestly, I'm glad I did." After resisting Drake's and Lane's offers to help for years, admitting she needed it hadn't been easy.

"I'm glad, too."

"Then what is it that's bothering you?"

"I've let you down. I should have been beside you, helping you, not out there acting like I didn't have a stake in the business side, too." Drake wasn't a fatalist. She took life one day at a time, not worrying about tomorrow until it arrived. Sharing she might no longer feel that way startled Ryan.

She grasped her forearm. "You did no such thing. We jumped on this bandwagon intent on making our own way in the world by doing what we enjoyed. We've both worked hard and put in safeguards to make sure the business, our employees, and own lives survived it all. The more successful we are, the harder we work. It's the natural way things go." Ryan squeezed then let go. "Giving up control of even a small part of it isn't easy for me, but it was the right thing to do." She considered maybe Drake was done with servicing women, though she doubted it. "If you're not happy, if what you're doing isn't working for you anymore," she said, and shrugged. "It's okay to tell me you want to do something else."

"Hell, Ryan," Drake said with conviction. "I hope I never want to give this up." She leaned back and blew out a breath. "But fuck, you're a tough act to follow."

"Then don't. Be you. Take care of things the way you want to, and I'll do my best to stay out of your way. We're doing this together. It's not like I'm going to disappear."

"Oh, I don't expect that will happen. That's not who you are, but that's okay. I love you just the same. The biggest thing is learning how to navigate less time escorting."

"Maybe you need a night with Trish." Ryan fingered her glass, wishing there was more.

"Yeah. Or Trish and Carol at the same time." Her eyes sparkled with mischief.

"Ha. I don't know who'd come out alive with that combination." Visions of Dani working Jill was both arousing and disconcerting. She didn't want Dani anywhere near another woman. "Go home or go get laid. Or both. Just remember it's okay to question things every so often. Either way, the future is up to you, and you can change it whenever you want."

Drake stood. "Care to join me?"

"Thanks. As tempting as it sounds, I've got a bit more to do here, then I'm going to pick up dinner on the way home before crashing. It's been a long week."

Once alone, Ryan began to pace. She ordered food, closed down her computer, and locked her office. The nagging feeling of restlessness continued to follow her down the ten floors and into her car. She wanted to see Dani. Against her better judgment, which was the case a lot lately, Ryan took a slight detour from the most direct route to the restaurant and drove past the salon. Standing on the sidewalk, Dani and George were shouting at each other. She slowed to a stop across the street and watched the heated argument unfold. Then George grabbed Dani's arm, and she was out and moving toward them.

"Let her go," she said.

George pulled back, and Dani rubbed where his fingers had been.

"Ms. Lewis, how nice of you to drop by." George's smile was predatory and fake.

"It's not a social visit." She turned to Dani. "Are you all right?" When Dani nodded, she faced George again. "An assault complaint wouldn't look good for your business." She took a step closer, forcing George to look up at her. "But that would hurt your employees more than you. I hope we understand each other."

George took a step back, his face red. He turned his attention on Dani. "You're done. Get your shit and don't come back."

She took a breath. Anger coursed through her. He'd touched Dani, and she wanted to be the only one to touch her. "Are you sure you're okay?"

"What are you doing here?" Dani's face was hard to read. She wasn't sure if it was gratitude or not.

"I was on my way to pick up dinner and saw you and George arguing."

"I didn't need rescuing." Dani stepped back like she needed space. "Aren't you going in the wrong direction?"

Maybe she'd made a mistake by interfering, but she couldn't stand by and watch George grab her like that. She'd wanted to punch him for touching her. "I really did order dinner." She met Dani's probing gaze. "And decided to ask you to join me."

"Thanks, but you heard him. I have to pack up and leave."

"Let me help you."

Dani shook her head. "I need to figure out what I'm going to do. It's something I have to do on my own." She started inside and Ryan took a step forward, but Dani waved her off. "I'm sorry, Ryan."

Numb, she made it to her car and slumped into her seat. Ryan didn't want to go. Her natural instinct was to go inside and make sure George stayed away from Dani. That wasn't what Dani wanted, though. She said she needed time to figure things out and that's what she had to give her, even if walking away went against everything she felt.

Chapter Thirty-one

Self-recrimination. Disappointment. Regret. Each emotion hit Dani with the force of a tidal wave, knocking her down, not letting her recover. George had accused her of slacking off and not working as fast or as hard as she could. While her extracurricular activities had slowed in the last month and she was able to trim a few hours from her schedule, she still brought in a big share of the clientele. Just because she was no longer killing herself didn't mean he wasn't getting his money's worth. She'd tried to explain the drop was as much due to the season as it was to other circumstances, but it was like talking to the proverbial brick wall. He'd followed her outside, threatening to fire her when her knight swooped in to save the day.

Ryan's voice had sent chills up her spine, the look on her face dangerous. Almost as feral as she looked in bed, but with the murderous anger she could read in her eyes when George had grabbed her. She appreciated Ryan's willingness to step in, though she wasn't sure if it had helped matters or made George angrier, but Dani loved the idea of Ryan's fearlessness when she stood up to her boss.

Ryan was the epitome of noble, and it came forth in everything she did. Ryan certainly treated her like she was special. She loved being pampered, wined, and dined as though she were the only woman to garner Ryan's attention, but that wasn't true. Was it? Just because Ryan said she was the only client she was seeing didn't mean she wasn't dating others, like the woman at the fundraiser. She hated admitting she'd been jealous of her being chosen to accompany Ryan to what had probably ended with them in bed and Ryan doing all those wonderful, exciting, and mind-blowing things she did when she made love. But it was entirely her fault. She'd pushed Ryan away using the same bogus excuses as before, like Ryan was out of her league. Or Ryan could have any woman, so why would she want her? But time and again Ryan had sought her company outside of the bedroom.

Dani pressed a few buttons on her steering wheel. When the connection kicked in after two rings, she didn't give the person on the other line a chance to speak. "Mark, I need you. Bring reinforcements and come to my apartment as soon as you can."

"I'm on it. Any special requests?"

It wasn't going to be an early night, not with the mixed emotions coursing through her. "Tequila and a pizza."

"Got it. I'll see you in forty-five minutes." Mark disconnected.

She pictured him already dialing for the pie as he raced around gathering supplies. Dani pulled up to her apartment, turned off the car, and took her first full breath since seeing Ryan. She stripped in her bedroom and headed for the shower. Mark had a key and would let himself in if she wasn't out before he got there. The hot needles pelted her skin as she tried not to think about the implications of being unemployed. She wouldn't…couldn't…go back to her parents. Her future included women, and that wasn't something they'd ever accept. But she wasn't about to go backwards.

After drying off and ruffling her hair, she pulled on sweats and a long-sleeve T-shirt. The doorbell rang and she smiled. She called out and pulled the door open to find Mark juggling a huge pizza, a shopping bag at his feet and a duffel bag slung over his shoulder.

"If we're going to be soul-searching, I'm spending the night." Mark's smile assured her the world, while crazy and unpredictable, still contained what she needed most.

She took the box, placed it on the coffee table, and turned to the kitchen. "You cut the limes. I'll get the rest." Dani didn't want to think until she had at least one shot to steady her and a slice of pizza for fortification. A few minutes later, she and Mark settled on the floor around the coffee table.

"To problems that can be fixed." Mark raised his shot glass, and she mirrored the move.

Lick, slug, suck. The slight burn and pure heat spread from her belly outward.

"Tell me what happened." Mark flipped up the cover and served them each a slice of pizza with the works.

"I've been fired." She probably should have started differently since she feared she might have to do the Heimlich maneuver, but Mark managed to recover and she went on, filling him in on George's rant, and how he'd grabbed her, and Ryan's reaction.

"You sent her away?"

"Yeah. I don't need her rescuing me," she said. Mark stared at her. "What?"

Mark wiped the corners of his mouth and poured more tequila, then motioned her to partake. The burn and grimace subsided after a few seconds. "As someone looking from the outside in, I could have sworn you wanted her in your life." He wasn't wrong.

"I do, but…" What *did* she want from Ryan?

"But only the way *you* dictate and only when *you* want sex. Is that it?"

She waved her half-eaten slice of pizza at him. "She's the one who's so into sex, and with anyone she wants."

"That's not true and you know it. How about the dinners she's made you and the pampering she showed? Did she ever once tell you to do something, or give her opinion when you didn't ask for it?"

"No."

"Have you ever wished you didn't have to make an appointment to be with her?"

Her chest tightened. Ryan *had* shown her there was more between them then exchanging money for sex. The impromptu dinners gave her a glimpse of the life Ryan was capable of providing. Did she really believe the only reason she'd been invited was for sex? And what about tonight? Ryan hadn't thought twice about stepping in when things got physical. Maybe she'd seen them going at it for a while and had hung back until then. Did Ryan act in an attempt to control the situation, or to protect Dani? Guilt washed over her. Ryan had never once told her what to do or how to respond. The times she'd stepped in outside of the Agency's realm had been acts of kindness and concern for her well-being, nothing more. She'd been a jerk in every way, putting her baggage onto Ryan, who had only ever been exactly what Dani needed.

"Yes." She held her head. "Jesus, Mark."

Mark stood, went to the kitchen, and returned with sodas. "We need to be clearheaded while we talk this part out." He popped the top on the cans and handed her one. "Do you have feelings for her, other than sexual?"

The weeks she hadn't seen Ryan had been awful. It wasn't just Ryan's particular way of making love, or how they played out scenes. She missed Ryan. Her even temperament and her genuine concern. Her chivalry and her charisma. Her intense blue eyes that focused only on her no matter how many women were around. The obvious flare of jealousy when Jill had kissed her and shown interest in Dani. And even more than that, her laugh, her smile, her wit, her charm. There was so much about her that Dani adored. "Oh, God. I might have blown my chances of even trying to have a relationship."

Mark wrapped his arm around her shoulders. "I think you may still have a chance, but don't jerk her around. Be sure what you want because if she cares about you as much as I think she does, sending her away may make her withdraw, and the last thing you want to do is let her think she's just a plaything to you."

They talked until the tequila kicked in, then they snuggled on the couch to watch some comedy neither was really watching. She dozed in and out, and whenever she closed her eyes, bold and beautiful Ryan was there. Somehow, she had to fix this.

"Is that really what you want to do?"

Ryan wasn't sure what she wanted anymore. At one time she'd thought there'd never be another woman who could get inside and touch her as deeply as Dani had. She'd tried to remain professional, aloof, knowing all the while that her cold and hardened heart was warming, changing into a beating, feeling thing again. "I don't know, but I have to try." She replayed snippets of conversations when Dani had been emphatic about not being controlled, about finally feeling the freedom to be who she wanted to be. Right now she needed help to stay there, and she could think of only one thing that would do that. "I'm going to see if I can convince her to meet with me."

Drake sat back. "She'll think you want sex."

"Not if we meet here in the conference room."

"That might work, though it might be better on neutral territory." Drake stood, then moved to the credenza and began to fix espressos.

"No. I want her to see she has control no matter where she is. I think she needs that." Ryan took the offered beverage and inhaled the rich aroma. "Thanks."

"What's your plan?" Drake sat back in the chair, one bent leg resting over the other, her long golden hair flowing around her, green eyes reflecting the light from outside.

"I'm going to proposition her."

Drake's brow shot up in response and she laughed.

"I'm going to offer to help set her up in her own salon." Ryan hadn't spoken to Dani since the scene with George two days ago, but she'd taken full advantage of the time by researching and having their real estate agent find an adequate location. She spent hours laying out a plan for start-up funds, and an equipment budget, barely sleeping or eating while she worked.

"You think she'll accept?" Drake asked.

In the past month, Drake had been by Ryan's side while she lamented over the loss of her connection with Dani. She shrugged. "I hope so. If independence is what she wants, I don't see any reason why she wouldn't."

"Except that she'd be relying on you for one more thing in her life. She might see it as you trying to control her next steps."

"You're a killjoy." Ryan scrubbed at her face.

"Maybe. I'm looking at all the angles."

Ryan stood. "I knew I picked the right person to be VP."

"Sweet talker." Drake batted her outrageously long lashes and smiled. "I'll leave you to it then." She strode to the door, her swagger on full display. Before she left, she half turned back. "If you need anything..."

"Thank you, Drake. I know I can always count on you."

She picked up her office phone, thinking Dani would be more apt to answer if she wasn't sure it was Ryan calling her. After three rings, she almost hung up, but Dani's low voice gave her impetus to talk though her heart raced. "Dani, it's Ryan."

"I can't talk to you right now."

"Please, Dani. It's important." Ryan wasn't going to plead, but her idea needed to be heard.

"No, not that. I mean, I'm in the middle of something. Can I call you back in an hour?"

She breathed a little easier. "Of course. I'll talk to you then."

"Okay. Bye."

Dani didn't sound angry or upset. In fact, she sounded pretty upbeat. Ryan wasn't sure if she should be happy or disquieted that Dani was getting along just fine. Maybe she didn't need Ryan's help after all. She had an hour to kill and hoped she didn't lose her nerve while she waited.

Dani dried her hands and grabbed a diet soda before sitting on a barstool to make the call. She scrolled to the contact information for the Agency and pressed the number. When she'd heard Ryan's voice, her center warmed. She'd been sorting through her emotions and had made up her mind to reach out to Ryan.

"The Agency, this is Anna speaking. How may I help you?"

"Hi, it's Daniella Brown. Ms. Lewis wanted me to call her."

"Of course, Ms. Brown. I hope you're well. Please hold."

Music played in her ear while her insides churned. Ryan's call had been unexpected, and she'd been happy to hear from her. Since sending her away she'd replayed moments in her head, splicing together the bits and pieces that rose in stark relief. Through them all one thing stood out...Ryan cared for her. She'd begun this journey with one goal in mind—to enjoy her freedom and explore her sexuality. Then, she'd been exploring her kinky side with Ryan's guidance because she trusted her. And not long after she'd begun feeling safe in Ryan's arms, making her realize she wanted those things in her life on a permanent basis. Ryan's voice sent a shiver of excitement through her.

"Dani, thank you for returning my call. Is everything okay?"

She laughed. "You mean aside from not having a job? It's as good as it can be."

"Good, but it sounded like there was something happening when I called."

"A neighbor found out I was no longer at the salon, and she wanted me to color and cut her hair. I was doing it in my tiny bathroom, which wasn't optimal, but I made it work."

"Ah." Ryan cleared her throat. "I would like you to come to the office to discuss a proposition."

"Are you going to hire me for the Agency?"

It was Ryan's turn to laugh. "As much as I would love to see you more often, I'm afraid not. I don't want to go into the details over the phone, but I hope you'll hear me out."

Dani wondered what was so important she wanted to see her at the office rather than her home. "I guess so. When is good for you?"

"Most of tomorrow is free. Thursday won't work because we're interviewing all day."

She chewed her lip. Seeing Ryan and being close to her was going to be a test, but after everything Ryan had done for her, she couldn't say no. And she didn't want to. "Tomorrow is good." They settled on a time and disconnected.

She'd escaped her overbearing parents to pursue her own sexuality and taste the freedom of being her own person. The salon had provided a venue for her to let her creative flair blossom in the cuts and styles she gave. When she cut, the end result rested solely in her control.

And that's where her control issues had spilled over into her everyday life. She'd feared Ryan wanted her only for sex, as her plaything, but nothing Ryan did was controlling. Even when she wielded power in the bedroom, Dani had learned she still had ultimate control over what happened. She sighed, tired of denying she wanted Ryan in her life on a regular basis.

Dani couldn't conceive what Ryan would say. If she let herself hope too much her disappointment would bury her. She didn't believe Ryan would have her come to the office for personal reasons, but that didn't stop her from hoping.

Had she ever wanted anything more in life? Ryan was a perfect partner in every way that should matter. What she did for a living, one that she was good at and made her happy, shouldn't be a reason not to pursue digging deeper to see if they could make it work. Lord knew, they were hot together.

The low thrum that had started turned into a beehive of activity, nerves twitching as muscle memory kicked in. Ryan's mouth knew the places to seek for her pleasure. Ryan's hands touched her in just the right way every time, teasing her along the path to orgasm. And Ryan's cock...well, what could she say except she wielded it with precision, like a swordman trained for battle. She knew when to fuck her slowly, or harder and deeper, until she cried out.

"Jesus," she said to the empty room. Wet and wanting, Dani wished she could go to Ryan and ask her to do all those things to her. For her. She needed to get a grip. Yes, she wanted Ryan and would like to explore more of the connection between them, but Ryan had issues and they needed to clear the air, otherwise she'd have to give up the freedom she'd just found, and that was a price she wasn't willing to pay.

"Ms. Brown is here to see you."

Ryan took a deep breath. "Show her to the conference room. I'll be right there."

"Certainly," Anna said.

Ryan stood, put her suit coat on, then took it off. She rolled the sleeves of her white dress shirt midway up her forearms and glanced in the mirror to straighten her tie. Her attire said business casual instead of formal. She nodded once, picked up the tray, and made it out the door without dumping it. The conference room was open, and when she walked in her breath caught. Dani stood at the window, silhouetted in golden sunlight, her features softened by the brightness. She wore a lacy, mid-thigh sundress with small blue and yellow flowers, that hugged her curves perfectly. She was gorgeous, and when she turned and smiled, Ryan was reminded again why she craved her company. She would do anything to see Dani smile.

"Hi," Dani said.

"Good morning." Her voice was rough. The need spread from her center as her clit began to pound between her thighs. This was *not* how she wanted their meeting to start, but she'd known it would happen. Fortunately, her emotions were on high alert too, and she needed to deal with things other than the physical. Ryan set the tray down. "Would you like a cup of coffee? I could get a pot of water if you prefer tea."

Dani touched her hand. "Coffee is fine."

Ryan's body shot into overdrive, and she clenched and released muscles, attempting to relax. She poured them both a cup and took the opportunity while Dani added sugar and cream to remember why they were both there. She pulled a folder from the side of the table.

"Thank you for seeing me."

Dani blew across her cup, then took a sip. "It wasn't a hard decision, Ryan. In spite of how we parted, I've missed you. And I'm sorry for the things I said. I was out of line, and frankly, I was wrong."

Unsure how to respond, she nodded. She hadn't considered Dani might have regretted her words and the way things were left between them. "I've missed you also."

"Now that we have that out of the way, what's your proposition?" Dani turned her chair sideways to face her, crossed her shapely legs to reveal smooth, creamy thighs, and sat back looking completely relaxed.

"Would you go back to your former employer?"

Dani's jaw clenched. "Not even if it was the last place I could find work."

She suppressed a smile. "I didn't think so." Ryan opened the folder. "How would you feel about opening your own salon?" She slid the sketch of a well-equipped, modern salon in front of Dani.

"Are you opening another business?" Dani glanced at the rendering, lightly running her fingers over the images.

"No. You are. That is, if you're interested."

Dani stared at her for a long time. "I don't understand."

Ryan leaned closer, hands clasped on the table because what she really wanted to do was touch her. "I'm offering to financially back you to open your own salon. Whatever you need, whoever you want to employ." The small packet of paper containing all the information was next. "You have full autonomy in decisions concerning the layout, services, and fees. The only thing I ask in return is to review expenditures, but only because I have a lot of business connections and I'd want you to get the best deals. And of course, we'd refer our escorts to you, which would help give you a solid client base to start with."

Dani flipped through several pages, taking her time. Finally, she glanced up. "Why are you doing this?"

"You deserve to have something to call your own and not be lorded over by an unappreciative employer. I've done my homework. There's nothing easy about the profession you've chosen, but many are successful, and I can help you get there. I know how good you are at what you do professionally, too." She waited, afraid Dani would decline her offer. "No strings attached, Dani. If you never want to see me again personally, I'll honor your wishes. Our relationship isn't part of the business proposition."

Dani's gaze moved to her mouth, then back again. "Would my business be tied to the success of the Agency?"

Hope, a feeling she hadn't had since being adopted, filled her heart. "No. This venture would be backed solely from my personal funds."

Dani grinned. "You have that much available?"

"The Agency has provided a very lucrative income. I assure you, I can afford it. And like I said, I want to invest in your future." Ryan's clit surged forward when Dani bit her bottom lip.

"We have to hammer out the details. If I say yes, I'll want your input for the logistics and the financial impact, but I have to have singular decision-making power. This business would have to succeed or fail due to my actions."

"Of course."

Dani stood and went to the window, her arms crossed in front of her. Her reflection showed her concentration was obviously focused inward. "And what do you want, Ryan?"

No one had asked her in so long, the words were foreign, and it took her a minute to respond. "I want you to be happy." Even though her heart was breaking at the thought of Dani wanting only the business part of what she offered, she would do everything she could to help her.

"No." Dani shook her head, her arms down at her sides, and turned to face her. "What do you want for yourself?"

She gazed into her eyes with such steadfast attention, Ryan felt her touch her soul. It was now or never. "I want you always by my side. Not behind me or in front of me, but as my equal, in all things. I want a relationship with you because you're beautiful, and intelligent, and insanely sexy. Because you make me want more out of life." Ryan went to her. "No matter what you decide about us, please say yes to the salon." She had fought the urge to touch her as long as she could and held her hands. Shadows of light and dark turned her eyes from honey brown to deep chocolate. For the first time since meeting her, Ryan was unsure what it meant.

"I'd be a fool not to."

"Not if you aren't positive it's what you want to do."

"I am, but where does that leave us?" Dani leaned into her as though seeking comfort.

"Where do you want it to leave us? You have all the control, Dani. You've always had the control, whether you knew it or not."

"There was a time I questioned your motives. When I wondered why you were pretending to care and thinking your actions were based on the sex we had." Dani took a breath and gestured to their chairs. "I was wrong, Ryan. When you stood outside the bank that day, your brow creased with concern..." she said as she smoothed the spot. "I had a glimpse of something more." Dani laughed. "But you're so damn hard to read."

"Sorry." She meant it.

"No. Don't be sorry. That's a part of you I love. That you don't fly off the handle. That you are in control of your emotions, and now I know why. Being shuttled around had to have been hard on you. It was your survival mode." Dani took Ryan's hands and pressed their knees together. "I don't want you to be surviving when you're with me, Ryan. I want and need you to be you. All of you."

Ryan's eyes were glassy as she took Dani's face in her hands and kissed her. It was a kiss full of promise, of trust, and, most amazingly, full of love.

Chapter Thirty-two

Dani's heart pounded in her chest as she stood beside the bed. They hadn't been together physically in almost a month, and she understood the significance of the moment

"I want to make love with you, Dani." Ryan began placing soft kisses along her chin. "Please tell me I can."

She was so wet already. "Yes." Ryan took her time undressing them both, then carried her into bed. She lay over her, her tanned skin silken and warm against hers.

"Mmm." Ryan moaned before sliding her hands under her shoulders and covering her lips with her mouth.

"There's so much I want to say." She traced the ridges of Ryan's collarbone and gently sucked the butter soft skin of her neck. "I know I'm stubborn and frustrating." Ryan must have sensed her need to tell her things and she moved off onto her side, resting her head in her palm.

"A little."

She play-poked her, making her flinch. "Okay. I get it." She laughed at Ryan's exaggerated eye roll. "Once I got out of my own head and realized you weren't trying to control me at all, that is."

"Never."

"You were taking me on a journey and you wanted me to be okay with each nuance and touch and…God, you made me feel so damn good."

The kiss that followed was tantalizingly slow, and she opened to her, letting Ryan's tongue enter to caress hers. When she could no longer breathe, she broke away, panting. She traced Ryan's lips with her fingertip. Then she traced the fine bones of her cheeks, her strong jawline, and along her throat. Ryan's eyes fluttered. She remembered the shift between them the last time they were in bed. She hadn't known what it was, but maybe she did now. "Do you love me?"

Ryan trembled under her touch. "Yes. I think I have from the first time I saw you. The first time I touched you." Ryan's breath shuddered.

"Show me."

"I want you so much it's painful. For years I've gone without needing anything for myself. Without anyone special in my life. You're more than special. You're the one my heart has been waiting for." She kissed her again. "You're it for me, Dani. The only woman I want to sleep with."

"That sounds really nice, but you have a business to run."

Ryan pressed her lips to Dani's wandering palm. "And I will, but Drake is the VP now and I'm ready to step back." Dani cocked a brow. She laughed. "Yeah. I promise not to work more than ten hours a day."

Dani lightly scored her sides and she groaned. "That's okay, babe. With a new business to run, I'll be working a lot myself. We just have to make time for each other." Dani nipped her lip. "What about being an escort?"

"I thought I'd keep it simple and only take on the rich ones." Dani's eyes grew big, and Ryan laughed. "Teasing. I've already pulled my profile picture. Like I said, only you." Dani looked sad. "I thought that would make you happy."

"I'm going to miss your kinky side."

"No, you won't. We can have all the kink you want."

"Good, because, you know, you're talented and I'm just starting."

"That's not the only thing I want, Dani." Ryan's hand smoothed over her hip, down her thigh. "I want your love. No matter how long I have to wait, that's what I want most of all."

"You don't have to wait. I'm right here and I love you."

She sucked in air, not believing what she'd heard. "You don't have to say it because—"

"Shh…I'm in control, remember? I'll tell you a thousand times if I need to." Dani pulled her down and kissed her hard, not the tender kiss she expected. Dani's mouth was hot and demanding, her tongue exploring and needy. She moaned, then broke away. Dani's lips at her ear. "Just in case. What's your safe word?"

This was one of the many reasons she'd fallen in love with Dani. Dani *knew* her. Knew what she needed and wasn't afraid to give it to her. As night turned into day, they'd gone from making sweet, passionate love to playing out scenes that proved *Dani* was in control, making her scream and finally making her beg for Dani to stop. Her body was spent, her heart content, and with Dani in her arms for the first time in her life, Ryan had found a place to call home.

Epilogue

Six months later...

Dani tapped her pen on the stack of applications to review and invoices to rectify. The renovations on the salon were nearly completed and the tradesmen were putting on the finishing touches with paint and trim work. The storeroom was full of supplies and Pam was coming later to help her stock stations and set up for the opening. Ryan and Mark offered to do the heavy lifting and she'd taken them up on the offer. The two had forged a friendship based on their mutual love for her, as she had with Drake because she loved Ryan. She was grateful for the absence of awkwardness when they were together. She stood and leaned in the doorway and thought about how far she'd come in the last few months.

True to her word, Ryan had helped her find the perfect space and had negotiated with the owner for a reasonable purchase price. They discussed the pros and cons of owning vs. renting, and it made perfect sense to buy. She could do what she wanted and assure the maintenance would never be a concern. The logistics of supplies and personnel fell to her, as did the interior design, although she asked Ryan's opinion due to her sense of style and fashion, as evidenced by her home. Their home, now.

Time had flown by. Next week was the grand opening, and excitement and butterflies coursed through her. Not in a million years had she thought one day she'd be the sole proprietor of a business. Ryan never had a doubt, and any time Dani had doubted herself,

Ryan had been right there, cheering her on. The small fortune she invested would be paid back in full, otherwise Dani would have never agreed. But it was hers, and she loved it.

Pam came through the front door loaded with bags. "Oh my God, this looks fantastic." She did a small spin as she took it all in.

"What have you got here?" Dani rushed to help her.

"Stuff for my station and a bunch of little things that you can either keep or give back. I know this is your place and I don't want to rain on your parade, but...well, you'll see."

They carried the bags to her office and Dani gawked at some of the items. Frames for each of the stylists' licenses. Mesh cups to hold various things on the stations. All in colors that matched the salon palette. "This was really sweet of you." She hugged Pam, so happy she'd agreed to come work for her.

Pam let go, her face beaming. "So when do we get to start?" She clapped her hands.

"Soon. Ryan and Mark promised to be here by two." She glanced at the clock knowing Ryan was always on time. "I'm sure—"

"Dani, where are you?" Ryan called out.

She couldn't stop her heartbeat from speeding up, or her body coming alive at the sound of Ryan's voice, the way it had since the night they'd promised themselves to each other. When she reached the work floor, she stopped.

"I know it's not the official opening, but I wanted these here early to remind you how beautiful you are." Ryan set a huge vase of deep red roses on the floor where her workstation would be.

Dani threw her arms around Ryan's neck and kissed her soundly. "I'll remember."

Mark came breezing in as they broke their embrace. "You didn't start the party without me, did you?" He was carrying a smaller vase of yellow roses and brought them to Pam. "Hi Pam, I'm Mark." He handed the flowers to her.

"For me?"

"Of course. I couldn't let Ryan show me up any more than she already has." He gave Pam a peck on the cheek, making her blush and giggle.

"Thank you." She inhaled before putting them on the floor in the space next to Dani's.

"Okay," Ryan said. "Let's get to it."

The painters folded their drop cloths and packed up their supplies. "That's it, Ms. Brown. If you notice anything that needs a touch-up, just give us a call."

"Thank you, Jack. It looks fabulous."

She turned and smiled at the group waiting. "Now we can get to the real work." Pam volunteered to stock the storeroom racks with product while she directed Ryan and Mark. Once the seating area was done, they placed the workstations according to the drawing she and Ryan had made. Six of the eight stations, four on each side, would be occupied before the month's end. At the back were two sinks and four hoods. With the furniture in place, it finally hit her that the dream was real, and she stood stock-still, her bottom lip trembling as she fought back tears. Ryan wrapped her arms around her from behind.

"What's wrong, baby?"

Dani shook her head. When she got her emotions under control, she turned in Ryan's embrace. "I never could have done this without you."

Ryan's fingertips traced her cheek. "Of course you could have. I was lucky enough to be able to speed things up, that's all." She kissed her slowly, passionately. She heard Mark in the background and smiled against Ryan's lips.

"They're at it again. Let's go make a food run. Neither one of us needs to see this."

"I think it's kind of sweet," Pam said before Mark pulled her away and they left through the back door.

Gently ending the kiss, Ryan held her and gazed into her eyes. "Tell me what else is going on."

"I'll be okay. It's a bit overwhelming, but in a good way."

Ryan brushed back her hair. "I know, and before long you'll forget all about being nervous and beg for things to slow down." Her mouth quirked.

"Is that how you were when you started the Agency?"

"No. We just wanted to have a lot of sex back then." Ryan laughed when she hit her.

"Do we have to wait for them to return?"

"Why?"

"I was thinking we should christen your office."

She was going to answer when Pam and Mark came barreling through the front door. Ryan swore. Dani laughed. "Hold that thought for another time."

"Perfect timing, you two. What goodies have you brought us?" Ryan asked.

Dani looked at her lover and the friends she was happy to have made. Mark hadn't wanted to see it before it was done, but he'd caved. He'd helped with a lot of the advertising and promotional stuff, too. She hadn't told her parents yet because the most important thing in her life wasn't the salon. It was finding Ryan and falling in love. If they couldn't accept her, there really wasn't any reason to tell them about the rest. Ryan looked up and caught her gaze, and in her eyes all she saw was adoration. She knew in her heart whatever the future held, they'd make it work together.

About the Author

RENEE ROMAN lives in upstate New York where she embraces the change of seasons. She is passionate about living an adventurous life and writing lesbian romance and erotica. Her latest works include *Body Language* and *Hot Days, Heated Nights*.

Renee is writing her eighth novel, *Glass and Stone*, and has several more ideas taking form.

You can find Renee on Twitter @ReneeRoman2018, and Facebook at https://www.facebook.com/renee.roman.71/ or you can contact her at reneeromanwrites@gmail.com

Books Available from Bold Strokes Books

Boy at the Window by Lauren Melissa Ellzey. Daniel Kim struggles to hold onto reality while haunted by both his very-present past and his never-present parents. Jiwon Yoon may be the only one who can break Daniel free. (978-1-63679-092-3)

Deadly Secrets by VK Powell. Corporate criminals want whistleblower Jana Elliott permanently silenced, but Rafe Silva will risk everything to keep the woman she loves safe. (978-1-63679-087-9)

Enchanted Autumn by Ursula Klein. When Elizabeth comes to Salem, Massachusetts, to study the witch trials, she never expects to find love—or an actual witch...and Hazel might just turn out to be both. (978-1-63679-104-3)

Escorted by Renee Roman. When fantasy meets reality, will escort Ryan Lewis be able to walk away from a chance at forever with her new client Dani? (978-1-63679-039-8)

Her Heart's Desire by Anne Shade. Two women. One choice. Will Eve and Lynette be able to overcome their doubts and fears to embrace their deepest desire? (978-1-63679-102-9)

My Secret Valentine by Julie Cannon, Erin Dutton, & Anne Shade. Winning the heart of your secret Valentine? These award-winning authors agree, there is no better way to fall in love. (978-1-63679-071-8)

Perilous Obsession by Carsen Taite. When reporter Macy Moran becomes consumed with solving a cold case, will her quest for the truth bring her closer to Detective Beck Ramsey or will her obsession with finding a murderer rob her of a chance at true love? (978-1-63679-009-1)

Reading Her by Amanda Radley. Lauren and Allegra learn love and happiness are right where they least expect it. There's just one problem: Lauren has a secret she cannot tell anyone, and Allegra knows she's hiding something. (978-1-63679-075-6)

The Willing by Lyn Hemphill. Kitty Wilson doesn't know how, but she can bring people back from the dead as long as someone is willing to take their place and keep the universe in balance. (978-1-63679-083-1)

Three Left Turns to Nowhere by Nathan Burgoine, J. Marshall Freeman, & Jeffrey Ricker. Three strangers heading to a convention in Toronto are stranded in rural Ontario, where a small town with a subtle kind of magic leads each to discover what he's been searching for. (978-1-63679-050-3)

Watching Over Her by Ronica Black. As they face the snowstorm of the century, and the looming threat of a stalker, Riley and Zoey just might find love in the most unexpected of places. (978-1-63679-100-5)

#shedeservedit by Greg Herren. When his gay best friend, and high school football star, is murdered, Alex Wheeler is a suspect and must find the truth to clear himself. (978-1-63555-996-5)

Always by Kris Bryant. When a pushy American private investigator shows up demanding to meet the woman in Camila's artwork, instead of introducing her to her great-grandmother, Camila decides to lead her on a wild goose chase all over Italy. (978-1-63679-027-5)

Exes and O's by Joy Argento. Ali and Madison really only have one thing in common. The girl who broke their heart may be the only one who can put it back together. (978-1-63679-017-6)

One Verse Multi by Sander Santiago. Life was good: promotion, friends, falling in love, discovering that the multi-verse is on a fast track to collision—wait, what? Good thing Martin King works for a company that can fix the problem, right...um...right? (978-1-63679-069-5)

Paris Rules by Jaime Maddox. Carly Becker has been searching for the perfect woman all her life, but no one ever seems to be just right until Paige Waterford checks all her boxes, except the most important one—she's married. (978-1-63679-077-0)

Shadow Dancers by Suzie Clarke. In this third and final book in the Moon Shadow series, Rachel must find a way to become the hunter and not the hunted, and this time she will meet Ehsee Yumiko head-on. (978-1-63555-829-6)

The Kiss by C.A. Popovich. When her wife refuses their divorce and begins to stalk her, threatening her life, Kate realizes to protect her new love, Leslie, she has to let her go, even if it breaks her heart. (978-1-63679-079-4)

The Wedding Setup by Charlotte Greene. When Ryann, a big-time New York executive, goes to Colorado to help out with her best friend's wedding, she never expects to fall for the maid of honor. (978-1-63679-033-6)

Velocity by Gun Brooke. Holly and Claire work toward an uncertain future preparing for an alien space mission, and only one thing is for certain, they will have to risk their lives, and their hearts, to discover the truth. (978-1-63555-983-5)

Wildflower Words by Sam Ledel. Lida Jones treks West with her father in search of a better life on the rapidly developing American frontier, but finds home when she meets Hazel Thompson. (978-1-63679-055-8)

A Fairer Tomorrow by Kathleen Knowles. For Maddie Weeks and Gerry Stern, the Second World War brought them together, but the end of the war might rip them apart. (978-1-63555-874-6)

Holiday Hearts by Diana Day-Admire and Lyn Cole. Opposites attract during Christmastime chaos in Kansas City. (978-1-63679-128-9)

Changing Majors by Ana Hartnett Reichardt. Beyond a love, beyond a coming-out, Bailey Sullivan discovers what lies beyond the shame and self-doubt imposed on her by traditional Southern ideals. (978-1-63679-081-7)

Fresh Grave in Grand Canyon by Lee Patton. The age-old Grand Canyon becomes more and more ominous as a group of volunteers fight to survive alone in nature and uncover a murderer among them. (978-1-63679-047-3)

Highland Whirl by Anna Larner. Opposites attract in the Scottish Highlands, when feisty Alice Campbell falls for city-girl-about-town Roxanne Barns. (978-1-63555-892-0)

Humbug by Amanda Radley. With the corporate Christmas party in jeopardy, CEO Rosalind Caldwell hires Christmas Girl Ellie Pearce as her personal assistant. The only problem is, Ellie isn't a PA, has never planned a party, and develops a ridiculous crush on her totally intimidating new boss. (978-1-63555-965-1)

On the Rocks by Georgia Beers. Schoolteacher Vanessa Martini makes no apologies for her dating checklist, and newly single mom Grace Chapman ticks all Vanessa's Do Not Date boxes. Of course, they're never going to fall in love. (978-1-63555-989-7)

Song of Serenity by Brey Willows. Arguing with the Muse of music and justice is complicated, falling in love with her even more so. (978-1-63679-015-2)

The Christmas Proposal by Lisa Moreau. Stranded together in a Christmas village on a snowy mountain, Grace and Bridget face their past and question their dreams for the future. (978-1-63555-648-3)

The Infinite Summer by Morgan Lee Miller. While spending the summer with her dad in a small beach town, Remi Brenner falls for Harper Hebert and accidentally finds herself tangled up in an intense restaurant rivalry between her famous stepmom and her first love. (978-1-63555-969-9)

Wisdom by Jesse J. Thoma. When Sophia and Reggie are chosen for the governor's new community design team and tasked with tackling substance abuse and mental health issues, battle lines are drawn even as sparks fly. (978-1-63555-886-9)

A Convenient Arrangement by Aurora Rey and Jaime Clevenger. Cuffing season has come for lesbians, and for Jess Archer and Cody Dawson, their convenient arrangement becomes anything but. (978-1-63555-818-0)

An Alaskan Wedding by Nance Sparks. The last thing either Andrea or Riley expects is to bump into the one who broke her heart fifteen years ago, but when they meet at the welcome party, their feelings come rushing back. (978-1-63679-053-4)

Beulah Lodge by Cathy Dunnell. It's 1874, and newly engaged Ruth Mallowes is set on marriage and life as a missionary…until she falls in love with the housemaid at Beulah Lodge. (978-1-63679-007-7)

Gia's Gems by Toni Logan. When Lindsey Speyer discovers that popular travel columnist Gia Williams is a complete fake and threatens to expose her, blackmail has never been so sexy. (978-1-63555-917-0)

Holiday Wishes & Mistletoe Kisses by M. Ullrich. Four holidays, four couples, four chances to make their wishes come true. (978-1-63555-760-2)

Love By Proxy by Dena Blake. Tess has a secret crush on her best friend, Sophie, so the last thing she wants is to help Sophie fall in love with someone else, but how can she stand in the way of her happiness? (978-1-63555-973-6)

Loyalty, Love, & Vermouth by Eric Peterson. A comic valentine to a gay man's family of choice, including the ones with cold noses and four paws. (978-1-63555-997-2)

Marry Me by Melissa Brayden. Allison Hale attempts to plan the wedding of the century to a man who could save her family's business, if only she wasn't falling for her wedding planner, Megan Kinkaid. (978-1-63555-932-3)

Pathway to Love by Radclyffe. Courtney Valentine is looking for a woman exactly like Ben—smart, sexy, and not in the market for anything serious. All she has to do is convince Ben that sex-without-strings is the perfect pathway to pleasure. (978-1-63679-110-4)

Sweet Surprise by Jenny Frame. Flora and Mac never thought they'd ever see each other again, but when Mac opens up her barber shop right next to Flora's sweet shop, their connection comes roaring back. (978-1-63679-001-5)

The Edge of Yesterday by CJ Birch. Easton Gray is sent from the future to save humanity from technological disaster. When she's forced to target the woman she's falling in love with, can Easton do what's needed to save humanity? (978-1-63679-025-1)

The Scout and the Scoundrel by Barbara Ann Wright. With unexpected danger surrounding them, Zara and Roni are stuck between duty and survival, with little room for exploring their feelings, especially love. (978-1-63555-978-1)

Bury Me in Shadows by Greg Herren. College student Jake Chapman is forced to spend the summer at his dying grandmother's home and soon finds danger from long-buried family secrets. (978-1-63555-993-4)

Can't Leave Love by Kimberly Cooper Griffin. Sophia and Pru have no intention of falling in love, but sometimes love happens when and where you least expect it. (978-1-636790041-1)

Free Fall at Angel Creek by Julie Tizard. Detective Dee Rawlings and aircraft accident investigator Dr. River Dawson use conflicting methods to find answers when a plane goes missing, while overcoming surprising threats, and discovering an unlikely chance at love. (978-1-63555-884-5)

Love's Compromise by Cass Sellars. For Piper Holthaus and Brook Myers, will professional dreams and past baggage stop two hearts from realizing they are meant for each other? (978-1-63555-942-2)

Not All a Dream by Sophia Kell Hagin. Hester has lost the woman she loved and the world has descended into relentless dark and cold. But giving up will have to wait when she stumbles upon people who help her survive. (978-1-63679-067-1)

Protecting the Lady by Amanda Radley. If Eve Webb had known she'd be protecting royalty, she'd never have taken the job as bodyguard, but as the threat to Lady Katherine's life draws closer, she'll do whatever it takes to save her, and may just lose her heart in the process. (978-1-63679-003-9)

The Secrets of Willowra by Kadyan. A family saga of three women, their homestead called Willowra in the Australian outback, and the secrets that link them all. (978-1-63679-064-0)

Trial by Fire by Carsen Taite. When prosecutor Lennox Roy and public defender Wren Bishop become fierce adversaries in a headline-grabbing arson case, their attraction ignites a passion that leads them both to question their assumptions about the law, the truth, and each other. (978-1-63555-860-9)

Turbulent Waves by Ali Vali. Kai Merlin and Vivien Palmer plan their future together as hostile forces make their own plans to destroy what they have, as well as all those they love. (978-1-63679-011-4)

Unbreakable by Cari Hunter. When Dr. Grace Kendal is forced at gunpoint to help an injured woman, she is dragged into a nightmare where nothing is quite as it seems, and their lives aren't the only ones on the line. (978-1-63555-961-3)

Veterinary Surgeon by Nancy Wheelton. When dangerous drugs are stolen from the veterinary clinic, Mitch investigates and Kay becomes a suspect. As pride and professions clash, love seems impossible. (978-1-63679-043-5)